The Outlaw's Twin Sister

The Outlaw's Twin Sister

STEPHEN BLY

CROSSWAY BOOKS

A DIVISION OF
GOOD NEWS PUBLISHERS
WHEATON, ILLINOIS

The Outlaw's Twin Sister

Published by Crossway Books
        a division of Good News Publishers
        1300 Crescent Street
        Wheaton, Illinois 60187

Cover design: Cindy Kiple

Cover illustration: James Griffin

First printing 2002

Printed in the United States of America

Library of Congress Cataloging-in-Publication Data
Bly, Stephen A., 1944-
  The outlaw's twin sister / Stephen Bly.
    p. cm. — (The Belles of Lordsburg; bk. 3)
  ISBN 1-58134-359-0 (tpb : alk. paper)
  1. Women pioneers—Fiction. 2. Businesswomen—Fiction. 3. New Mexico—Fiction. 4. Outlaws—Fiction. 5. Twins—Fiction. 6. Aunts—Fiction. I. Title.
Series: Bly, Stephen A., 1944-   .
PS3552.L93 O98   2001
813'.54—dc21   2001005556
                                     CIP

15	14	13	12	11	10	09	08	07	06	05	04	03	02
15	14	13	12	11	10	9	8	7	6	5	4	3	2

for
Kris Bearss

For whosoever shall do the will of God,

the same is my brother,

and my sister,

and mother.

MARK 3:35 (KJV)

One

Guadalupe, Mexico—*Wednesday, September 5, 1884*

"You have forsaken me."

"I alone have stuck with you."

"You have denied the faith."

"I have never denied my Lord."

"You have rejected our church."

"I attend my church every week, as you know."

"You have turned your back on tradition."

"Some traditions need to be left behind."

"The Bible says to help those in prison."

"The Bible says to visit those in prison."

"You have deserted your family."

"I welcome my family with open arms."

Guillermo's thick black mustache drooped lower. "You are too rigid to forgive."

"I *have* forgiven you, Guillermo, a thousand times." Her narrow, taut lips revealed no emotion.

"You think only of yourself." He clutched the iron bars, his knuckles white.

"I have risked my life for you on more than one occasion."

His gaze dropped, and the swagger in his voice disappeared. "This will be the last time I ask you."

"On that we both agree."

He rubbed his chin, eyeing her. Anger flashed across his unshaven brown face. "You never did like me."

"There is no one on earth who has shed more tears for you."

"Tears do not get a man out of jail. I need more than tears."

She stared through the small, high window behind him into the pale Chihuahuan sky. "No one has prayed for you more fervently."

"You would pray for *El Diablo* if you thought it would do any good. Perhaps you do not love me."

She looked away as she tried to rub the tension from her forehead. "I will carry love for you to my grave."

His words snapped like a bullwhip. "God will punish you for not helping me."

She backed away from the jail door. "I will someday walk the streets of heaven, but I am not sure you will be there."

"May you never marry and your womb be barren!" he shouted.

She turned to leave. "Yes, that is the order in which it usually works."

He shook the iron bars. "Julianna, are those your last words to me?"

She studied his wild brown eyes. "No, Guillermo, my last words are, 'May the Lord have mercy on your soul, my brother.'"

"You cannot leave me here to be shot! You are my sister!"

"I am your twin sister," she murmured. "We are from the same womb, but I am fearful we do not have the same heart."

Julianna Naomi Ortiz tugged on the cuffs of her long beige gloves and walked the long corridor of the Guadalupe jail amidst the insinuating remarks of a dozen prisoners. The odors of cigar smoke, sweat, and urine swirled in the air inside the building.

When she stepped outside into the hot Rio Grande Valley sunshine, her eyes squinted, and the dry, bitter air grated in her throat. She swept her long, thick black hair over her shoulders so she could no longer see the streaks of gray out of the corners of her eyes. Julianna glanced down at her full black skirt that now had a yellow-brown tint.

Will I ever live in a place where there is no dust, where clothes stay clean, and the air is fresh, and the grass stays green all year long?

Her boot heels marked a steady rhythm on the wooden boardwalk. *El Señor, it is absurd for me to be here worrying about the dust on* my dress. *In a few days my brother will be executed for the murder of two men. I just do not know what to do anymore. I do not know what to think. I do not even know how to pray. You must help me to pray. It was not always this way. I must remember better days.*

"Hermana, venga aquí."

Julianna glanced up to see a tall, sweaty man in a gray cotton shirt. His black eyebrows drooped like his mustache. "Mr. Alvarez, I am surprised to see you so close to the jail."

"I am takin' a chance, that is true, but we need to talk to you."

"We?"

Alvarez's black felt hat had a shallow, flat crown and turquoise band. "Laredo and Jack are back down the alley. We need to talk to you."

She slipped the strap of her brown leather purse up to the bend of her elbow. "Why should I go into an alley with the three of you?"

Alvarez leaned so close that she could smell his bad breath. "You want to help your brother surely?"

Julianna watched an empty stagecoach weave through the parked rigs along the street. "I want the Lord's best for my brother."

"Then you have to help us, *hermana.*"

She noticed that his shirt had a rip near the elbow. "Roberto, would you please tell me why my brother is the only one in jail? When you held up those Mexican freighters, there were four of you. When you shot at the driver and guard, there were four of you."

"We fired in the air, *hermana.* We just wanted them to halt. The old man should have stopped like the other wagon instead of trying to outrun us. No one would have died."

She took a deep breath. The dark green blouse stretched tight against her shoulders. "When the driver lost control, and the rig plunged down into Little Cougar Arroyo, killing both himself and the *alcalde's* nephew, there were four of you. When you tied up the other driver and guard and drove off with the wagon full of goods, there were four of you. When you were captured at Montoya Raton, there were four of you. Why is it that only my brother is going to be shot by the firing squad?"

"Because Guillermo put up such a fight at his capture that we managed to escape. Do you want us all to be shot?"

"My concern is for justice, Mr. Alvarez. Getting what you deserve is a fair system, don't you think? And the fact that you three deserted my brother and ran away does not exactly seem fair."

"Who would help him if we allowed ourselves to get caught? Besides, no one gets what they deserve, *hermana*. Not the *alcalde*, not the *generales*, not the *padre*. No one. Not the Texas Rangers. Not the rich mine owners in San Francisco. Not even the unmarried sisters like you. Why should we be different? In this life we are all struggling to get better than we deserve. Now are you coming to talk with us?"

"You are a philosopher, Mr. Alvarez. I do not see that it would make any difference in Guillermo's fate if I talk to you."

Alvarez pulled off his black hat and ran his fingers through his short, dark hair. "Your brother is down to his last three friends. I think we ought to at least hear how he is doing."

She rubbed her forehead, and the fingertips of the beige gloves revealed the yellow-tinged dust of Guadalupe. "Yes, I suppose so. I would want to hear from you if the roles were reversed. But I am not comfortable in a dark alley. Can we meet somewhere else?"

"Julianna, we treat you as if you were our own *hermana*."

"I do not know how you treat your sisters."

Alvarez pointed down the shady path between the two adobe-walled buildings. "Besides the alley is not all that dark."

The shops and stores on Calle Nueve contoured along the once-barren hills of the mountain pass. The alleys followed no logical order or pattern. By day they presented a challenging maze. At night too often they provided violent traps. Julianna followed Roberto Alvarez around the crates, barrels, and garbage piles to a spot that had been roofed over with used lumber and canvas. It offered shade for those who chose not to show their faces on the streets of Guadalupe. A cloud in the thin blue sky dawdled above the heat-reflecting adobe, and the aroma of lost lives clung to the dark red stains smeared across weathered, battered wood backdoors.

Julianna recognized the silver conchos on Jack Burkeman's black sombrero.

"I knew she would come for me. She cannot keep her eyes off me," he laughed.

Julianna spun around and crashed into Roberto Alvarez. He grabbed her shoulders.

"Do not touch me," she growled.

Roberto yanked his hands back. "He did not mean anything by that, *hermana*. We always tease you—you know that. Stay just a moment and hear us out."

Julianna slowly turned around, crossed her arms, and glared at Burkeman. He shoved his hat back and flaunted a straight, white-toothed grin. "With a scowl like that, your side could have won at San Jacinto," he remarked.

"My side *did* win at San Jacinto!" she snapped.

"I meant no offense, Señorita Ortiz. What's the plan? What did Guillermo say? Are you smuggling him a gun? Do we use dynamite? Where is the weakest wall in the jail?"

Alvarez studied the alley. "Where is Laredo?"

Burkeman pulled off his sombrero and waved it to the south. "He went lookin' for tobacco."

"He does not have any money."

Burkeman shrugged and grinned. "You know Laredo. He has a way with words. What about Guillermo?" His eyes seemed to be staring at everything about her except her eyes.

Julianna fought the urge to yank the scoop of her neckline up even higher. "We did not discuss escape plans."

"The Federales had him guarded close, did they?" Burkeman pressed.

"No, we had a limited amount of freedom, but I did not discuss escape with him. That was not the purpose of my visit."

Burkeman jammed his hat back on. "Shoot, what did you talk about?"

"His eternal destiny."

Alvarez's shoulder pressed against hers. "He is goin' to be shot unless we do something!"

Julianna stepped back. "What better time to speak of heaven and hell."

"You ain't goin' to help him escape?" Burkeman asked.

"I will pray for him, and I will talk to a very good Santa Fe lawyer, Jefferson Carter, about the case. That is all I can do."

"All you can do? You could find out when they let him outside, when he goes to the privy, where we can stash a gun, and whereabouts we should blow a hole in the wall!" Burkeman fumed.

She stepped out into the middle of the alley away from them. "I will not be a part of a violent jailbreak."

"What kind of sister are you?" Alvarez challenged.

"A long-suffering one, as you both know. Now if you will excuse me, Paco is waiting, and I need to get back to El Paso and catch the train."

"Are you comin' back to see him again?" Roberto asked.

She stared at a trash pile where the broken head of a porcelain doll lay beside a rotting turnip. "Only if I can be of some assistance. I do not care to watch my brother die."

"Then why aren't you goin' to help us?"

"Jack Burkeman, how many times have I fed you and given you a place to sleep when you were on the run?"

Two dimples flashed in his boyish grin. "Maybe three dozen times."

"There is nothing more I can do. Two citizens of Mexico were killed, including the mayor's nephew. The freight belonged to a cousin of the president of Mexico and was bound for the governor of Baja California. I cannot change any of that. I am somewhat amazed that my brother has not been executed before now. I will do whatever is legal, compassionate, and possible. That is all."

"How about what is illegal and compassionate?" Alvarez pressed.

She scooped up the little porcelain doll head and positioned it on top of the empty crate. "I will not commit a crime. You all know that." *El Señor, sometimes this is exactly how I feel. Like a broken doll on a garbage pile.*

"You don't have to do nothin'. Jist pass word back and forth," Burkeman insisted.

"That makes me an accomplice."

"Not unless we get caught," Alvarez argued.

"I have said my last words to my brother."

Burkeman rubbed the light beard on his chin. "You givin' up, *hermana*?"

"I am always ready to do what is right."

A crash and a curse came from around the bend in the alley. Roberto and Jack yanked out their revolvers. There was a shout, another curse, a scream, and then the report of two gunshots fired at almost the same time.

Laredo Nisqually hurdled over two broken potato crates and a brown dog as he crashed into the alley near them. "Run . . . run . . . *amigos*!"

Roberto grabbed Julianna's hand and sprinted toward the street. She held up her long skirt. Jack Burkeman ducked behind a broken barrel, fired two quick random shots, and then followed them.

"What did you steal?" Roberto shouted.

"Just some saddlebags and some silver. There was not even any tobacco!" Nisqually hollered.

"How much silver?" Burkeman called out.

Nisqually fired another shot down the alley at the unseen pursuer. "*¿Quién sabe?*" He grinned. "Not a lot. I do not know why he is so angry. It must be the principle."

"Just one man?" Roberto asked as he took a shot.

"He is enough," Laredo said.

Jack Burkeman fired two more shots and then shoved more bullets into the chamber of his revolver. "Who did you steal it from?"

Laredo Nisqually retreated down the alley with the others. "Now that is the bad part. It was DelNorte!"

"You fool!" Alvarez shouted.

"How did I know it was him? He was washing up at the tub with a towel covering his face. The saddlebags were lying there. They begged me to take them."

"Get to the horses and ride for the river," Roberto shouted at Burkeman.

"He will follow," Burkeman warned.

"Not for a little silver," Laredo replied.

"You do not know DelNorte!" Roberto hollered. "You can ride with me, *hermana!*"

Julianna jerked her arm free. "I will go nowhere with you. I committed no crime." She staggered back against the front of the Bogota Cantina. A crowd gathered in the doorway, staring out at the commotion in the dusty street.

Leading two saddled horses, Burkeman galloped to the alley where Nisqually and Alvarez held the pursuer back with a volley of bullets. Burkeman squeezed off several shots as the other two mounted the panicked, prancing horses.

"Come on, *hermana!*" Alvarez shouted and offered his hand.

"I will have nothing to do with you," she yelled.

"You will see us again. We will find you."

"If DelNorte doesn't shoot us first," Burkeman bellowed.

Steel-clad hooves thundered in a low fog of dust as they galloped up Calle Nueve.

Julianna strode along the sidewalk as shouts rolled up the alleyway. *I should never have come to Mexico. I do not like it down here. El Señor, just being near my brother causes me turmoil. I do not understand how You could put us in the same family, much less in the same womb.*

"Where did they go?" a man shouted.

"*¡Ellos fueron allí!*" another replied.

She hurried faster down the boardwalk.

"*¿Cuantos hombres?*"

"*Tres, y la mujer.*"

"*¿Mujer? ¿Dónde?* Where is the woman?"

"*¡Vaya! ¡Allí está la hermana!*"

"*¡Señora, espere!*" She heard boot heels crash on the boardwalk behind her, but she didn't slow down or turn around. "Lady, I'll either tackle you or shoot you, so you'd better stop!"

Julianna spun on her heels and folded her arms across her

chest. "Mister, I have nothing I want to say to you. The three men you are pursuing went north."

The man had silver hair and matching neatly trimmed beard. His narrow, steel-gray eyes looked younger, and they danced with anger. "The old man said they went east."

"The old man is wrong. I believe they will ride to El Paso." She turned and stomped away.

A large, strong hand grabbed her shoulder. This time when she spun around, her purse sailed at the end of its strap. The thick, engraved leather bag caught the man on the ear.

He staggered back, stumbled over his feet, and sat down hard on a bench in front of the Maricopa Saloon. Muted laughter tumbled out of the crowd huddled at the door.

He jumped up and rubbed his ear. "I reckon I deserved that."

"Yes, you did. I will not submit to harassment by the likes of you!" She stomped along the boardwalk and down the steps to the dirt street.

He trotted after her. "Woman, whose sister are you? The man said they called you 'sister.' Whose sister? One was named Laredo. Are you his sister? Who were the other two?"

She crossed the street behind a boy leading a firewood-laden donkey.

"Woman, did you hear me?"

She stopped so abruptly that he stumbled to keep from crashing into her. "DelNorte, I believe it is, my name is Señorita Julianna Ortiz. My brother did not rob you. He is in jail. I came to visit him. Now I am going home to New Mexico."

"Is your brother Guillermo Ortiz?"

"Yes, he is."

"Then those other two were Roberto Alvarez and Santa Fe Jack Burkeman."

She continued across the street. "Woman . . . lady . . . Señorita Ortiz, I can have you arrested for being an accomplice to a crime."

"And I could sue you for false arrest."

"Not in Mexico," he said.

"Oh? Are you an expert on Mexican law?"

"Sort of. Harvard class of '69."

Julianna slowly turned back. His wool trousers were tucked into black stovetop boots. For the first time she noticed that he packed two revolvers, the second tucked under his long coat in a cross-draw holster.

"You look surprised," he said.

"Your Virginia accent does not sound like Cambridge, Massachusetts."

"Just as yours reveals no Hispanic dialect."

"Now that we have equally astonished each other, I trust that you will cease to harass me."

"I will not. I expect you to help me get my saddlebags back."

"Then you will be disappointed. I have no intention of complicating my already enigmatic life." She thought she saw his eyes relax, almost dance. "I bewildered you again?"

"Señorita Ortiz, I'm puzzled. I'm standing in the middle of the street of a small Mexican town a hard ride south of El Paso after being robbed of my poke, talking to a very attractive Spanish lady about her 'enigmatic life.' It does seem rather bizarre."

"Is your name really DelNorte?"

"That will do for now."

"There is one thing that puzzles me. Three men, all of whom are worthless scoundrels and openly afraid of the great DelNorte, steal his poke by accident and then run off, thinking they will be chased down and shot by the legendary gunman. But he instead accosts and harasses an American lady and lets the men escape. Why do you suppose he did that?"

He shoved his revolver back into his holster and shook his head. "You know, Miss Ortiz, I've been wondering that same thing myself." He stared down the road. "They're going north?"

"I am sure they will head toward El Paso. That type usually hides on whichever side of the border is safest at the moment."

"How about you, Miss Ortiz? Which side of the border is home for you?"

"I told you I live in New Mexico."

"That's a large territory."

"Are you trying to find out where I live so you can come and harass me there as well?"

"Harass you? Lady, you were with the men who robbed me."

"Now I am a lady? At least you stopped calling me 'woman.'"

"My point still stands."

"Those three were *compañeros* of my brother. He is awaiting a Mexican firing squad. They wanted to know his condition. I was not happy to talk with them, but they are his friends. Laredo was not with them. I was told he went to buy tobacco. He stole your saddlebags, and they fired a few shots at you and then galloped out of town."

"Why didn't you tell me that sooner?"

"You did not take time to ask."

"You ran like you were guilty."

"Or merely concerned about my safety in a gunfight."

"It wasn't much of a gunfight."

"They do better in the dark."

"They did all right in daylight. They stole my money."

"I am sorry you lost your silver, but I was not in a position to stop them. I merely wanted to get away from them."

"Like you want to get away from me now?"

"Precisely," she snapped.

"Do you always run away from men?"

"What is that supposed to mean?"

"Just wondering."

"Mr. DelNorte, I do believe this conversation is over. Good day."

It was a soft, easy grin. "Did I offend you?"

"You most certainly did."

He tipped his black hat. "My apologies." He strolled alongside her as she marched down the dusty street. "May I ask you a question without offending you?"

"I doubt it."

"As do I. Miss Ortiz, could you tell me the town in which you live?"

"Why do you want to know?"

"So that by all means I can avoid it and never cause you duress again."

"That would be very kind of you. I live in Lordsburg."

"Is there a street address so I will know which street to avoid?"

"Perhaps it would be best if you avoided the entire town."

"Yes, I suppose so."

"DelNorte, now I have a personal question to ask you."

"That sounds fair."

"Could you tell me which town you live in?"

"Do you want to know which town to avoid?"

"No, I would like to know which town to send your body to, because if you show up in Lordsburg, I will probably shoot you on sight."

His laugh was low, pleasant, like soft rain on parched ground. "I spend several months of the year in Brownsville, some time in El Paso, and some in San Diego."

"Thank you."

"You're welcome."

"I assume you need to keep on the move to avoid legal complications."

"You may assume whatever you wish."

"When I shoot you, to which location would you like your body sent?"

"Whichever is closest to the point of death would be fine."

"Is there a particular person I should address the coffin to?"

"No, you have my permission to send it to the entire town," DelNorte roared.

"Then that is what I shall do."

"Are you headed back to Lordsburg now?"

"Yes. I will catch the train in El Paso. And I suppose you are going the same direction to retrieve your silver?"

"The thought had crossed my mind. I can rent a carriage, and we can ride together if you'd like."

"How considerate, DelNorte, but I already have a carriage, thank you."

"Do you need a driver?"

"No, my driver is quite proficient."

"You have your own driver?"

"Now you look surprised again, Mr. DelNorte."

"Anything about the enigmatic Señorita Ortiz should surprise me."

"Good, because my driver is my ten-year-old boy."

DelNorte stopped walking, but she continued to stroll. Julianna chuckled. "DelNorte, too many surprises, I surmise."

"But I just thought . . . Señorita . . ."

"You see, you have judged me and rejudged me several times. Yes, I am *Miss* Ortiz. Yes, young Paco Ortiz belongs to me. Now how does that set in your Harvard-educated mind?"

"Well, I, eh . . . you don't have to explain your private life to me."

"That is good because my private life is extremely complicated."

"Would you be offended if I rode alongside your carriage back to El Paso?"

"I am not sure. Paco will insist that I carry the shotgun in my lap. He says there are dangerous men in Mexico."

"You have a very wise son."

"I did not say Paco was my son."

The Rio Grande trickled along a wide riverbed of brush and scrub alamo trees. The roadway paralleled the course of the river and in the spring was sometimes flooded. In September it was difficult to see the water some fifty yards from the roadway. The appearance of the shallow, brushy riverbed belied its historical significance as an international boundary.

The black leather carriage was pulled by a single horse whose trotting gait never varied. The ten-year-old holding the reins in his hand wore a white long-sleeved cotton shirt and brown canvas coveralls. He had neither hat nor shoes. His brown skin was so dark that he made the woman riding next to him look almost pale.

"You did not get Tío Guillermo out of prison?" he pressed.

"No. That was not the purpose of our visit."

"Why did they not let me go in? Is it an awful place?" Paco asked.

"Yes, it is. I do not think I want to come back."

"While I held the carriage, I heard shooting. Did you hear shooting?"

Julianna nodded. "I believe I did."

"You should have carried your shotgun. Guadalupe is a dangerous place."

"Paco, they would not let a lady from New Mexico carry a shotgun into the prison."

"They would have thought you were Ramona Hawk!"

Julianna cringed. "She is in prison."

"Yes, and you do not look like her," he quickly added.

She bit her lip and remained silent.

"Ramona Hawk is quite a beautiful woman, you know, for an outlaw."

Ramona Hawk's demonic glare flashed through Julianna's mind. "Nothing like me," she murmured.

"Oh, I did not mean that you are not beautiful. I mean, you are *mi tía*. Aunts are neither beautiful nor ugly, you know."

She bounced along to the rhythm of the rig. "Oh, I did not know that."

"Yes," Paco informed her, "they are like mothers. They stand above beauty."

"Your mother was very beautiful, Paco."

"Yes, but I did not know that until after she was killed. Now when I look at her photograph, I see a very beautiful woman. But when she was alive, all I saw was a mother. Perhaps it will be the same with you. After you are dead, you will become very beautiful."

Julianna laughed. "Paco Ortiz, you are such a charmer!"

"Yes, that is what Gracie and Lixie always tell me."

"How about Bonita? What does she say about you?"

"She says I am very crude. But what does she know? She is an Apache."

"But she is a very bright girl, other than her evaluation of Mr. Paco."

He sighed and shook his head. "She is young. She will learn."

"I do believe she is a few months older than you."

"Have you noticed that I seem to attract older women who have an urge to get married after they meet me?"

She studied the ten-year-old. "You mean, Grace Parnell and Lixie Miller?"

"Yes. You are the only one who is not married. I am very concerned."

"For me or for you?"

"For you, of course. I do not intend to marry until I am governor of New Mexico," Paco asserted.

"Perhaps I also will not marry until after you are governor of New Mexico."

"But you will be very old by then, and the best years of your life are passing you by."

She wiped the dust out of her eyes with a linen handkerchief. "Where did you come up with that?"

"That is what everyone says."

"And just who is talking about me like that?"

"Lixie says you are too beautiful to spend your nights alone."

"She said that?"

"She said you are too beautiful to spend your days alone too. But you do not spend your days alone. You run your jewelry store. So I suppose she meant your nights."

"Hmmm. It is a little disheartening to be the topic of such conversations."

"She says she knows several fine gentlemen in the army who would make excellent husbands."

"What? She is talking to you about a husband for me?"

"Did you know Bonita wants to get her hair cut?" Paco glanced back over his shoulder.

"Are you changing the subject?"

"I think someone is following us."

"Are you trying to avoid my question?" she pressed.

"No, really. Someone *is* following us."

"Paco!"

"And he is gaining. Grab the shotgun."

"Paco Ortiz, you . . ."

"Then you hold the reins!" He shoved the leather straps into her gloved hand, reached under the carriage seat, and yanked out a double-barreled shotgun.

Julianna slapped the reins on the horse's rump. She peered back at the cantering rider in the black hat. Paco cracked the shotgun open, examined the two shells in the chambers, and then snapped it shut.

"Do you think we will need that?" she questioned.

Paco glanced back at the oncoming rider. "He looks dangerous."

"Does he have gray hair, a neatly trimmed full beard, tanned face, and square shoulders?"

Paco flopped down in the seat. "You know this *hombre?*"

"No, I have never seen him before in my life." She grinned.

"You are teasing me. Who is he?"

"I do not know his real name."

"Is he a jewelry merchant?"

"No, I do not believe so."

"How do you know so much about him?"

"He was standing very close to me."

"What is his unreal name?"

"They seem to call him 'Of the North.'"

"His name is Mr. North?"

"Well, in Spanish they call him—"

"DelNorte! He is DelNorte?" Paco gasped.

"Yes, I believe that is it."

Paco yanked back the huge hammers on both barrels of the shotgun.

The man on the gray horse trotted up on Julianna's side of the carriage and tipped his black hat. "Señorita Ortiz."

"Mr. DelNorte, this is my nephew, Paco Ortiz."

DelNorte grinned and let his hat slip to his back. It dangled by a woven horsehair stampede string. His gray hair flared out where the hat had been. "Señor Ortiz, do I have your permission to ride alongside your carriage and visit with your aunt?"

Paco looked the man over. "Are you the real DelNorte?"

"I'm afraid so. Are you disappointed?"

"You are old."

"Paco!" Julianna lectured.

DelNorte roared with laughter. "Yes, but I was gray-headed before I was thirty. I am forty years old now, and that, son, is very old."

"My aunt is not exactly young. She is thirty-two."

"Paco!" Julianna sighed.

"Well, you are. You are thirty-two years old and never married," Paco concluded.

Julianna shoved the reins into her nephew's hand and took the shotgun from him. "Excuse me one moment, Mr. DelNorte, while I dispatch my nephew."

A blank stare on his face, Paco shrugged at the man on the horse. "I do not understand women."

"I certainly know how you feel, son."

"Every day she tells me to tell the truth and never lie. Then when I tell the truth, she glares at me as if I had picked my nose in public."

"Well, son, sometimes it's better not to speak at all."

"Are you the DelNorte that stopped fourteen rustlers from driving twelve hundred head of stolen cattle across the Rio Grande?"

"Nope, that wasn't me. I only stopped eight drunk cowboys from stealing 964 head."

"Are you wanted by the law?"

DelNorte grinned. "No, are you?"

"Of course not!" Paco grinned.

"That's good. Now will you let me ride alongside your carriage for a while?" DelNorte asked.

"Are your intentions honorable?"

DelNorte stared at Paco and then glanced at Julianna and grinned. "How old is this *niño*?"

"He has just turned ten. Paco takes very good care of me."

"My intentions are merely social. It's a long ride to El Paso, and I thought the trip would go more quickly if I have someone to visit with."

"What do you want to talk about?" Paco asked.

DelNorte sat tall in the saddle. "We can visit about horses, outlaws, the weather, the Apaches, or even about your Aunt Julianna."

Paco sighed. "I trust I will not get bored."

Two

"How many notches do you have on your gun?"

DelNorte's left hand held the reins. His right cradled a Winchester '73 carbine across his lap. "None, Paco."

"You have never shot a man?"

"I've never wanted to ruin a good walnut grip."

"You do not want to answer?"

"It's a question you should never ask a man."

Paco rubbed his flat brown nose and wiped his hand on his shirtsleeve. "You mean, it is okay to ask a woman how many notches she has on her gun?"

DelNorte grinned. "No, partner, you especially shouldn't ask that."

"How come you pack two pistols?"

"How do you know I pack two pistols?"

"You have two holsters—one at your right and one with a cross-draw."

"How do you know I don't have three pistols?"

"Three? You have a sneak gun?"

"Now that's a secret a man has to contemplate, doesn't he?"

"DelNorte, did you ever have a shootout with Billy the Kid?"

"No, but I had supper once with Pat Garrett."

"Did you know Jesse James?"

"I visited his brother Frank in jail."

"Are you a pal of the Earp brothers?"

"I know Virgil pretty well, but I know Stuart Brannon better."

"Did you ever rob a train while it was moving?"

"No, but I jumped off a train while it was moving."

"You did?" Paco's round brown eyes widened. "Did you break your neck?"

"No, but I tore an embarrassin' hole in my trousers."

"Aunt Julianna says that if I jumped off a train, I would break my neck."

DelNorte rubbed his gray beard. "That's probably true. A man has to know how to land without hurting himself."

"Can you teach me how to jump off a train?"

Julianna reached over and patted the boy's knee. "Paco, quit pestering DelNorte."

"How am I going to learn anything?"

DelNorte surveyed the brush as they rode. "There are some things you only learn about in the midst of doing them, son."

"Like jumping off trains?"

"And understanding women."

"Don't you start in on women, DelNorte," Julianna snapped.

"No, ma'am." He pulled his hat back up on his head and turned his gaze away from the river. His voice lowered. "Don't either of you look toward the river. Were you expecting someone to follow you?"

Julianna smiled. "Only you."

"You figured I'd follow you?"

"You seemed persistent."

"Well, someone else is trailing us over in the brush near the river. One, maybe two men. Probably two. Think I'll circle back and take a look."

"I do not see anyone," Paco called out.

DelNorte scowled.

"That is, if I was looking at the river, which I am not . . . anymore."

Julianna glanced at the shotgun in Paco's lap. "Do you think it is Laredo and the others?"

"Do you?"

Julianna scooted back on the hard leather carriage seat and straightened her back. "No, I do not think they will stop until they get to El Paso."

DelNorte cocked the lever on the carbine. "I reckon I'll check it out."

"Do you want us to stop for you?" she asked.

"You keep right on rolling toward El Paso. The bridge across the border is just over that next rise. If you hear gunshots, race up there and cross over into the States."

"Do you want us to wait for you there?"

"I don't know who's out there and what they want or where I'm headed. No, don't wait for me. I might be tied up for a while. But it's surely been nice chattin' with you two."

"We are taking a train back to Lordsburg tonight at 7:12 P.M.," Paco blurted out. "Are you going to come with us?"

DelNorte winked at the boy. "No, your Tía Julianna has banished me from ever settin' foot in Lordsburg."

Paco slapped the lead line on the horse's rump. "You must have said a very, very naughty word. I said a word one time, and she told me if I ever said it again, they would kick me out of town!"

"Yes, come to think about it, I believe it did have something to do with my words. Have a good day, Miss Ortiz." He tipped his hat.

"Thank you, DelNorte. I do hope there is no trouble. I have some questions to ask you next time I see you."

He rode up alongside her. "Oh?"

"Legal questions."

He scratched his neck while watching the brush along the river. "Why would you ask me legal questions?"

She studied the creases by his eyes. "You said you studied law at Harvard."

He looked down at her. "No, I merely said I had gone to Harvard."

"I assumed that meant you studied law. What did you get your degree in?"

She watched his eyes dart from brush to tree to the riverbed. "I didn't say I got a degree," he mumbled.

"DelNorte, did you go Harvard University in Cambridge, Massachusetts, or not?" she demanded.

"Yep."

"Did you graduate?"

"Yep."

"What was your course of study?"

"Ancient history."

Julianna began to laugh.

Suddenly he was looking straight at her. "You find that funny?"

"I find that unbelievable."

He shrugged and grinned. "I've had the same reaction from other women."

"You are a mysterious man, Mr. Ancient History DelNorte."

"No, the mystery men are those over in the brush trailing us. Keep up the same pace as if you haven't seen them."

"I have not seen them," she said.

"I have." DelNorte turned his horse around and trotted south.

"He is going back to Guadalupe," Paco observed.

"No, he is going over in that brush. I believe he just wants anyone there to think he is going back to town."

"I guess I do not need this shotgun anymore."

"I think you should carry it until we get to the border."

"I will be glad to get back to Lordsburg. I wonder if DelNorte knows the Parnells? I forgot to ask him if he knew Colt. Everybody knows Colt." Paco turned around on the leather seat and stared back down the dirt roadway. "I cannot see him anymore."

"How about those in the brush? Do you still see them?"

Paco shrugged. "I never saw them in the first place."

"Them? What if it is only one man?"

"Or a woman," Paco added. "What if it is a woman?"

"Why would a woman be following us?"

"Maybe she is following DelNorte."

Julianna took a linen handkerchief from her sleeve and wiped dust and sweat from her forehead. "Now that could be."

"Or it could be nothing."

"I certainly hope so," she murmured.

At the sound of three quick gunshots, Julianna reined the carriage to a halt. Paco jerked up the shotgun. "You are supposed to race to the bridge," he reminded her.

"Can you see him?" she asked.

Two more shots ran out.

"I see nothing but gun smoke."

"Hang on, Paco. Let's get back to the United States."

The abrasive power of every bump, hole, and rock seemed magnified as the carriage wheel slammed into them. Julianna bounced from one side of the leather seat to the other as they rumbled along. The hills were barren of all but clumps of dry grass and occasional clusters of yucca. There were no trees to be seen except those that paralleled the Rio Grande. When they crested the next rise, the road turned straight to the river and three small adobe buildings. She slowed the rig. "Put the shotgun under the blanket under the seat."

"Why did you slow down?"

"It would not look good to race up to the border. They might think we had something to do with the gunfire."

"There is another shot. Did you hear that?"

"Yes, I did," she said. "Now be your charming self and turn around and sit down."

Two very dark-skinned, gaunt uniformed soldiers stood with rifles in hand at the first adobe building. The one with a thick mustache spoke first. "*¿Dónde van ustedes?*"

"We are going home," she reported.

"What is the gunfire?" the other asked.

Julianna looked over her shoulder. "I am not sure. We did not see anything."

"Were they shooting at you? This horse has been raced."

"I do not think so. The shots scared us. We thought we should hurry and find protection from the brave Federales."

The man with the thick mustache shouted some instructions in Spanish. A third man stuck his head out of the doorway of the smallest building. He held a half-eaten chicken leg.

"*Vaya a ver cual es el problema.*"

"*¿Yo?*"

"*Sí.*"

"*¿Ahora?*"

"*¡Ahora!*"

"*Pero este es el tiempo para . . .*"

The thick-mustached man waved his gun at the man, who handed the chicken leg to the other guard with a rifle and raced toward a string of three picketed horses.

"*¡La cincha!*" the mustached one yelled.

The man shifted his heavy broadcloth coat, threw his foot in the stirrup, and yanked himself up. The saddle swiveled on the tall stallion and dumped the man in the dirt. He struggled to his hands and knees. "*¿Qué paso?*"

"I said, tighten the cinch."

As the man adjusted the saddle, the mustached man hiked closer to the carriage. "Would you believe he is one of my best men?" he murmured.

The other uniformed man finished eating the chicken leg, tossed the bone in the dirt, and ambled inside the small, square building.

"I don't believe they really want the border guarded. I cannot leave my post, not in hands like these." He surveyed Julianna. "Where were you born?"

"El Paso."

"Which side of the border?"

"Texas."

"How about your *niño*?"

"I am her—"

Julianna's hand on his knee silenced him. "Paco was born in Silver City, New Mexico."

"Now we live in Lordsburg," Paco blurted out.

"I have been to Lordsburg," the man replied.

"Next time you come, you will have to shop at my jewelry store. I have some very lovely silver pieces made by the Zuni Indians."

"I might look you up if I get back that way," the soldier said.

"Yes, please do. May we go now?"

"No."

"Why?"

"You will wait until Marquez returns. I want to know what that shooting was."

"We must catch a train in El Paso," she insisted.

"Why were you in Mexico?"

"I was visiting family."

"Did you buy anything?"

"No."

Paco stood up and pointed back up the hill. "Look, here comes a horse!"

"A horse?" The officer trotted to the back of the carriage. "Garza!" he yelled. The other uniformed man came out of the building with a rolled tortilla in his hand.

"There is a man running!" Paco added. "I think he is trying to catch the black horse."

"Garza, ride out there and help Marquez."

"Did he get bucked off again?" the man mumbled.

"Knowing Marquez, he might have fallen off."

Julianna wiped her forehead with her handkerchief. "Sir, I am feeling a little faint in this heat. Do you have any ice?"

"Ice? I haven't seen ice since I left Monterey last March. Lady, go on and get across the border."

"Thank you, sir. And if you are ever in Lordsburg, you will get a 10 percent discount on any jewelry in my store."

"Good day, señora."

They rambled across the wooden bridge.

"Aunt Julianna, you give everyone a 10 percent discount."

"Yes, quite generous of me."

"Do you think DelNorte is all right?" Paco asked.

"If the Federales are his only threat, I am sure he is quite safe."

They paused for a moment at the American side of the crossing at the customhouse and then turned north on the road to El Paso. For the next three hours they talked to no one except a young girl selling tomatoes when they stopped at a small town to water the horse.

When they reached El Paso, Paco lounged by the livery gate

as Julianna returned the carriage. When she exited the barn, she carried a small lavender parasol over her head.

"Are we going to the train depot now?" he asked.

"The train does not leave until later. I want to go to Mr. Fieldman's to see if those jade pieces I ordered for Lixie's wedding have arrived yet. I'm afraid I waited too late to order them. The wedding is Saturday."

"He will not let me go in the store barefoot," Paco said.

"I told you to wear your shoes."

"I can just wait out on the front bench."

David Fieldman's wholesale jewelry store was a one-story adobe building with no windows facing the street. The only sign was a small one attached to the iron front door that read "D. Fieldman, Wholesale Only."

"You sit here and wait," she instructed.

"How long will you be?"

"Only a moment or two. I doubt if he could get those jade pieces from San Francisco by now, but it does not hurt to inquire."

She pushed the heavy door open and stepped inside. A spring forced the door closed behind her. She paused to let her eyes adjust to the dimness. The two-foot-thick adobe walls kept out the stifling September heat, and the swept tile floor was as clean as any she had seen. Rows of shelves were filled with marked and numbered velvet-lined oak flats.

I have no idea how Mr. Fieldman knows where everything is. And I have no idea how much inventory is in this one room. I thought it was difficult with my store at home.

"Mr. Fieldman?" she called out.

There was no answer. Julianna strolled to the display cases against the back wall of the store.

Mr. Fieldman, I have never known your big glass case to be so empty and your store so unstaffed. You must have sold a lot of merchandise recently.

"Mr. Fieldman?" she called out toward the open door to the storeroom.

She thought she heard noises in the back room and stepped

toward the open doorway. She paused to listen and could only hear the buzz of a horsefly. A drop of sweat trickled down her forehead and dropped to her cheek.

"Mr. Fieldman, you have a customer out here!"

It sounded like a board squeaked, but the red tile floor stretched from the showroom to the back room. She caught a whiff of Fieldman's pipe tobacco.

She stepped through the doorway. A large bare table filled the middle of the room. It was covered with green felt and looked like a pool table without rails or pockets. Several oak flats lay broken on the tile floor next to the table.

There's been an accident. He's . . .

A man's legs poked out from behind the table. David Fieldman lay on his side, his hands tied behind his back, his feet bound, and his tie yanked off and bound in his mouth.

"Mr. Fieldman, what happened?"

Fieldman's narrow, penetrating gray eyes reflected panic as she stooped by his side. He shook his head as if to toss the gag off by sheer force.

Julianna heard a deep guttural laugh behind her.

A woman's laugh.

A familiar laugh.

Then several other voices.

Then she saw and heard nothing at all.

When she turned her neck, the pain shot up from the small of her back and exploded at the back of her head. Sweat dripped off her forehead, but her cheek felt very cold. She blinked her eyes open and tried to roll over, but the pain in her head was so great she had to close her eyes and grit her teeth. Finally she managed to raise up on one elbow and open her eyes again. David Fieldman lay bound only two feet from her. She reached over and tugged down the gag.

"Señorita Ortiz, I was afraid that blow from the rifle barrel had killed you."

"I am alive, but I think I will have a headache and ringing in my ears for the rest of my life." She tried to look around the room, but most things were a blur.

"They are gone. Can you untie me?" he asked.

She crawled across the cold, hard tile floor. "Of course. Who were they?"

"Two well-dressed Mexican men and a strange-looking lady. They said they were opening a store in Deming. But as soon as I turned my back, they pulled guns." With his hands free, he sat up and untied his own feet. "Señorita, should I get a doctor to look at your head?"

She gingerly touched her head and then examined her fingers. "No blood. Other than having a large bump, I suppose I will survive."

Fieldman stood and offered her a hand. "May I help you up?"

"I believe I will just sit here a minute. You will excuse me for not looking ladylike?"

"Miss Ortiz, you may sit there all you want. Can I get you a washrag and some water? Some smelling salts?"

"You better find the sheriff. How much did they steal?"

Fieldman surveyed the room. "The more expensive pieces, of course, but they left when you came in. They didn't get to the raw gems. They were looking for a quick resale, I'm sure. I always have several clerks here for this very reason, but today both of them needed to be off. Do you think that's suspicious, or am I just imagining things?"

"Perhaps the sheriff can check it out."

"Oh, dear, I hate to leave the store and you in such a condition while I fetch the sheriff. I can wait a few minutes while . . . "

Julianna took a deep breath and struggled to her feet. "Send Paco to find the sheriff."

"Where is he?" Fieldman asked.

"Out on your front bench. He will not wear his shoes, so he does not come in."

"I'll go tell him. Oh, I do hope you're all right. This sort of thing is a risk I take being in this business, but I'm appalled that you have been injured, Miss Ortiz."

While Fieldman rushed to the front of the store, Julianna

brushed down her dress and tried to carefully straighten her hair. She paused in front of a glass case and used it as a mirror.

El Señor, this has not been a good day. I did not want to come down here. I did not want to leave Lordsburg. I will never leave home again. I will order the jewelry by mail and buy only from those who send salesmen to my little store.

"I can't find him. He must have wandered off," Fieldman called out as he returned to the storeroom.

"What?"

"Your Paco is nowhere to be found."

"No!" she moaned. "He was right out there. He said he would wait on the bench."

She rushed through the showroom. Her head throbbed with every step on the hard tile. Fieldman followed her. With the sun low in the west, shadows filled the dirt street. A slight drift of air chilled the perspiration that clung to her face and neck.

The bench was empty.

A long carriage carrying two large women and a barking black dog rolled by, but there was no other movement in the street.

Julianna whirled around. "She took him!"

"Who took him?"

"Ramona Hawk took Paco from me!"

"My word, I thought she was in jail in the States somewhere."

Julianna put her hands on her cheeks. "She is the one who just robbed you," she moaned.

"That was Ramona Hawk?"

"Yes. I know her."

"But this woman snuck up behind you."

"I will never forget her laugh."

"What does Miss Hawk look like?" Fieldman asked.

"She is my height."

"This woman looked taller, but it could have been the boots."

"She has long dark hair like mine without the streaks of gray."

"This woman had yellow hair."

"She was blonde?" Julianna questioned. "Hawk is very thin."

"This woman was plump. I would guess she is great with child."

"You were robbed by a pregnant woman?"

"She caught me off guard."

"She always wears long, dangling earrings," Julianna continued.

"This woman had no jewelry at all. I notice such things."

"She is almost ten years older than I am."

"This woman was younger," Fieldman said.

"She has a small, slightly upturned nose and a narrow, rather pointed chin."

"As does this woman."

"See, it is Ramona Hawk. She kidnapped my Paco."

"You took a nasty blow to the head, Miss Ortiz."

"She took Paco!" Julianna cried out.

"Why on earth would she do that?" Fieldman challenged.

"To get back at me." She scurried to the street corner and shouted, "Paco!" *El Señor, I believe I could withstand the loss of all things but not Paco! Not my precious Paco! I could not live through that. I am a weak woman—You know that. You know how weak.*

Julianna trotted to the alley and called out once again, "Paco!"

From deep in the alley she heard a honk.

"Paco?"

From behind a barrel a huge ring-necked goose came waddling out. Then stumbling over a pile of mesquite firewood, Paco scampered after the goose.

"Paco Ortiz!" Julianna cried.

"Hi, Tía Julianna. Are you ready to go? Hi, Mr. Fieldman."

She squatted down, threw her arms around him, and cried, "Where have you been?"

"Playing tag with that goose."

"Tag?"

With a quick dart forward, the goose bit Paco on the seat of the pants, honked, and ran down the street.

"Stop it. I had time out. That didn't count!" Paco yelled.

She stood up. "Why did you not stay on the bench like I said to?"

"I, eh, well, the goose wanted to play, and you were taking a long time."

"There was some trouble inside."

"What kind of trouble?"

"A robbery."

"And I missed it? You never let me see anything!"

"It is a long story. I want to go home. Let's go to the train." She turned to the businessman. "Mr. Fieldman, I trust you can take care of things with the sheriff. We have a train to catch."

"Did you come for the jade pieces?"

"Yes."

"I'm very sorry."

"What do you mean?"

"They arrived yesterday, and those three just stole them."

"She took my jade?"

"I will order more." Fieldman pulled gold wire-framed spectacles from his vest pocket and carefully slipped them on his long nose. "Are you sure you don't need a doctor, Miss Ortiz?"

Julianna reached over and patted his hand. "I just need to get home, Mr. Fieldman."

Julianna spent half an hour in the depot back room washing her face and recombing her hair. Her head still throbbed. She walked slowly over to Paco, who wiggled his toes in the dust on the depot floor. A man reading a newspaper sat next to him.

"Look, Aunt Julianna, I wrote your name and my name in the dust with my big toe. I think I am left-footed. Can a boy be right-handed and left-footed?"

She sat down on the worn oak bench next to him and read the writing. "'Paco & Julianna Ortiz.' Yes, you probably can."

"*Hermana*, are you leaving town without talking to us?" It was a low, deep voice that filtered up from the newspaper.

"Roberto! I am surprised that you showed your face. Although I suppose hiding behind a newspaper is not exactly showing your face."

"You did not answer my question."

She folded ungloved hands in her lap. "I answered your question in Guadalupe. I will not be a part of helping my brother break out of jail. If you have a legal suggestion, please let me know."

"There is nothing legal we can do in Mexico."

She leaned her head back against the wall, felt pain, and slumped forward. "And you have already done all the illegal things."

"*Hermana*, we just need you to smuggle a gun to him and tell him what time we will be there to bust him out. It should not be difficult for you to hide a gun."

"Roberto, this is a useless conversation. You know how I feel about that. Your greatest fear should be your safety. Paco and I saw DelNorte, and he is on his way to El Paso. He might already be here. He will be looking for you. You need to go into hiding. Perhaps you could move to Idaho. I understand no one can find you in Idaho."

"The great DelNorte is probably dead by now," Roberto announced.

Julianna sat up and clutched Paco's warm, sticky hand. "What do you mean, he is dead?"

"Sometimes luck rides with you," Alvarez boasted. "We had just snuck across the river, and who did we meet but Laredo's cousin and the four Iturbe brothers."

"I thought there were only three Iturbe brothers."

"Big Chat got out of Leavenworth and joined up with them again. He pretended to be insane, and they let him out early."

"He is insane."

"Maybe so, but he is not dumb. They owed us over two hundred dollars all told and had come up here to rob a bank. They had no more than got to town, but some wild-eyed deputy marshal spotted them and started hollerin' and shootin', so they lit shuck for the border."

"And you met them going one way, and they were going the other?"

"Yep, so we told them that an old boy on a tall gray horse would be following us, and if they finished him off, we would forget about their debt."

"So you sent them after DelNorte?"

"Yep."

"And you did not tell them it was DelNorte?"

"We did not want to discourage them."

"That was risky."

"Laredo never liked that cousin anyway," Roberto added.

"How do you know they succeeded in killing him?"

"You should see Laredo's cousin. He makes *El Diablo* look like a saint."

"He can kill people with his looks?" Paco challenged.

"He is a very tough *hombre*."

"So you are confident of DelNorte's demise?"

"Yes, they would be able to ride right up to him because he does not know what they look like. Then one shot to the brain, and DelNorte is ready for the buzzards."

"It is nice to have someone do the work you are afraid to do yourself," she huffed.

"We are not afraid—merely prudent." Roberto kept his face behind the newspaper. "Perhaps opportunistic. Why stoop to such petty business when others will do it for you?"

"A true test of leadership, no doubt."

"Yes, and that is why I am sitting here in the depot in the open and DelNorte is nowhere in sight. That proves that he has been disposed of."

"Then why do you hold the newspaper up to your face?" Paco asked.

"There might be others who want to find me," Roberto replied.

"I say you have doubts," Julianna challenged.

Alvarez lowered the newspaper to his lap.

"If DelNorte is still alive, I think he will be very, very angry at you," Paco remarked.

"You are right, Paco," Julianna added. "Why, he could be coming to the depot right now."

Laredo raised his newspaper in front of his face.

"*Hermana*, we will be in Hachita. We must act fast. Guillermo has only a few days at most."

"If you go to Hachita, stay out of Millie's," she warned. "Guillermo has a better chance with the Federales than you three do at Hachita."

Roberto stood. "*Hermana*, we will wait for a word from you."

Paco continued to write with his big toe in the dust on the depot floor. "What word do they want to hear from you, Aunt Julianna?"

"I believe the word is *repent*."

Paco sat next to the window clutching a basket in his lap. Julianna's green carpetbag was tucked back under her legs. She sat with hands folded in her lap as the train pulled out of the station.

"The train is moving. Can I eat my cheese sandwich?"

"What is in the basket must last us until we get home," she instructed. "That will be at midnight."

"But I am hungry now."

"Why not eat half a sandwich and see if that fills you up."

"That is a good idea. Which half shall I eat—the large half or the small half?"

"By all means, the large half."

"Yes, that is what I was thinking. Do you want the other half?"

"Not yet. My head is still hurting."

"Do not worry, Aunt Julianna. I do not think Laredo's cousin and the others killed DelNorte. He snuck up on them."

"But Laredo was right. DelNorte did not show up at the depot."

"Perhaps he did show up. Just because we did not see him come to the depot does not mean he failed to arrive."

Julianna sighed. "Yes, that is very true."

Paco leaned forward and rubbed his backside. "Aunt Julianna, have you ever played tag with a very smart goose?"

"I do not believe so."

"They cheat."

She glanced out the train window as the lights of El Paso disappeared and the train picked up speed. "I will remember that."

"The day turned out to be less boring than I expected," Paco said.

"That is nice." She closed her eyes. "Which event was the least boring?"

"Meeting DelNorte." Paco dug through the food basket. "He reminds me a lot of Colt Parnell. Can I have an oatmeal cookie?"

"Just one. He does not look like Colt."

"I mean, he is a lot nicer than his reputation."

Julianna brushed crumbs off Paco's round brown cheeks. "Colton Parnell has the most sterling reputation in southern New Mexico. DelNorte is known as a feared gunfighter with a mysterious past and unknown alliances."

"Other than that, they are very much alike," Paco mumbled.

"Wipe the mustard off your chin."

She watched him wipe his mouth on the sleeve of his shirt.

Julianna leaned back against the leather seat of the railroad car and closed her eyes. *Dear Margarita, my sweet sister, had you lived, what would you think now of your darling Paco? Not a day goes by that he does not remind me of you. I know that if you were with me, you would urge me to marry. But there is too much sadness in this world. We must hold onto the faith and ride it like a wave to glory. Remember how mother used to tell us that? You were so young when she died. Now you two are together, and I alone am left. It does not seem fair. The one who survives is punished with loneliness. I have Guillermo only for a few more days. I do not know what else to do for him. It was not easy to walk away. I can exhort him today, but if he is shot by the firing squad, I will mourn the rest of my life for him. I do not know, Mama, I just do not know. How can I sin and risk my life for a horse thief and murderer? Yet how can I abandon my twin brother? On the one hand, I will fail my heart, and on the other, I will desert my soul. Life is very hard, El Señor. I will raise Paco. He is my purpose in life. He will be governor someday. Then I will have completed my course and kept the faith.*

Her eyes flipped open. Paco's nose was pressed against the window glass.

"Why are we stopping?" she asked.

"There is a man back there loading his horse," Paco announced.

"But there is no depot out here."

"I guess he flagged the train down."

"Can a person do that?"

"This one can."

"Does he have a gray horse?"

"Yes, and there is a bandanna around his head."

"Over his face, like a holdup man?"

"Over his forehead like a hat, like a man with a busted head. Can I yell at DelNorte?"

"No. Perhaps he does not want others to hear his name shouted."

"I wonder if DelNorte has any new notches on his guns—you know, if he carved notches?"

"You are not supposed to ask him that question."

"There are many rules to follow when you are young," Paco sighed.

"And many when you are old too."

"But you get to make up the rules when you are old."

The train chugged forward. Most of the passengers in the car settled back into their routines. Then the train door opened, and a rush of hot September air blasted the back row. The man with a gray silk bandanna around his forehead and black hat in hand slipped into the empty seat behind them.

Paco turned around and stood on his knees in the seat. "What happened to your head? How many did you fight? We heard there were four and that they killed you."

DelNorte spun his hat in his hand. "Yes, it's true."

"Which part?" Paco asked.

"The part about Laredo's cousin and the four Iturbe brothers."

"You know them?" Julianna inquired.

"Roberto bragged that you are dead," Paco reported.

"They came closer than I like to think. I did not know there were four Iturbe bothers until today."

"I hear one is crazy," Julianna said.

DelNorte held the bandanna against his head. "They are all crazy."

"But you whipped all five of them!" Paco exclaimed. "One time Stuart Brannon took on thirty-six Moroccan sailors and a killer squid."

"I must have missed that story."

"It was in *Stuart Brannon Lands at Tripoli and Other Maritime Adventures.*"

Julianna noticed blood oozing through the gray silk bandanna. "DelNorte, what happened to you?"

"I circled back and cut the trail of three riders following us. I tracked them along the river and then waited to see if I could spot the third Iturbe. As soon as he showed his hand, I made my move."

"But there were four Iturbes," Paco reminded him.

"A lesson I quickly learned. The fourth one jumped me as I approached the others. It had been a trap all along."

"We heard shots," Julianna said.

"I had two wounded and two pinned down when the other Iturbe jumped me with a knife at least twelve inches long. Got a little cut on the forehead before I subdued him."

"You captured five of them?"

"I left 'em hangin' from a tree."

Paco's mouth dropped open. "You hung them all?"

DelNorte glanced at Julianna. "By their ankles."

"Will their feet fall off?" Paco asked.

DelNorte scrunched down until he could lean his head on the back of the seat. "No, it was a low limb. Their shoulders and heads rested on the ground. But they can't get loose until someone stops and cuts them down."

"They might be there a long time," Paco remarked.

"The Federales will come find them. I would imagine at least three of them are wanted for something in Mexico, and the government soldiers will get the credit for 'capturing' the *banditos*."

"Is your head injury serious?" she asked.

"It will heal."

"You have not told me why you got on this train," she quizzed.

DelNorte closed his eyes. "To see you, of course." His hands still clutched the Winchester '73 carbine.

"Aunt Julianna said you could not come to Lordsburg."

"Perhaps I'm going to ride up to Hachita," he added. "I suppose that's where Alvarez and the others went."

"Why would you go there?" she asked.

"To recover my poke."

"No one ever left Hachita with a penny. It is best to go there broke," Paco announced.

"Then I qualify."

"DelNorte, Hachita is an awful place. You should take Colt Parnell and Jefferson Carter with you," Julianna urged.

"Some things a man's got to do alone," DelNorte mumbled.

"Why? Who made that rule?" she demanded.

"Señorita Ortiz, we live out here on the frontier. I can't let anyone walk off with my poke. They have to know that I'll personally defend it with my life. I couldn't ask others to make that sacrifice."

Julianna glanced around to see if any other passengers were listening to their conversation, then proceeded. "You will need a place to stay in Lordsburg."

He opened one eye. "You makin' an offer?"

Her back stiffened. "No, I most certainly am not."

"He can sleep in my bed," Paco suggested.

"He most certainly cannot. But I will check with Mary Beth Holden. They have a very lovely guestroom."

"I'll just put up in a hotel," DelNorte said.

"I would think a wounded man would need a little more privacy than that."

"Are you actually going to let me into Lordsburg?"

"It is September. If you die, I will send your body to San Diego. It should be nice there this time of year."

"There was a moment or two this afternoon when I thought I was close to doin' just that. I don't like knife fighters who sneak up when you're fighting someone else."

"I am glad you are safe," she murmured.

He opened both eyes but continued to slouch against the seat. "Now are you going to tell me about that lovely lump on the back of your head?"

Three

The desert at night is like a symphony. Black sky and low-hanging stars meet the heat rising off the pale brown desert floor, but they do not blanket the sounds the way a fog muffles river bottomland. They mute all noise night creatures make, like a mother raising her finger to her lips to still an anxious child.

Horses step more lightly.

Night birds restrain their calls.

The creatures of the night slink and saunter and slither. They do not stomp, smash, and shriek. Like a cymbal crash added for emphasis, the desert tranquility is at times punctuated by a coyote's yip or a wolf's mournful howl, but always at a distance—anesthetized reminders that all is at rest.

The sounds of the steam engine's churning gigantic pistons and the rumble of steel on steel of the railroad cars disturb the serenity of the southern New Mexico night.

But not much.

The undeviating rhythm of the rails plays as a counter-melody to the desert symphony. As if complementary pieces by the same composer, they blend with amazing congruity. The effect inside the dimly lit railroad car is to gently rock its passengers to sleep.

At least most of them.

Paco wanted to stretch out on the seat, so he traded places with DelNorte. Julianna described the robbery at Fieldman's, but she didn't mention her suspicions concerning Ramona Hawk. Some memories were too painful to dredge up, and the thought of Hawk was always painful.

DelNorte sank down with his knees against the seat in front of them, his head leaning against the backrest. From time to time he entered the conversation with a nod or a smile.

A few rows ahead of Julianna a man with a pipe had his window slightly open, and the rush of air sent the smoke around her head. Her legs warmed to a sweat where they rested on the leather seat.

Julianna's headache eased from pulsating pain to a dull constant throb. She stared out at the black desert and watched her own reflection in the glass.

Miss Ortiz, if you dyed your hair, you would look younger. She glanced at the reflection of DelNorte. *Some, of course, look fine with gray hair. Why is it that men look distinguished with premature gray hair, and women merely look old? I am not old. I will not wear my hair up until I marry.*

Julianna sucked in a deep breath of smoke-tainted air and bit her lip.

I will not marry. This world is not my home. I do not like my life, my situation. I could never ask another to like it either, and for that I have chiefly my father to thank. She turned back and sat straight up in the seat.

El Señor, I must trust that You designed our families for our own good, but I must confess I have many questions to ask You in heaven about mine. I have a father, two stepmothers, and eight siblings, though only Guillermo is a full brother, and I feel totally alone.

Julianna reached back to the seat behind her and stroked Paco's bangs off his eyes. She lifted his smooth, warm chin to close his gaping mouth.

Forgive me, El Señor. I am so ungrateful. I have my Paco. He is my deliverance. One day at a time, sweet Jesus. And one night at a time.

She studied the other people in the train car.

Twenty lives suspended until they reach their destination. It is the story of my life—suspended until I reach the destination. For the others, a time to sleep. For me, it is the silence I dread. There is nothing to do but think and think and think.

She stared at the man sleeping only a foot away from her.

What kind of name is DelNorte? "From the north." North of what?

North of the border? North of Richmond? Was he in the war? Of course he was. He would have been in his teens. Yet he went to a northern college after the war. Harvard. Or did he? Why do I believe him? A gunman of mysterious background with violent innuendoes, who wanted to shoot me when we first met, and I am letting him sit next to me. Am I that desperate for company?

She held the front of her blouse away from her body and fanned herself with it. *I must take one crisis at a time. The authorities can take care of the holdup at Fieldman's. Mr. DelNorte will take care of Alvarez and the others, I am sure. I must talk to Jefferson Carter about my brother. A lawyer will know what to do. Of course, he and Lixie are getting married on Saturday. That might slow down his interest in legal work.*

Why is it I can never tell Guillermo how I really feel? When we are together, he always brings out the worst in me. It has always been that way. I just do not understand.

I may not sleep like the others, but I can close my eyes.

She peered over at DelNorte and then closed her eyes.

And at least I will be the only one in the car without my mouth gaping open.

Her chin was on her chest; the pillow was warm, hard, and bristly. The train slowed again. She reached up and wiped the corner of her mouth without opening her eyes. She heard the conductor's low, sonorous voice, like a mother's first call for breakfast. "Mister, time to wake the wife and boy. This is Lordsburg."

Wife and boy?

Julianna's eyes blinked open to a view of a scarlet-stained gray silk bandanna and matted gray hair. There was a head on her shoulder.

She tapped his shoulder. "DelNorte, we are here in Lordsburg." He didn't move.

"I do hate to wake you. You must need the rest, but we have to get off here. You seem to have slipped over on my shoulder."

With slow determination she eased him over until he sat

straight up, his chin on his chest. She leaned back and rubbed Paco's shoulder. "Time to wake up, *niño*. We are home."

The young boy's eyes blinked open in unison, but he didn't move his head. "I will sleep here tonight. You can have the bed."

"We are on the train, young man. You must carry my bag for me."

"Let me sleep. I will get off next time the train comes through Lordsburg."

"It will go to San Diego before it turns around."

"That will be nice. I have never been to California."

"You are not going tonight. Sit up, baby. I need you to help me wake up DelNorte."

Paco sat up with the seam line from the leather seat across his cheek like a scar. "Do we have to walk home?"

"We live one block from the depot. Of course we will walk."

"I suppose I am too big for you to carry."

"Yes, you are." She turned and tapped DelNorte on the knee. "We are in Lordsburg. Time to wake up."

"I am glad we are home," Paco mumbled. "When I am governor, I will make Lordsburg the capital."

"The people in Santa Fe might object."

"They will love me and do anything I say."

"You are still dreaming, Mr. Governor." She poked DelNorte in the ribs with her elbow and found nothing but hard muscle and bone. "It is Lordsburg. I believe you wanted to get off here."

"Mr. DelNorte, you have to wake up so you can go to Hachita and beat the tar out of Laredo and the others," Paco blurted out.

Several stirring passengers looked back at them.

"Paco, keep your voice down."

"I was just trying to wake him up."

"You woke up everyone in the car."

"For this they should thank me."

"They are not all getting off at Lordsburg." Julianna studied the sleeping man's face. Then she bit her lip, reached out, and put the palm of her hand on his bristly gray beard. "Mr. DelNorte?"

His mouth dropped open.

"Oh, no!" She sat straight back against the window and gasped for breath. Her heart raced.

"Is he dead?" Paco sputtered.

The passengers began to murmur as the train pulled into the station.

"Señora, do you need some help with your husband?"

She glanced up at the man with the pipe several rows ahead of her.

"Please get the conductor," she called out.

She furiously tugged on DelNorte's sleeve. "Mr. DelNorte, you must wake up!"

"Is his heart beating?" Paco asked.

Julianna slipped her fingers under the stained silk bandanna that circled his forehead. She pressed her fingertips to his temples. The rhythmic thump seemed ten times slower than her own.

"Yes!" she replied. When she pulled her fingers back, they were covered with warm, sticky blood. "Oh, dear Lord."

"He is bleeding, Aunt Julianna. I think he is hurt very bad."

The conductor rushed to her side. "What is the trouble, Señora?"

She fought to control her words. "DelNorte is severely injured. He needs a doctor."

The conductor leaned over and stared. "DelNorte? Your husband is the legendary border gunman?"

"He is not."

"Is he able to get off the train?"

"He has passed out," Julianna replied.

"Do you need some help with your husband?" the man with the pipe asked.

"Could you assist us, please. I need to get him to a doctor." She turned and motioned to the boy. "Paco, you carry my bag."

"It is very heavy."

"I know, but I need to assist these men."

The air on the platform at Lordsburg felt cool as Julianna stepped down ahead of the men.

"Put him over on this bench. I will go get a doctor."

"This train has to pull out on schedule," the conductor insisted. "What about his horse?"

"I'll unload him for you," the man with the pipe offered.

"Thank you. You have been very kind." She strained to see in the darkness. "I believe you got a little blood on your suit."

"My word, señora, don't worry about my suit. I hope your husband comes through okay. I'll tie his horse in front of the depot."

"May El Señor reward you for your kindness."

"He already has. Many times over," the man replied and then disappeared into the darkness.

She took the satchel from the boy's hand. "Paco, run and get Dr. Richardson. He is staying at Mrs. Sinclair's. And be careful in the dark."

The express office door swung open just as the train began to pull out. The silhouette of a tall, well-dressed, tawny-haired woman appeared in the doorway.

"Julianna, is that you?"

"Gracie? Oh, thank you, Jesus."

The woman left the door open and scurried out to the dark platform. "What is it? What's wrong? Is that Guillermo? Has he been shot?"

"Gracie, this is DelNorte."

The taller woman arched her dramatic eyebrows. "*The* DelNorte?"

Julianna fanned the man's face. "Yes. He was injured in a knife fight in Mexico and passed out on the train. I sent Paco for the doctor."

Gracie slipped her arm around Julianna's waist. "You have become a nurse to gunfighters?"

Julianna patted Gracie's hand. "It is a long story."

"I'll look forward to hearing it . . . tomorrow. What can I do for you?"

"I need to get him to a room." Julianna could see the concern in Grace Parnell's flashing eyes. "What are you doing working tonight? I thought you had retired from the telegraph business."

"Ethan and Mary Beth took Rob to California. He's going back to college. I'm filling in while they are shorthanded. But poor little Ruthie is sick, and my dear Colt is home with a crying toddler."

Julianna stared off at Railroad Avenue. "I sent Paco to find Dr. Richardson."

"He's gone!" Gracie said.

"Where?"

"There was an explosion at a mine in Pinos Altos. Every doctor in southern New Mexico was summoned to Silver City."

"But I—I mean, DelNorte needs help."

"I'll get Lixie," Gracie said. "She's patched up more soldiers than an army surgeon."

"But I can't ask you to abandon your station."

Gracie flipped her hair back off her forehead. "What can happen to me? They can only fire me. I just want to know one thing."

"Yes?"

"Is DelNorte a nice man?"

"What do you mean, nice?"

"Julianna Ortiz, you know exactly what I mean by that."

Julianna looked down at the injured man. "Yes, he is. I do not know him very well. But I would like to know him better."

"Honey, that's all I wanted to hear you say. Let me lock up. I'll see if I can find someone to haul him to your house."

"Oh, not my house. What will it look like?"

"Julianna, it's the middle of night. We'll figure out something when morning breaks and moral concern wakes up. You stay by your man. I'll get Lixie. She'll know what to do."

Julianna's jewelry store had prime footage on Railroad Avenue, but it was one of the narrowest stores in town. Just sixteen feet wide, it stretched back to the alley 111 feet. Julianna had furnished the back half of the building as an apartment for her and Paco. From the alley, her door looked like a backdoor to the jewelry shop. Instead, it led to a small patio with vines trellised overhead and black iron chairs in the shade below.

The showroom was one long room with glass counters on both sides. The apartment was one long room as well. At one end, near the curtain that served as a door to the store, were a woodstove, sink, cupboards, a counter, and a small table with two benches. In the middle of the room stood an iron-framed bed with a lumpy feather mattress. It was covered with cotton sheets, with two wool blankets folded neatly and stashed under it. This was Paco's "room," as he called it. An enormous brown leather sofa occupied the far end of the room—the only piece of furniture Julianna owned that had belonged to her mother.

Julianna slept on the couch, read in the rocker, relaxed on the patio, cooked at the stove, and worked in the store. Some weeks she hardly got beyond her long, narrow world.

A neighbor named T-Bang drove the Hernandez brothers' bell wagon down the alley, an unconscious DelNorte in back. T-Bang and fellow boarder Nobby-Bill Lovelace toted the wounded man inside.

Lixie Miller, fully dressed with hastily applied makeup, led the men inside. "Wait a minute, boys. Julianna, do you have any old sheets to put down on the sofa? He's a dirty mess. I presume he was rolling in the dirt."

"Five men attacked him. I do not know how old the sheets are."

"They will look old by tomorrow," Lixie commented. "Paco, go build a fire in the kitchen stove and warm up some water."

Julianna stretched out the white muslin sheets on the sofa and scrunched a buffalo hide pillow at one end.

"Put a pillow slip on that cushion."

"It is old—it is not . . ."

A glare from Lixie's fiery eyes sent Julianna to the cedar closet. When the pillow was encased, T-Bang and Nobby-Bill eased the man down on the couch.

"I cannot thank you enough," Julianna said.

"We was playin' whist with the Berry sisters. It was a delight to escape from them," T-Bang announced.

Lixie ushered the men to the little patio. "Remember, you are not to breathe a word to anyone about DelNorte being at Julianna's. You know how an injured wolf is attacked by every member of the pack. Well, that could happen here."

"Yes, ma'am, we won't say a word," Nobby-Bill assured her.

As the two left, Lixie closed the door and moved over to the injured man.

"Julianna, get your sewing kit. Paco, bring me the water as soon as it's hot. Where is that bottle of iodine?"

"What do you need with a sewing kit?" Julianna asked.

Lixie held the lamp close to DelNorte's forehead. "You've seen his skull?"

"Yes."

"I need to sew him up so that you can't see it."

Julianna held her chest and took a deep breath. "Lixie, I cannot thank you enough for coming out like this."

"Honey, this is Lordsburg. We are exiles at the edge of the world. We take care of each other, and you know it. You would do the same for me."

"Yes, I would come out in the middle of the night, but I would not sew up a wound." *Nor would I take time to fix myself up as nice as you do, Lixie Miller.* "And your wedding is on Saturday."

"I'm over fifty years old. I was married to the general for almost thirty years. It's not like this wedding is the most dramatic event of my life."

Julianna grinned. "You are lying, Lixie Miller."

Lixie rolled her eyes. "Yes, I am. I'm as nervous as a schoolgirl," she confessed. She looked down at the wounded man. "DelNorte is prematurely gray. I don't think he's as old as I am."

Julianna offered, "I think he is at least forty. I believe he was in the war."

"His forehead is going to look seventy-five if we don't get it stitched up soon." Lixie toweled the perspiration off DelNorte's face. "Rev. and Mrs. Howitt are staying with me. He's going to candidate at the church and has agreed to perform the ceremony on Saturday."

"Will your house be furnished by then?"

"I certainly hope so. It was very convenient of the Holdens to go off and allow me to use their place until then." Lixie turned toward the kitchen stove. "Is that water hot yet?"

"It is hot enough for your face but not hot enough for your hands," Paco responded.

"Bring some here," Lixie ordered. "Your aunt can bathe him."

Julianna's hand went to her mouth. "I can what?"

Lixie's white-toothed grin flashed in the dim lamplight. "I meant bathe his hands, arms, and face, of course. I wondered what kind of reaction I would get when I said that."

"What kind did you get?"

"It was priceless." Lixie paused a moment. "When Gracie knocked on the gate and said Julianna Ortiz had DelNorte in her arms, I said, 'Yes, of course. It's only right.'"

Julianna rubbed the man's dirty hands with a damp cloth as Lixie untied the silk bandanna. "What did you mean by that?"

"I meant, you are a very uncommon woman, and I would expect you to attract a very uncommon man."

"I did not say I was attracted to him or him to me. We met by chance. We happened to be at the same place at the same time. I had no idea that he was going to stop the train and—"

Lixie interrupted, "Now you are lying to me, Julianna Naomi Ortiz."

"Yes, I am. I trust you will keep my secret."

"Honey, Gracie and I know all about it, and Mary Ruth is gone to California. There is no one left to blab to." Lixie studied DelNorte's forehead. "Oh, my, would you look at this. I've seen scalped soldiers who looked better."

Julianna looked at the gash across DelNorte's forehead. The deep cut ran from just above his left eyebrow across his forehead in a slanting fashion, until almost parallel with his right ear. "He must have lost a lot of blood."

"That will be the key. If we can patch him up and keep him quiet through the fever and infection stage, perhaps his body will rebuild the blood supply," Lixie explained.

Julianna turned her head. "We should have stayed back on the trail and helped him. He told us that if there was shooting, we should race to the border. But we should have stayed."

"This is a man who knows what he's doing. You did what he

asked you to. Now which do you want to do—wash out the wound or sew him up?"

Julianna plucked up the jar of iodine. "I will wash. I am not very good with a needle and have never sewn a person."

Lixie helped clean the bloody wound. "It's quite simple when they are unconscious. Just think of it as a rip in the pants that needs mending. It's more difficult when they are awake."

It took almost an hour for Lixie and Julianna to clean, sew, and dress DelNorte's wounded head. Paco had fallen asleep on top of the feather mattress by the time Julianna walked Lixie out to the patio.

"Lixie, you are a jewel of a friend."

"You might have some doubts next week when Bonita comes to stay with you while we are on our honeymoon."

The night air felt fresh and comfortable compared to the stuffy apartment. "Bonita is a very bright, delightful girl."

"Yes, but her Indian ways will catch you by surprise."

Julianna took Lixie's arm and walked her to the alley door. "Paco spends his days thinking of ways to impress her. But her Apache skills often far outweigh his talent."

"The feeling is mutual, I believe. Bonita will never tell Paco, but she is convinced that he will be governor. She asked me on Sunday afternoon if I thought New Mexico would ever elect a Mexican governor and if an Apache could ever become a governor's wife."

"Oh, no!" Julianna giggled. "They are only ten."

"They are both quite grown up in some ways. And they have both lost their parents. But they're still very much children in other ways."

"Not unlike the rest of us."

Lixie stood at the alley door. "Do keep an eye on DelNorte. The fever will hit him sometime in the next twenty-four hours. That seemed to be when we lost the soldiers who had been tomahawked."

Julianna bit her lip. "It is amazing how you can talk of such things, as if discussing a baby with a cough."

"Honey, I'm an old army wife. If you don't get tough, you spend your days in total depression and tears until they lock you away. But I trust I'm not calloused."

"I am sorry I have to send you out in the dark alone."

"Keep your eyes on him. We certainly want to keep him alive long enough to know his real name. Gracie and I will need more to gossip about than just some mysterious, handsome man called DelNorte. She said she will check on you when she gets off at six in the morning."

"Lixie, I would rather you did not tell the new preacher about me having a man in my house. It is too complicated to explain, and I would not want to prejudice his judgment."

"Julianna, there are two things in this town you can trust: There will be gunfire on Railroad Avenue on a Saturday night, and, second, the belles of Lordsburg will stick together."

"I did not know I was one of the belles."

"You are a sincere Christian lady with a mysterious past who has a notorious man on your sofa. Honey, you are one of the belles. Welcome to the club."

Julianna waited until Lixie strolled out of the alley. Then she bolted the backdoor and hurried across the darkened patio. She left the door between the patio and apartment open. Julianna stopped near the unconscious DelNorte.

Mysterious past? They think I have a mysterious past. It is Gracie who has the mystery—a senator for a father, a baby sister to raise, daring exploits to write home about. And everyone in the States has read about Lixie Miller, the lady who can slay her philandering husband with a look of scorn. They are the ones books are written about. There is no mystery about me. Perhaps I should tell no one about my past so that they will continue to allow me into the "club." If they knew, they would be bored.

Mr. DelNorte, you are my ticket to social acceptance in this town. So strange. Living on the frontier is quite different from anywhere else. Out here the more mysterious and notorious, the better.

She paused near Paco, who slept shirtless in his ducking

trousers on top of the sheet on the feather mattress. One arm had flopped down to the floor. His mouth was wide open.

Look at him. Not a care in the world. Tomorrow he will wake and view the world as a brand-new adventure. No matter how hectic things were tonight, there is sweet, pleasant sleep. He has confidence that the entire world was meant for him to enjoy. El Señor, is that the childlike faith You demand? Perhaps it is best seen not in our professions or acts of charity but in our sleep. I did not have a long enough childhood. I was eight when Daddy left and nine the winter Mama died. Just about Paco's age.

But he was only five when Margarita, my sweet Marga, and her Carlos were killed. Oh, Paco, we are alike—you and me—related by sorrow as well as by blood.

Julianna turned off the lamp near the kitchen table and left on the lantern near the sofa at the far end of the room. She shoved open the heavy green drapes that hung from brass rings and served as a door to the jewelry store. Then she padded out into the darkened display room. She cranked open the small window above the front door and felt a slight rush of night desert air as it washed into the store and flowed toward the open patio door at the back of the building. Julianna paused in the shadows behind a display case of turquoise and silver jewelry. She stared out at the starlit shadows of Railroad Avenue.

Five years ago this was just a barren piece of desert abandoned to smugglers and scorpions, just a flat spot on the road between Shakespeare and Silver City. Then the railroad came, and a town was birthed like a child untimely born. Now people come and go, live and die in this little place. Insignificant people in an insignificant town. None of us greatly impressing our generation or ourselves.

She let out a deep sigh.

I think too much, El Señor. I know it. Marga always told me so. "You need a husband, big sister! He will fill your life with children, confusion, and challenges. Then you do not have time to think."

Oh, sweet Marga . . . how I miss our talks, our giggles. You were the only one on earth who could make me laugh. It was a horrible day when the Apaches killed you and your Carlos.

Someone staggered out of the saloon next door in the night shadows. She watched him cross the street and wander off to the railroad tracks. A rider came slowly down the street from the east. He stopped his horse in the middle of the street and stared at the saloon next door. He motioned to someone behind him and waited. Two other riders appeared. Hidden in the showroom of the jewelry store, Julianna spied only dim silhouettes.

But it was enough.

A woman? One of them is a woman! She has on men's clothing, but it is a woman.

Julianna scooted across the store to try to follow their progress, but they quickly disappeared into the darkness.

Why would a woman dress like a man and ride straight through town without stopping at two in the morning? Was she fat? Was she pregnant? Was her hair gray? Or white? Or yellow? Or was it just the dim light? There are mysteries all around. I am merely a minor enigma.

Julianna Ortiz dragged an oak rocking chair over to the side of the couch and tugged a huge buffalo robe from the top of the wardrobe closet to line the chair. She sat down and unlaced her high-top shoes.

If you wake up tonight, Mr. DelNorte, you will see bare feet. If you look in a mirror, you will see your forehead stained red with iodine and stitched like a seam on a baseball. I do not think you will wear a hat for a while.

She rocked back and forth. The smooth tile floor felt comfortable and cool to her tired feet. "This would be a nice time to sit and visit. You could tell me about your past, and I would tell you about mine. Why not start by telling me your actual name and why it needs to be such a secret."

She shoved the sleeves of her blouse up past her elbows and folded her hands in her lap.

"Okay, I will start. I was born in El Paso, Texas, on August 29, 1852, to Trubidicio Villa Ortiz and Naomi Parkinson Ortiz. My mother's family was from Georgia by way of New Orleans. They moved to Texas with Mr. Austin. She was Protestant and refused to convert to Catholicism, a fact that often caused her sorrow. As you know, I have a twin brother, Guillermo. My dear precious sister, Margarita, and her husband were killed by Apaches four years ago, and now I raise their son."

She took a big, deep breath and rocked back. "Am I boring you? By all means interrupt me if I seem repetitive. From the time Guillermo and I were three or four, Daddy would take long trips looking for Spanish gold that he was sure was buried in caves. He would take Guillermo with him because my brother could crawl into places my father never could reach. They would be gone for several days or several months—we never knew. Mother sold off her jewelry and furniture to keep us alive during the times he was gone. She hid some of her jewelry so that he would not use it to finance his trips. I do not think he ever forgave her for that.

"The winter I turned nine was very cold, and mother did not have much left to sell. Father had been gone since the second of November. He did not make it home for Christmas or New Year's. Mama took sick on a Friday and died Sunday night. We never knew what it was. Later Marga and I decided she had starved herself just to keep us alive.

"Father did not make it home for the funeral, and we had no way to contact him. A visiting Methodist preacher did the service. He was very comforting, and we knew Mama was in heaven. He let Marga and me stay with his family until he contacted Mama's cousin Ellen in Santa Fe. She came down on the stagecoach and took us home. Her children were grown, but she treated us very well."

She stopped rocking. "DelNorte, do you hear anything I say? Because if I thought you could hear, I would stop immediately."

She rocked back and forth awhile and then dozed. When she woke up, she fanned her sweaty neck. "Now where was I? Oh, yes, we had been with Ellen for three months when my father showed up in Santa Fe without Guillermo. He screamed and yelled at Ellen for 'stealing' his children and demanded that we move with him to Mexico. He said he did not want to take sides in the Civil War, and we would sit it out in Mexico. Ellen cried, but there was nothing she could do. When we got to Mexico, we found that my father had married a woman named Rachel Madera two months before. He knew mother was dead, but he did not come for us until April. He asked us over and over where mother's jewels were. I do not think it ever dawned on him that she had sold them all to feed us.

"Our new stepmother was expecting a child when we arrived, and Father said we could not go to school. We needed to stay home and help her. Then he and Guillermo took off. He came home right before the baby was born, and on Christmas Day my sister and I packed our belongings in a basket and stole across the river. We hiked along the Rio Grande until we got to Santa Fe. We skirted the battle at Valverde and made it into Santa Fe to Ellen's house in time to watch it fall into Confederate hands."

She stopped long enough to study the wounded man's face. "With your Virginia accent, perhaps you were with General Sibley's troops. . . . Father did not come for us after that. Ellen said it was dangerous to move about, and the Southern army might conscript him into service. Marga and I thought he just was not interested in us because we could not produce poor Mama's jewelry.

"Ellen made us write to him every Christmas and on his birthday. Oh, how we hated to write, but we did just to please her. So we grew up in Santa Fe. We went to school there, and Ellen's husband, Paul, taught us both the jewelry business. About the time I turned twenty, I got a long letter from my father. He told me Guillermo was out on his own, working for John Chisum over on the Pecos. His wife, Rachel, had left him and taken their boys—Roberto, Pasquel, and Chappa—with her. The church would not give him a divorce, so he moved to Texas and married a lady named Tullina. They had four girls and lived a hundred miles southwest of El Paso. It was a very chatty letter for a father we had not seen or heard from in ten years.

"We worked for Paul and Ellen in their jewelry store until the Southern Pacific opened this line. Paul said it was a good time to start a new business. He and Ellen helped us open this store. But my blessed Margarita met Carlos and ran away to Socorro to get married. Paco was born a year later, and we all lived in this room for a while. Finally Carlos had a chance to start a jewelry store in Tombstone, Arizona. He and Marga went to check it out and left Paco with me. They never came back."

Tears rolled down her cheeks. She didn't bother drying them as she continued to rock. When she finally opened her eyes, she didn't know if she had slept, but she did know the tears were dry.

She cleared her throat. "Father did not come to Marga's and Carlos's funeral even though I wrote to him. But he did send a beautiful granite marker with their names on it. It is perhaps the finest marker in the cemetery.

"Now he writes once a year, and I write to him. He sends Paco a present on his birthday, but, of course, he never sends anything to me. I have not seen him in over twenty years. Someday perhaps, but not now. Every Christmas Paco and I take off a few days to spend with Ellen and Paul. They sold their store and are talking about moving to San Diego. I have a large family that I do not know. Paul and Ellen are the only ones I feel close to."

This time when she woke up, she could see daylight breaking on the patio. She stepped over and put her hand on DelNorte's forehead. It was blazing hot.

"Now, Mr. Mystery, we will see how clever you are at fighting a fever." She soaked a towel in cool water, wrung it out, and placed it on his forehead. "I trust that will not adversely affect the stitches."

She started a fire in the woodstove and put on a pot of coffee. Then Julianna closed the window in the front of the store and swept the wooden sidewalk outside. Freight wagons bustled at the railroad yard across the street. Two men slept on benches in front of the saloon. She stared down Railroad Avenue to the west.

I have no idea if I dreamed that I saw riders last night or if I actually did. I wonder if they just kept on riding? A woman and two men. They could have gotten here that soon after the train if they had started earlier and taken a shortcut. They could be near the Arizona border by now.

When she reentered the store, she locked the door behind her and closed the curtain between the store and the apartment. She moved the boiling coffeepot to the side of the stove and then studied her sleeping nephew.

I do not believe you moved all night. You are a very tired young man.

Julianna carried a basin of water to the small rawhide table next to the sofa. She resoaked the rag and positioned it back over DelNorte's forehead.

"Now you know everything about Julianna Ortiz, the outlaw's twin sister. Well, not everything. There are some things to be kept secret . . . forever!"

There was a light rap at the backdoor. Julianna stared at her bare feet and then went out into the patio barefoot.

"Julianna, it's me—Gracie Parnell."

She swung open the door, and the telegraph operator burst in with a sheaf of papers. "You look like you slept in your dress," she observed.

"And you look too fresh to have been working all night."

"Has he awakened?"

"No, but he has not died either."

"I thought I heard you speaking to someone."

"I was talking to myself."

"Ah, saying things to him you'd like to say if he were awake, but you don't have the nerve? Hmmmmm." Gracie strolled across the patio.

Julianna scurried behind her. "What do you mean, hmmmmm?"

"Julianna Ortiz, you know perfectly well what I mean," Gracie giggled. She marched into the living quarters and up to the sofa. "He looks better without blood in his hair."

"Do you want to see Lixie's sewing project?" Julianna motioned toward his forehead.

"Heavens no! Leave the towel alone." Gracie glanced around the room. "And how's our Paco?"

Julianna tried to straighten her hair. "He is a sleepyhead. Usually he is up by now."

"And waiting for me to come off shift. Do you have any tea?"

"I have cocoa and coffee. Which would you like?" Julianna asked.

"Both," Gracie replied.

"Together?"

"Yes, my sister says it's quite the rage at the Brazilian Embassy in Washington."

Julianna poured two cups of hot coffee as Gracie plopped down at the table and spread the papers out in front of her. Julianna passed her a cup of coffee and a tin canister. "Here is the chocolate. You can mix your own. What are all the telegrams?"

"Not official telegrams. It was very slow last night, and I did a little snooping."

"Snooping about what?"

Gracie nodded at the man on the couch. "About the mysterious DelNorte."

"Oh?"

"I telegraphed some old friends and found out a few things."

"Like what?"

Gracie sipped the coffee mixture and tapped on one of the papers. "He was born in Virginia. Went to Harvard in the early '60s but didn't graduate until '69 with a degree in—"

"Ancient history. Yes, I already knew that. Did you find out his real name?"

"That is the strangest thing." Gracie took a sip of her drink and grimaced. "There is absolutely no record of any other name anywhere. Just DelNorte. Even his army papers call him DelNorte." She stirred more cocoa into her cup.

Julianna attempted to read the papers upside down. "Which side did he serve on?"

"Both."

Julianna rubbed the back of her neck. "What?"

"It seems he was a spy."

"For which side?"

"Both say he worked for them." Gracie's eyes danced as if giving out Christmas presents. "He was in the North when the war broke out, and the Union sent him back to Virginia to look around.

Seeing that the North would give DelNorte free passage, Jefferson Davis seemed to personally convince him to serve the Confederacy. He was awarded citations for bravery by both sides."

"You found all that out in one night?"

"That's not all. Since the war, he's been working along the border where he has built a reputation as quite a shootist."

"We all know that."

"But right after the war, before he went back to Harvard, he worked at the customhouse in Baltimore and was for a while engaged to—are you ready for this?" Gracie teased.

Julianna held her breath.

"Miss Ramona Hawk," Gracie triumphed.

"What?" Julianna felt her knees weaken. "Ramona Hawk!"

"It seems they met while spying for the Confederacy or double-agenting or something."

"He was engaged to Ramona Hawk!" Julianna mumbled.

"Which reminds me, sweet Julianna, read this." Gracie shoved a yellow telegram toward her.

Julianna held the telegram toward the window. "She—she escaped from prison in Detroit!" she gasped.

"Seems that she was on her way to teach French to the warden's daughters and just disappeared. Someone saw a couple of well-dressed Mexican men near the wall, but it's unknown if they were a part of it."

"Over two weeks ago, and they are just getting word out?"

"The rumor is that they thought they could capture her and get her back in prison before anyone knew she was gone."

"Capture Ramona Hawk?"

"Yes, well, they are naive. And now I have the delightful duty of telling this to Colt. He will be livid."

"And rightfully so," Julianna said.

Gracie folded up the telegram. "I had better take it by the marshal's."

"Tell Marshal Yager to stop by and see me today. I might have some information on Hawk myself," Julianna said.

"You know where she is?"

"Maybe. I thought I heard her voice in El Paso . . . but I'm not sure."

"Once this gets into the newspapers, there will be Ramona Hawk sightings all over the West."

"That is very true. People are still seeing Billy the Kid at cantinas along the border several years after his death."

"I must run along to the marshal's and then relieve Colt from tending a sick baby," Gracie reported. "If it wasn't for the wedding on Saturday, I think he would go on a trail drive just to get some rest."

"I have seen Colt with Ruthie. He makes a wonderful daddy."

"He makes a wonderful everything! I intend to give him more experience with fatherhood. Oh, my word, I can't believe I almost forgot the most important news of all. This isn't an official telegram, but Sparky—that's the third-click telegrapher in El Paso—said that there was an older Mexican gentleman at the depot late last night. He took Sparky over to the waiting room and pointed to the dirt on the floor where someone had written 'Julianna & Paco Ortiz.'"

Julianna laughed. "Yes, Paco practiced writing with his big toe. What did the old man want?"

"He said he wanted to go see his daughter and his grandson, but he was afraid to do so because it had been a very, very long time. He had decided not to buy a ticket and was about to leave, but when he saw those two names in the dust, he knew it was a sign from El Señor because those were the names of his daughter and grandson. Julianna, your father is coming to see you tomorrow!"

Four

The egg yokes crumbled like sawdust.

The coffee tasted bitter.

The ham was blackened and flavorless.

Only Mrs. Martinez's tortillas were edible. Julianna had bought them from the woman next door.

Paco ate three jam-and-butter tortillas and then splashed water on his hands, face, and the floor.

"Can I go see Bonita? I want to tell her about DelNorte!"

"Paco, you cannot tell anyone about him being here."

"But why? He is a very well-known man."

"Yes, and I would think he has enemies who would try to finish him off if they knew he is wounded. You want him to have a chance to recover surely?"

His round brown eyes widened. "Oh, yes. You are right. That is a good reason. For a minute I thought you did not want anyone to know you had a man at your house."

"Paco Carlos Ortiz, I do not want anyone to know. You must understand that my honor and dignity are very important to me. I do not want anyone to be suspicious of my character."

"I know, Aunt Julianna. That is why they call you The Gemstone."

"Call me what? Who calls me that?"

"The men at the saloon. They say, 'Like a gemstone in a glass case, we can only view Señorita Ortiz through the windows of her jewelry store.'"

"They say that?"

"Sometimes."

"Why did you never tell me before?"

Paco shifted from one foot to the other. "I thought you would yell at me and tell me never to go into the saloon again."

"*Niño*, have I ever yelled at you?"

"No, but you have wanted to many times. I have seen it in your eyes." He charged to the doorway. "Can I go see Bonita now?"

"Do not make yourself a pest. Lixie was up most of the night. They might all be very tired."

"You look very tired. Your eyes look old."

"Thank you, young man."

"You are welcome." He flung open the door to the patio.

"And do not talk about DelNorte," she cautioned.

"What if Lixie already told Bonita about him?"

Julianna glanced back at the sleeping man. "Then let Bonita bring up the topic. I want you home by ten o'clock. You need to have a bath."

"Today?" Paco waved his arms. "But it is Thursday! No one takes a bath on Thursday."

"You will. We have company coming."

"Who?"

"You are in a hurry. I will tell you when you come back."

"A bath at ten in the morning? I have never had a bath at ten in the morning in my life!"

"You did for Gracie and Colt's wedding."

"Yes, perhaps for a wedding." Paco changed directions and scurried toward the backdoor. "Tía Julianna, are you going to marry DelNorte?"

She felt her shoulders and neck stiffen. "Why did you ask that? I do not even know the man."

"He is sleeping on your couch."

"Paco Ortiz!"

"You see, your eyes say you want to yell at me right now."

"I will explain things to you when you get your bath. I am not going to marry DelNorte."

"Never?"

"Go see Bonita."

"You did not answer my question."

"Be back by ten, or you will be in hot water."

"Either way I am in hot water. Can I take a tortilla to Bonita?"

"Of course, but I am sure Lixie has fixed them breakfast."

"But she tries to make her own tortillas. They are not very good. She is not as smart as you."

"Yes, I buy mine from Mrs. Martinez next door."

"I will be back by ten."

"And do not go into the saloon."

"I knew you were going to say that."

"Look at my eyes. Do I look like I am about to yell?"

"No, they look very happy that I am leaving before I ask you more questions about DelNorte."

"Paco!"

"Now they want to yell. Good-bye!" He fled out the backdoor, across the small patio, and into the alley.

She walked out on the patio and bolted the alley door behind him. *I know, El Señor, I should have told him about his grandfather coming today. I am still in shock. I do not know what to tell Paco. He knows so little about my father. I never mention him unless Paco asks, and then there is so little to say. Perhaps Paco and I will go to Silver City. I will close the store, and we will run away and hide until he goes home.*

She sauntered back inside and stopped by the man on the couch. She lifted the towel and studied the stitches. "You are no longer bleeding, DelNorte. That is good. It either means Lixie did a good job of sewing you up or that you have no more blood. I trust it is the former. There is no swelling at the seam. I think that is good as well. But your forehead is very hot."

I cannot run away from my father and leave DelNorte. This is getting complicated, El Señor—very, very complicated.

She noticed her hand still lying on the injured man's forehead. She yanked it back, soaked the towel, and replaced it on his head.

"You do not look comfortable, Mr. DelNorte. Your clothes are filthy. You still wear your boots. Your hat and guns are on the table. I do not feel at ease removing anything else; so you will remain a collapsed gunman. I have seen better-looking men passed out on the bench in front of the saloon next door. No, that is not true. I have seen cleaner and neater men passed out in front of the saloon next door."

It took an hour for her to clean the kitchen, wash up, and put on a fresh dress. With her long black hair carefully combed and held behind her ears with silver clips, she opened the store.

The first person through the door wore a suit, vest, and tie. "Good morning, Señorita Ortiz. How is the jewelry store business?"

"I was closed yesterday while I went to El Paso, and I am hoping to make up for it today. How is the newspaper business, Mr. Gorman?"

"Always the same, always hunting for a story. How was El Paso?"

She glanced back at the curtain that separated the back room from the front. "It is growing. Did you know that the wholesale district now covers two entire blocks?"

"How is Guillermo?"

"Why do you ask?"

"He is a local man who runs a business in our town. Now he is in a Mexican jail. That's a story of local interest."

"My brother is a border bandit who got caught. He is alive and wishing very much he was back in Lordsburg."

"Is there any chance of his being released soon?"

"Not that I know of."

"Is he to face a firing squad?"

"I believe that is common knowledge. You printed that fact in *The Outlook* already."

"There is some talk around town by certain elements that a bunch of the boys will ride down there and bust him out of jail. Do you know of these plans?"

"I do not, and I cannot condone any plan that is illegal."

"Off the record, Señorita Ortiz, do you have any plans for helping him yourself?"

"This will not be in the newspaper?"

"No. I promise."

She stepped closer. "I do have one plan for helping my brother," she whispered.

He pulled out his pencil and notebook. "And that is?"

"You said it would be off the record."

He shoved the notebook back into his pocket. "And the plan is?"

"Prayer."

"What?"

This time her voice boomed. "You do believe in prayer surely, Mr. Gorman."

"Yes, I do."

"So do I."

"That's all you are doing?"

"I will pursue every legal, moral, and biblical avenue afforded me."

"Have you enlisted any others to help you 'pray'?"

"I believe so, but you would not want me to divulge their names."

"'Lordsburg Businessman Rots in Mexican Jail While Twin Sister Prays.' I suppose it's a little long for a headline."

"There must be other news."

"I will be forced to write more stories about Lixie Miller's upcoming wedding or the strange death of Sylvia the duck," Gorman mused.

Julianna folded her arms and stared at the large glass case and the silver necklaces. "I thought you would be writing about the latest prison escape of Ramona Hawk."

Peter Gorman dropped his arms. "Hawk escaped? When? What happened?"

"Now I can see you were unaware. Perhaps you should go visit with Marshal Yager and get more details. Gracie Parnell was headed that way with a telegram."

"My word, I trust Ramona Hawk is not headed back to Lordsburg."

"I am surprised at you, Mr. Editor. If Hawk comes back here, think of the great stories it will make."

"'Ramona Hawk Escapes!' Now that's a headline. Señorita Ortiz, you've put a smile on my face."

"Would you like a pair of earrings for your wife? Then you can put a smile on my face," she countered.

"I must return later and look for a brooch. I always get her one for her birthday. She has quite a collection."

"You know, Mr. Gorman, I have never seen your wife wear a brooch."

"Come to think of it, neither have I. I wonder why that is?"

Nobby-Bill Lovelace shoved open the door and stomped in. His clean-shaven face was as round as the bowler he wore. "Well, how is he?" he called out.

Julianna scooted around between the two men. "I was just talking to Mr. Gorman about him. My brother is in good health but much worried about his future. A Mexican jail is not a lovely place to be."

"Your brother?" Nobby-Bill blurted out. "Who's talkin' about—"

"Did you see this brooch, Mr. Lovelace?"

"Brooch? Why would I want to see a brooch? I was talkin' about—Oh! You stabbed me with that thing!"

"I am very sorry."

"She seems to be in a mood to sell brooches," Gorman replied.

Nobby-Bill glanced over at the newspaper editor and then back at Julianna. "Oh . . . your brother! Yes. I reckon he'll be wantin' justice to take place."

"I believe he wants better than justice."

"I have to go find Marshal Yager," Gorman said.

"I seen him over at the depot not more than ten minutes ago," Nobby-Bill reported.

The newspaperman had just hurried out the front door when Julianna heard someone bang on the backdoor.

"Sorry, Miss Ortiz. I almost spilt the beans on DelNorte."

"Please keep it to yourself today while I figure this out."

The pounding at the backdoor continued.

"Is he doing all right?"

"He is still unconscious. Mr. Lovelace, would you watch the store while I open the backdoor? It is probably Paco. Normally I do not lock it, but with a celebrated injured man, I thought it might be safer."

"Yep. I'll watch it for you. Don't you worry about a thing. I ran a store in Grammarton . . . that is, until the town blew up."

The pounding continued as she approached the backdoor. "I am coming," she called out. "Quit pounding. Paco, my eyes will tell you I am very close to yelling at you."

"Yell all you want, but open the door, *hermana*. We would rather not get caught." The voice was deep, anxious.

Julianna leaned her ear to the door. "Roberto?"

"Yes, and Laredo and Jack as well."

"We need to talk to you," a higher-pitched voice called out. "Open the door, *hermana*."

"Just a minute. I need to straighten up a few things."

"What are you waiting for? You would have opened it up quickly if it had been Paco."

"Paco lives here. Just wait."

Julianna raced back into the apartment and grabbed her corset from the dirty clothes basket. She tossed it in the basin of water near the sofa and then wrung it out and stretched it over the back of the oak rocker near the backdoor. She closed the door behind her and scurried across the patio.

She took a deep breath, tossed her hair back over her shoulders, and swung open the door. Laredo Nisqually, Roberto Alvarez, and Jack Burkeman shoved their way into the patio.

"What took you so long, *hermana?*" Roberto asked.

"I have a customer in the store. Remember, I do have a business to run."

"We will wait in your apartment. It is more private," Laredo said.

"You will wait right here in the patio," she demanded.

Burkeman glanced toward the doorway. "Are you hiding something in there?"

"Yes. My undergarments are hanging to dry. I will not have the likes of you three gawking at them!"

"I've seen undergarments before," Burkeman said.

"You have not seen mine," she snapped. "What do you want?"

"We have bad news. When we got to Hachita, we found out that my cousin and the Iturbe brothers did not kill DelNorte after all," Roberto reported.

Julianna noticed a bruise on his jaw. "Why does that not surprise me?"

"He left them tied upside down to trees. I believe he is part Apache," Nisqually complained.

"If he were Apache, he would have hung them by their heels instead of letting their shoulders rest on the ground and would have built a fire under their heads. They would not still be alive in some Mexican jail, no doubt. What does this have to do with me?"

"How did you know their shoulders were on the ground?" Burkeman quizzed.

"Was I right or not?"

"You didn't answer my question," Burkeman probed.

"Nor did you answer mine. Why are you here?"

"We wanted to warn you about him," Nisqually insisted.

"I am not the one running from DelNorte; so what do I care?"

"But you talked to him coming out of the alley. Perhaps he will try to contact you," Roberto added.

"If that is true, then you do not want to be here," she said.

"Aye, but we risk it just to warn you," Laredo insisted.

"That is hogwash, and we all know it." Julianna folded her arms and stared at the six-foot-tall Roberto Alvarez. "What do you really want?"

"We need you to lend us a little cash for some groceries," he muttered.

Julianna paced the small patio. "You had DelNorte's silver when I saw you last."

"Yes, well . . . we had a slight difficulty when we got to Hachita." Roberto had dirt and sweat smeared across his forehead.

"They stole our poke," Laredo said. "I mean, DelNorte's poke."

"There was a gunfight, and we were nearly out of bullets," Jack Burkeman reported. "If we had had more cartridges, we could have stood 'em down."

"Yet you escaped?"

"Our horses were too fast," Roberto explained.

"You are luckier than most," she remarked.

Laredo rubbed his narrow, pointed chin. "Yes, I have friends in Hachita."

"It was your friends that robbed us!" Burkeman fumed.

"Yeah, but they did not shoot us in the back!" Laredo countered.

Julianna tugged on her earrings and then bit her lip. "I will not give you money that you have not earned. You know better than to ask for that."

"Just a meal and a place to stay until dark, *hermana*," Roberto pleaded. "After that we can be on our way."

"You cannot stay here. I cannot have you endangering Paco and me."

"*Hermana*, you worry too much." Roberto stepped toward her. She stepped away. "We will just stay here on the patio. Perhaps you could bring us something to eat. Then we can all decide how to get Guillermo out of jail."

"You will have to leave after you eat. I have a business to run. I will not have you out here."

"Señorita Ortiz?" The voice was muted as it filtered down from the front of the store.

Jack Burkeman drew his revolver. "Who's that?"

"It is my customer. Remember? I must go take care of him."

"We will wait here," Roberto said.

"If we waited inside, we could fix our own meal," Laredo suggested.

"You will wait back here. I will bring you something to eat as soon as I deal with this customer. The first man who sticks his head inside that door will be shot, and no one in this town will fault me for it."

She closed the door behind her and trotted up to the front of the store. "Nobby-Bill, is everything all right?"

"Who was at the backdoor?" he asked.

"Some drifters wanting a handout."

"Mrs. Sinclair gets that type at the boardinghouse all the time. She makes them shovel out the yard and wait by the side door. If she has food left over after a meal, she feeds them."

"Why did you holler at me?"

"I made you a sale and didn't know what to do with the money." He handed her a ten-dollar bill.

"My goodness, what did you sell?"

He rocked back on his heels with a wide smile. "One of them rings."

"A ten-dollar ring? Which ring?"

"In that glass case by the front door."

"Show me."

She followed the short man to the front of the store.

"Right there. It was silver and turquoise, sort of like that one."

She pulled out the oak tray lined with red wool felt. "Those are not ten-dollar rings. They are one-dollar rings. Look, right on top of the tray—'$1.00.'"

"Well, I'll be. I must have been in a hurry. I thought for sure it said '$10.00' That must have been why the man seemed a little taken back."

She shoved the tray back into the glass case and pressed her fingertips hard on her temples. "I can't believe this. I was gone for a minute, and you overcharged a customer by 1,000 percent."

Nobby-Bill rubbed his chin. "I guess I'm a natural-born salesman."

She waved the ten-dollar bill in front of him. "I have to return the man's money to him."

"That won't be all that difficult. He's coming back in a few minutes. He's the new reverend staying at the Holdens. At least he hopes to be the new reverend. Seems like a pleasant fellow."

The air in the store reeked of burned ham. "The reverend is coming back by here?" Julianna propped the front door open.

"Yep. He said he wanted to meet all the folks in the church before he makes his final decision about coming here."

"And he is coming back this morning?"

"Yep. He and the missus was goin' to step down and introduce themselves to some others and then come back here."

"His wife is with him?"

"Yep. A very smart-lookin' lady, but she could use some color in the cheeks and some lipstick and put on about fifty pounds. Maybe some earrings would help. You might offer her some suggestions. We wouldn't want folks to think that only sour-lookin' ladies go to church, would we? Did you want me to stick around a bit and help out some more with the store?"

"I believe you have done plenty."

"You know, that's exactly what they told me when Grammarton blew up. You don't have to thank me, Señorita Ortiz. I didn't have much else to do this mornin'." He meandered to the open door.

Julianna caught his sleeve. "Wait. On second thought, just watch the store for a few minutes more. I need to go feed those drifters. I will feel more confident with you here."

"Yes, ma'am. Be happy to oblige. I reckon there are some times when it's nice to have a man around the place."

And there are some times when there are too many men around the place. "Be sure and check the price carefully if you sell anything."

"Don't worry. Nobby-Bill Lovelace don't make the same mistake twice. Except maybe last Tuesday," he mumbled.

"I'll be right back." Julianna buzzed into the kitchen area and grabbed up the stack of tortillas. She tossed them into a basket, along with two airtight cans of California peaches, some wild cherry jam, and a thick hunk of ham. She carried them past DelNorte and through the door to the patio.

"Did that customer leave?" Roberto asked.

"Not yet. Please keep your voices down. Here is some food. Take it with you and leave."

"We can just eat it here," Laredo insisted.

"I want you to leave."

"But we can't go traipsin' out in public carryin' a little Sunday school basket of fixin's," Burkeman protested.

"Then hurry and eat and leave."

Alvarez drew his knife and sliced off a large wedge of ham. "But we have not come up with a plan yet to help Guillermo."

"I told you I would not be a part of something illegal."

"Who said it had to be illegal?" Alvarez mumbled. "If you think of something legal, we are even open to try that."

"How wonderful of you."

"Do you have any beans?" Laredo asked.

"None that are soaked."

"Thank you, *hermana*, we knew we could count on you. We always thought of you as part of the gang, you know." Roberto flashed his dimpled smile.

"I was never, ever a part of anything you did."

Roberto bowed toward her. "That is true, but we think of you that way nonetheless."

Julianna retreated into the apartment and shut the door behind her. This time when she passed the unconscious gunman, she scooted the rocking chairs next to the sofa and draped the big buffalo robe over them so that anyone standing in either doorway could not see who was lying there. She then pulled out a couple of petticoats and stretched them out next to the corset.

Mr. DelNorte, I am not sure what you will think if you wake up. Perhaps it is best for you to stay unconscious for a while longer.

"Señorita Ortiz, you have company!" Nobby-Bill called out.

She brushed down the front of her dress and sashayed out to the store. A thin, blond-haired man wearing a dark suit stood at the front counter. Next to him a pale, tiny woman with sunken cheeks, straight auburn hair tucked up under a straw hat, and friendly green eyes stared at her.

"Señorita Ortiz, let me introduce you to Rev. and Mrs. Howitt," Nobby-Bill said.

"Oh, my," Mrs. Howitt stammered, "you are so . . ."

Julianna raised her eyebrows. "Mexican?"

"Eh, it's just that we have never met a Mexican of the Protestant faith before," the reverend explained.

"I was unaware that El Señor made ethnic distinctions."

"Oh, heavens, no," the reverend said apologetically. "I'm sorry. I only meant that in our sheltered town in Wisconsin, we had no members of your race. One of the reasons we want to move to New Mexico is because of the ethnic mixture."

The small woman held out her hand. "Señorita Ortiz, we are honored to make your acquaintance. Please accept our apology."

Julianna shook the woman's hand. It was cold but very strong.

"Let us start this over," the man said. "I am Rev. Luke Howitt. And this lovely woman is my wife, Posey."

"And I am Julianna Ortiz, and I owe you nine dollars."

"For the ring?" Mrs. Howitt probed.

"Yep, and it's all my fault, folks," Nobby-Bill confessed. "I read the tag wrong. I don't really work here. I was just helpin' out Señorita Ortiz while she . . ."

Julianna cleared her throat.

"While she was occupied with other business."

Julianna counted out nine silver dollars to the preacher.

"We thought there was a mistake but hesitated to ask, being so new in town. We thought perhaps . . ."

"That Mexicans count money differently?" Julianna smiled.

"Now we are never going to live down that comment, are we?" Howitt said.

"If I tease you about it, that means you are totally forgiven," Julianna explained.

"You are very gracious, as I would expect of your kind," Mrs. Howitt replied.

Posey, dear, you keep sticking your tiny, little shoe in your mouth. "What is your opinion of Lordsburg?"

"It is very, eh, rural," the man declared.

"The words *isolated* and *remote* come to mind," Julianna said.

"Indeed." Howitt nodded. "But I think this might be an ideal place for us. You can't tell, I'm sure, but my sweet Posey is a sick girl. The doctor said the dry climate would be good for her health."

"If you want a dry climate, you came to the right place," Nobby-Bill blurted out. "In Lordsburg we have to save up all week just to spit on Saturday night."

The Howitts stared at the bald-headed man.

"That was jist a figure of speech, folks. No offense," Nobby-Bill quickly amended.

"Do you have children?" Julianna asked.

Mrs. Howitt wrung her hands. "No, not yet."

The preacher slipped his hand around his wife's waist. "But there is plenty of time for the Lord to provide."

"Señorita Ortiz has a nine-year-old," Nobby-Bill declared.

Nobby-Bill, did the devil send you here to harass me? "I am raising my nephew Paco," she explained.

"Her sister Margarita and her husband was massacred by a band of renegade Indians," Nobby-Bill offered.

Posey Howitt's frail hand covered her narrow mouth. "Oh, dear!"

"When was that, Señorita Ortiz?" Rev. Howitt probed.

"About five years ago."

"Don't worry, ma'am, that was across the line in Arizona Territory," Nobby-Bill assured her. "Shoot, we ain't had Apache trouble over here in a couple years, not countin' last month."

"What happened last month?" Mrs. Howitt asked.

"Don't mind me; I talk too much. Think I'll go over and look at them silver conchos."

"The people seem so very nice here," Posey Howitt declared.

"Who have you met so far?" Julianna asked.

"We met the Holdens just briefly before they left for California. They graciously let us use their house even though they are Episcopalians."

"The Holdens might be the most hospitable people in America. We are thinking about making them honorary Mexicans," Julianna declared.

The Howitts stared at her.

"That was a joke."

"Oh, yes!" Howitt smiled. "Then we had supper with Elizabeth

Miller. She is such a jewel. She is not like the newspapers in the East make her out to be at all."

"And we met her Jefferson Carter," Posey Howitt continued. "My, he is such a gentleman. Rev. Howitt will marry them on Saturday."

"My Paco is the ring bearer, and Lixie's Bonita will be the flower girl."

"Is Bonita an Apache Indian?" Mrs. Howitt inquired.

"Yes, she is."

"But she seems like such a delightful, ordinary child."

"Children have a way of destroying conventional images."

"Quite so," Howitt said. "And we just finished a late breakfast with Mr. and Mrs. Parnell. Their little Ruthie is such a cutie. Did you know that up until his sudden illness forced him to retire, Ruthie's grandfather was a U.S. senator from Iowa?"

Rev. Howitt, he is Ruthie's father, not grandfather, and it is that fact that caused his sudden "retirement." "Gracie is a wonderful friend. She worked all last night, you know."

"Yes. The women of this town are all so interesting. It's quite different from boring, little Plainfield, Wisconsin."

Mrs. Howitt, you have met the Belles of Lordsburg. They are different from any women in the entire country. "I am happy to be here. It is the place El Señor wants me to be."

"We are hoping it's where He wants us to be as well," the preacher added.

"Please forgive me for not inviting you into my home at the back of the store. It is washday, and . . . well . . ."

Mrs. Howitt nodded. "You have some delicate things hanging out to dry? I understand completely. On such days I make Luke take his tea on the front porch!"

Your own husband? I do not think I am called to be a preacher's wife. "Next time you will have to have supper with Paco and me," Julianna insisted.

"Oh, yes," Mrs. Howitt beamed.

"I trust you like Mexican food." Julianna studied the frail

woman's expression. "I do not know why, but I have this special fondness for Mexican food."

Posey Howitt began to giggle. "You're teasing me again, Julianna!"

"Yes, and you are taking it very well, Posey."

"I like you, Julianna. I'm glad we met."

Nobby-Bill wandered back over. "Did you know Señorita Ortiz has the nicest jewelry store between El Paso and Tombstone?"

"I have the only jewelry store between El Paso and Tombstone."

A deep voice rolled out from the back of the store. "Señorita Ortiz, we need to see you for a moment."

"Julianna has panhandlers at the backdoor," Nobby-Bill explained.

"Panhandlers on wash day?"

"I have a small patio on the alley. Some transients without food or money came by and wanted a meal. I feel that it is my Christian duty to assist, don't you, Reverend?"

"Yes, quite so. A cup of cold water in His name," he replied.

"I will be just a moment. Please look around. I try to specialize in Indian and early Spanish period New Mexico jewelry. Some say this is more a museum than a store."

Julianna grabbed up three pottery handleless mugs and the coffeepot. The backdoor to the patio was open, but no one was near it.

"I do not appreciate your opening my backdoor."

"We called, and you did not answer," Laredo tried to explain.

"Here is some coffee. You really need to be going."

Roberto shrugged. "Where are we going to go?"

"That is of no consequence to me."

Jack Burkeman took a slurp of coffee and wiped his mouth on his sleeve. "If we are not around, who will help you with Guillermo?"

Julianna rubbed the dust from the corners of her eyes. "We have had this conversation a hundred times before."

"But what if we go back and convince the Federales that if they release Guillermo, we will lead them to Geronimo's camp in the

Sierra Madres? The Mexican government would do almost any-thing to capture that ol' Apache," Roberto suggested.

"Do you know where Geronimo is camped?" she asked.

"Of course not. But you could be waiting for us there with a relay of horses, and we could make a break for the border. The Federales get lost easily in the Sierra Madres."

"This is your 'legal' plan?"

"Perhaps *legal* is not the right word. This is the plan that requires no dynamite or gunfire . . . perhaps."

"When you finish eating, please leave and close the backdoor."

"You are abandoning us, *hermana?*" Burkeman pressed.

"Even a mother sparrow kicks her young out and makes them fly on their own."

"We should have stayed in Mexico," Laredo complained.

Burkeman finished off his cup of coffee. "If you hadn't taken DelNorte's poke, we would still be there."

"And we would be broke," Laredo said.

"We are broke," Burkeman replied. "But at least DelNorte wouldn't be looking for us."

"That is true." Laredo Nisqually shrugged.

"When you three little birds finish your worms, leave my tree," she demanded.

Julianna had turned toward the apartment when the alley door was flung open, and Bonita sprinted in, followed by Paco.

"I won!" Bonita shouted.

"You cheated!"

"I did not."

"I said, 'No alleys.'"

"That is not an alley. It is a street."

"It is not!"

"There are businesses on it."

"They are alley businesses, not street businesses." Paco's eyes darted to the men. Bonita scurried behind Julianna's skirt. "What are they doin' here?" he asked.

"Paco, is that any way to talk to your favorite uncle's best friends?" Laredo roared.

Roberto Alvarez pointed to the hidden Bonita. "Niño, you have a girlfriend now?"

Bonita stuck her tongue out at Paco.

"She is not my girlfriend," he reported. "She is my friend."

"That explains it," Jack Burkeman hooted.

"You children go inside."

"But you have personals hanging on that buffalo robe," Burkeman said.

"And you are to hurry, finish eating, and leave."

Julianna entered the apartment and closed the door behind her. When she got to the sofa, Bonita and Paco were staring at the injured man.

"Bonita wants to see the stitches."

Julianna pulled off the towel and resoaked it in the basin.

"I have seen this man before," Bonita announced.

Julianna wrung out the towel and draped it back on his head. "Where, honey?"

"In the Sierra Madre Mountains. He is a brave man."

"Why do you say that?"

"He carried a white flag to visit my grandfather without bringing a gun."

"Why did he do that?"

"And he gave my grandfather a ribbon with a medal. It was his favorite. Grandfather always had it around his neck. When he was killed, someone stole his medal," Bonita reported.

"Are you sure the man with the flag was this man?"

"Yes. Grandfather called him the 'young-old man' because of his gray hair. Is he going to die?"

"I hope not."

"Is Paco really going to take a bath now?" Bonita giggled.

"Not with you here!" he squealed.

"I am afraid things got very hectic here. There will be no bath this morning."

Paco hopped excitedly around the dining room chair. "That is an answer to prayer."

"But you have to wash your face, neck, arms, and feet."

"Maybe it is only half an answer to prayer."

"Paco, you clean up and stay here. I need to talk to you as soon as I finish visiting with Rev. and Mrs. Howitt."

"They are here?" Bonita asked.

"Yes, out front in the store."

"She is very skinny, like my mother right before she died," Bonita said.

Julianna stared at the girl's emotionless brown eyes.

Dear Bonita, you and I have so very much in common. You, me, and Paco. We have all lost our mothers much too soon. "Bonita, you watch him closely and make sure he scrubs with soap."

"Soap? You did not say I had to use soap," Paco whined.

Julianna dashed back into the showroom. "I am sorry, but Paco came home, and I had to get him to clean up."

"Julianna, I have a question I would like to ask," Posey Howitt ventured. "And I'm sincerely hoping it doesn't sound as thoughtless as some of my others."

"You want to know why I speak English without an accent and yet call the Lord El Señor?"

"Yes, you are right."

"My mother was an American. She told my father that she would not have Spanish spoken around the house, though she was quite fluent in it. Her only exception was to call the Lord El Señor. Somehow that appeased my father. But enough about my family. I will tell you more when you come to have supper with me."

"We will look forward to it." Rev. Howitt pulled out a small beige notepad from his vest pocket. "Now we must be off." He studied the notes. "We are scheduled to have tea and cookies with a Mrs. Sinclair and her son Buddy."

"Her son?" Nobby-Bill hooted. "Buddy is her pig!"

"Pig?" Mrs. Howitt gasped.

"He is quite the town character," Julianna informed them. "I am surprised you have not met him yet."

"Last November he got fourteen votes for mayor," Nobby-Bill reported.

"A p-pig?" Mrs. Howitt stammered.

"But Lixie—I mean, Mrs. Miller distinctly said we would have coffee with Mrs. Sinclair and Buddy," the preacher interjected.

"I do believe he likes coffee. Am I right, Nobby-Bill?"

"Yep, and you ought to see him dunk those little, round sugar cookies. Kind of cute—that little grunt he makes when he sinks his chops into them. Course, if he gets coffee up his nose and sneezes, it can be quite a mess. I remember one time . . ."

"Nobby-Bill, do not tell all of Buddy's secrets," Julianna cautioned. "Let Rev. and Mrs. Howitt discover a few for themselves."

"A pig?" Posey Howitt continued to mumble.

Just then a gray-haired man with drooping gray mustache burst through the door and strode over to Julianna. "Rumor has it you might have some information about Ramona Hawk."

"She's in a Detroit prison, Marshal," Nobby-Bill declared.

"There is a real Ramona Hawk?" Posey Howitt asked. "I thought she was just a character out of novels, like . . . like . . . Stuart Brannon."

The marshal, Nobby-Bill, and Julianna stared in disbelief at the preacher's wife.

"Mr. Brannon is a real person, dear," Rev. Howitt lectured, "although some of the stories are slightly stretched."

"What do you know about Hawk?" Marshal Yager asked.

Julianna held her laced fingers to her lips and tasted ham. "I believe it was Ramona Hawk who robbed a jewelry warehouse in El Paso yesterday."

"You saw her?" the marshal pressed.

"I saw nothing. I was in Fieldman's during a holdup and felt the barrel of a revolver across my head. I heard her laugh, and I know it was Hawk. I have heard that laugh before."

"Could Fieldman identify her?" the marshal continued.

"Put a blonde wig on her and wrap a pillow around that tiny waist of hers, and he could. At the time I did not know she had escaped; so I was puzzled by her voice. Now I am sure it was her."

"Do you think she'll be coming back here?" Nobby-Bill pressed.

"If she wants revenge, this is the place to come," the marshal reported. "She's not above shooting someone in the back."

Mrs. Howitt clutched her husband's arm.

"Sorry to frighten you, ma'am." Yager tipped his hat. "There's nothin' for you to worry about. Ramona Hawk is no threat unless you are rich or you crossed her."

A high-pitched scream from the apartment sent Julianna bounding into the back room. The big buffalo robe was stretched over the rocking chairs and flopped over the back of the sofa, making a tent that completely covered DelNorte.

Alvarez, Nisqually, and Burkeman stood just inside the backdoor. They and the marshal stared each other down.

Julianna hurried to Bonita, who sprawled on the tile floor, soaking wet.

"What happened?" Julianna asked.

"Paco poured the pan of cold water over me!"

He stuck his head out from the buffalo tent. "She was peeking at me."

"But you were just washing your face."

"And my feet."

"Julianna told me to make sure he did a good job," Bonita sobbed.

"You could wait and inspect me when I am finished," Paco said from inside the robe tent.

"Do you still have your duckings on?" Julianna asked.

"Of course!" he shouted.

Alvarez laughed. "He is a very modest fellow."

Julianna grabbed a cotton towel to wipe off Bonita's face.

Marshal Yager rubbed his chin and glared at Roberto and the others. "What are you three doing here?"

"I believe Señorita Ortiz was feeding the hungry," Rev. Howitt offered.

"We heard that Julianna's brother was arrested in Mexico. We were checking up on his health," Laredo declared.

"Ain't that nice of you? They say he had three accomplices in that freight wagon holdup. You wouldn't happen to know who was with him?"

"Now, Marshal Yager, you ain't a Federale; so what difference does it make to you? We don't even know who he's with right now."

"He's with murderers and cutthroats in a Mexican jail," Julianna replied.

"Okay, now you heard how he's doin'. I want you three to leave," the marshal insisted.

Julianna dropped down to her knees and continued to dry Bonita's thick hair.

"He shouldn't have poured water on me," Bonita whimpered.

"No, he shouldn't."

"I want you three to leave now," the marshal called out.

"Paco, tell Bonita you are sorry."

"You got no cause to run us out of Lordsburg, Marshal," Roberto protested.

Paco's response was faint, yet distinct. "I am sorry!"

"You three hang around much longer, and I'll think of a cause. Now go on!" The marshal marched straight through the apartment toward the men. "I'll make sure you can find your way out."

"Can I come into your lodge now?" Bonita called out.

"Yes," Paco replied.

Bonita giggled and dove under the buffalo robe.

Nobby-Bill offered Julianna his hand as she stood back up.

"It looks like another crisis is averted." Posey Howitt smiled.

"Yes, if only all the troubles of the world resolved themselves so quickly," Julianna agreed.

"She has the sweetest smile for an Indian girl," Mrs. Howitt added. "It's almost angelic."

"She hits like the devil!" Paco shouted from under the buffalo robe.

"We need to be off to Mrs. Sinclair's boardinghouse," Rev. Howitt announced.

"I'll walk with you," Nobby-Bill offered. "That's where I live."

"Oh, delightful," Rev. Howitt said. "You can introduce us."

"Say hello to Buddy for me," Julianna said. "If he comes by later, I will have some scraps for him."

"He'll be delighted to hear the news," Nobby-Bill remarked.

"No, he won't. Aunt Julianna burned the ham," Paco called out.

Julianna gathered up her petticoats and corset that had fallen to the floor during the tent-building. She folded them just as Nobby-Bill stuck his head back inside the curtained doorway. "You got a customer out here, Señorita Ortiz."

"Tell them I will be right there."

She continued to fold her clothes. "Paco, you and Bonita fold up the buffalo robe. It will be too warm for DelNorte."

"I will fold it up myself," Bonita called out. "It is a woman's job."

"You are not a woman," Paco declared.

"I am too," Bonita shot back.

"Hush, you two. I have a customer to take care of."

He was a tall, thin Mexican man in a suit too big for him and worn brown boots. His gray hair was neatly trimmed, as was his mustache. He had the look of one with a recent haircut and shave. His brown eyes were narrow, almost sunken, his chin pointed, his shoulders rounded, and yet his back was straight. His fingers were yellowed from tobacco. His face was lined with wrinkles—deep brown wrinkles.

"Hello, Julianna, you look quite lovely."

She took a long, deep breath and held it. She clutched her fingers until her knuckles were white.

"Hello, Papa . . . you look quite old."

Five

"Are you angry with me?"

"You haven't seen me in twenty years, and that is the first thing you say?"

"You look angry."

"Papa, how do you know how I look when I'm angry? I was angry when you stayed away all winter and let the sweetest woman on earth starve to death. I was angry when you were not there at her funeral. I was angry when you showed up pretending to care for us when all you wanted was Mama's jewels. I was angry when you abandoned us again with a bitter woman we hardly knew in Mexico. I was angry when Marga and I had to hike all the way to Santa Fe, sleeping on the cold ground at night and eating stolen raw eggs and corn to survive. I was angry every time someone asked what had happened to my mother and father, and I would run into the other room and cry all night because I could not tell them. I was angry when you did not come to our precious Marga's funeral even though I begged you. I was angry when I looked into Guillermo's remorseless eyes and wondered how you could have turned him into such a person, when we both started life in the womb of a wonderful Christian lady. Those were the days I was angry, Papa!"

"I am glad you are not angry today."

Julianna bit her lip. *For twenty years I have rehearsed what to say when I see him, and now I cannot remember the script! El Señor, help me say the right thing. Perhaps I have already said too much.* She rocked back and forth, clutching her waist.

The old man cleared his throat. His small dark eyes searched the room. His black tie hung loose around a shirt collar two sizes too big for his neck. His left hand was gnarled, fingers cramped against his palm.

He rubbed his narrow lips. "Are you going to say nothing else, niña?"

She took a deep breath. "There is nothing left to say. Perhaps the days for saying things has past."

The old man stared down at the top of his scruffy brown boots. "I sent a stone for Margarita's grave. It was the best one I could afford."

"It is a very beautiful marker. It is the finest in the cemetery. I thank you for that sacrifice."

For several moments Julianna stared out the window at Railroad Avenue, biting her lip. She could feel her eyes starting to tear, but she sucked in a deep breath and held it. When she glanced back, the old man's mouth was open, as if to speak, but no words came out. His shoulders slumped. His head hung down. He raised his thin hands and let them fall to his side.

She turned and threw her arms around his bony shoulders and sobbed.

Weak, timid arms held her as her tears flowed down on his dusty wool suit. *Within two minutes I have done and said everything I promised I would never do or say. The only thing I have not done is beg him to love me. This is horrible. Julianna Naomi Ortiz, you are not twelve years old. You are thirty-two.*

She stepped back. He instantly released her.

"Now I am glad I came," he said. "I knew the names at the depot were a sign from El Señor."

Julianna wiped the tears from her cheeks with her fingertips. "Actually they were a sign from Paco's left big toe."

"There are big brown eyes watching us from behind the curtain at the doorway," Mr. Ortiz said.

Julianna continued to wipe her eyes. "Oh, it is Paco!"

The old man cleared his throat again. "My grandson wears a dress over his jeans?"

Julianna spun around, saw the curtain wave, and heard receding footsteps. "That is Paco's friend Bonita."

"She looks Apache."

"Yes, but she graciously condescends to have a few Mexican friends. Come, let me introduce you." She started for the curtained doorway.

He gazed around as he strolled. "You have a very nice store."

"Uncle Paul and Aunt Ellen taught me well."

He peered into a glass case of silver belt buckles. "It was right for them to raise you. You would never have this if you had been with me."

She paused at the green-curtained doorway. "Papa, I need to say something before we take another step. I will try to be gracious today. I will try to treat you with honor because it is one of the commandments. I will feed you and let you drink my chocolate. But I will not lend you money. If you came here merely to get me to give you money, would you please leave right now."

He shook his head. "No, I did not."

"If you ask me for money, I will make you leave, and I will never see you for the rest of your life."

"I did not come to ask for your money."

"I needed to know that." She led him to the back room. "Well, this is my home." *DelNorte! I forgot about DelNorte.*

"You have a buffalo lodge inside the house?"

"The children are playing. Paco?"

A shaggy head popped out from the buffalo robe flap.

"Paco, this is my father and your Grandfather Ortiz."

"Hi." He faked a grin.

"Hello, *niño*," the old man replied.

"Good-bye."

"*Adios.*"

Paco's head was instantly replaced by one with thick, long black hair and straight white teeth.

"Bonita, this is Paco's Grandfather Ortiz."

"*Hola, niña*," he said.

"You are very old," she blurted out.

"Yes, I am."

"My grandfather is dead."

"I am sorry to hear that."

Bonita showed no expression on her round brown face. "He was killed by Mexicans."

"I am doubly sorry for that."

Bonita's head disappeared into the buffalo robe tent to a chorus of giggles.

"I think Paco needs a little time for this to sink in," Julianna said.

She sat her father across the table and served him thick, dark chocolate.

"How long do you plan to be here?" she asked.

"Would you like for me to leave now?" he replied.

"Papa, I do not know why you are here."

"Can we have some chocolate too?" Paco yelled from under the buffalo robe.

"You will have to come drink it at the table."

Paco scampered out, followed by Bonita. They sat on both sides of Julianna as she poured them some chocolate.

"Are you really my grandfather?" Paco questioned.

"Yes, your mother, Margarita, was my daughter."

"But my mother was pretty."

Mr. Ortiz laughed. "You are right. I am not pretty. Your mother looked like her mother."

"I look like my father. Isn't that right, Aunt Julianna?"

"Yes, you do. And Carlos was a very handsome man indeed."

"Did you know my father?" Paco attempted to lick chocolate foam off his upper lip.

"No, I did not know your father."

"Where do you live?"

"In the Sierra Hueco mountains east of El Paso."

"We were in El Paso yesterday."

"I know."

"The next time we are in El Paso, can we come to your house and visit you?"

"Paco!" Julianna cautioned.

"Can Bonita and me go to the depot and look for bandits?"

She took a deep breath. "Yes, that would be fine. Wipe your lips off."

The children ran to the backdoor.

"Good-bye, Grandfather Ortiz," Paco shouted.

"Good-bye, Grandfather Ortiz," Bonita giggled.

"*Adios, niño . . . niña.*"

He slowly finished sipping his chocolate. Neither spoke for several moments.

"What do you see when you look at me, Julianna?"

"A tired, old man."

His narrow, sunken brown eyes lowered. "When I look in a mirror, what I see is a failure. I do not look at mirrors much anymore. But when I look at you, I see success."

"Papa, I have worked very, very hard to get what I have."

"I am sure you did."

"I have sacrificed much in order to be independent and in control. It is not easy to succeed."

"Sometimes it is not easy to fail either. Julianna, I will not chronicle my failures as your father. We both know those quite well. Nor will I tell of how I have failed two other families that call me Papa as well. There are no excuses for my behavior. There are reasons but no excuses."

"Why did you show up now, after all these years? Why did you not let me know you were coming?"

"I did not warn you because I was afraid you would leave town just to avoid me."

"Yes, I might have done that."

"I came because of Guillermo."

Julianna sighed. Her shoulders slumped. *I should have known, Papa, that you did not come to see me. I was never important enough in your life to warrant a visit.* "We both know he is in jail waiting for the firing squad. We both know that he has spent his life in reckless pursuit of lawlessness. So what is there to discuss?"

"Have you seen him in prison?"

"I just got back. Have you gone to see him?"

The old man dropped his head. "I have not seen him in five years."

"Guadalupe is not too far from you. You should go and see him."

"Yes, that is what I want to do. I need you to come with me."

"Why, Papa? You have not needed me for thirty years."

"I need you now."

"Your present wife can go with you."

"She detests Guillermo."

"You have other daughters now."

"They refuse to go into Mexico."

Julianna stared across the room at the homemade buffalo robe tent. "There is nothing we can do for him."

"I know." Mr. Ortiz's voice cracked like a dry twig under a wagon wheel. "I want to see him one last time. There are things I need to tell him."

She felt her neck stiffen. "You were not there one last time for Mama. You were not there one last time for Marga. But you want to be there for your outlaw son?"

"Julianna, the weight of my mistakes and sins and failures crushes my spirit with every breath I take. I do not think I could live if I added to the burden."

She tapped her fingers on the tabletop.

"Will you go with me to see Guillermo?"

She bit her lip and looked away. "I will think about it."

"Sometimes the Federales move up an execution date."

She dusted the tabletop with her hand. "Yes, I know."

"I do not think we should postpone this too long."

"Papa, this is really too much for me to consider quickly. I must have some time."

"Yes." He stood up. "I will wait. The train does not leave for El Paso until 6:00 P.M."

"Where will you go now?"

"I want to give you some time to think. I have thought about this much in the past few weeks. So I will go to the depot, sit in the shade, and help the children look for *banditos*."

She walked him out into the showroom. "Paco is a very smart young man."

"I would expect nothing less."

"I cannot promise that I will have an answer for you by 6:00 P.M."

"I know."

She reached out and took his hand. It was bony and cold. They continued to stroll toward the front door. "*Niña*, none of this is easy for me either. I know your anger is well founded. I have explained every failure of mine to you a thousand times in my mind over the past twenty years."

"Papa, it would have helped me to hear it even once."

"It is too late for explanations." He shuffled out into the dusty dirt street and waited for a freight wagon pulled by eight mules to pass.

Julianna stood in the doorway and watched the old man. "I close the store between one and three. *Siesta*, you know. Would you like to have lunch with me?" she blurted out.

He looked up with a grin that revealed tobacco-yellowed teeth. "I would like that."

"Let's meet at 1:30 at the Sonoran Hotel. They have a good cook from Monterey. It is too warm for me to fire up the stove."

"I will buy our lunch. Don't worry, *niña*, I have a little money. I bought a new suit, and I will buy lunch."

She was watching him climb the steps to the train platform when the stagecoach from Silver City pulled in. Three of the eleven passengers headed straight for her store. It took an hour for them to conclude their purchases and leave.

Julianna buzzed into the apartment. "Well, Mr. DelNorte, I trust you have not baked in that buffalo sweat lodge. My life is usually not this hectic. My life is never this hectic. Let me pull off the robe and check your wounds."

She yanked back the heavy buffalo robe. The couch was empty. "But . . . I . . . you . . ."

He cannot be gone. He was here. He cannot get up. He . . . this . . .

She rushed out into the patio and spied the door to the alley wide open.

"He left?" She walked to the door and looked up and down the empty alley. "He woke up and just left? He cannot do that to me. El Señor, I do not understand. I tend his wounds, sit up the night with him, protect him, and hide him, and he just wakes up and leaves?"

She stepped out into the alley. "DelNorte, I had some things to discuss with you," she called out.

The voice was soft, fresh, like the first breeze of fall in the mountains. It sent a chill down her back. "Why don't you come back into the patio, shut the door, and lower your voice? Then we can talk all you want to."

Julianna slammed the door and locked it. She stalked to the corner of the vine-covered patio where a man with a towel across his forehead sat in an oak rocker.

"DelNorte, why did you not tell me you were out here before I blurted out foolish things?"

"I didn't want to interrupt your tantrum."

"How long have you been awake?"

"Since your father asked you to go with him to see your brother in jail. How long was I on your sofa?"

"Since midnight last night."

He gingerly patted his forehead. "Did you sew me up?"

"No, that is the work of Lixie Miller. Would you like to look at it?"

"Is it rather gruesome?"

"Let's just say that you would not make the top of the list on any woman's dance card."

DelNorte tried to laugh. "Señorita Ortiz, how many years have we known each other?"

"Less than twenty-four hours."

"No, no, I'm sure we've known each other for years."

"Is that meant as a compliment?"

"Yes, it is. You tease me with the easy, relaxed manner of old friends."

"The old part is correct at least." Julianna relaxed with a smile. "Now what can I do for you?"

"I would like some water to drink, a hot bath, and clean clothes," he announced.

"Yes, I imagine you would. We are definitely not that close as friends. This is a jewelry store, not a bathhouse. I will get you something to eat and drink."

"Just some water, please. I don't think I can eat yet. It took all my strength to make it to this chair. And maybe a basin of clean water to wash. I must have a fever. I feel like I've been baked in a charcoal oven."

She strolled back into the apartment. She heard the front door of the store open and peeked out.

"Oh, Lixie! Come in."

Lixie Miller's yellow satin dress framed her small figure. "It's after one. I was afraid you would be closed."

"It has been a hectic morning. Lock the door behind you. I do need to close up."

"How is your patient?"

"He is awake and sitting in the patio."

Lixie scooted over to her. "How delightful! What is he like? What is his real name? Has he been married? Why does he spend so much time in Mexico? Did he propose to you yet?"

"Lixie! I have not even had a chance to talk to him. He just got up."

"Oh, good! We can find out at the same time. Shall I pump him for answers, or do you want to?"

Julianna frowned.

"I was teasing, Señorita Ortiz. I will be on my best behavior, which, as everyone knows, is not all that sterling."

Julianna poured water into a basin and more into a red pottery jar. "He woke up thirsty, wanting a bath and clean clothes."

"Oh, yes, bath time. Now I'm sure I stopped by at the right time."

"Lixie!"

"You will need a chaperon, of course." She laced her fingers together in front of her waist. "I volunteer."

Julianna raised her eyebrows. "He is not taking a bath at my house."

"Why not? He is filthy and in no condition to go anywhere else to clean up."

"Then he will remain filthy, but I will not even jest about such matters."

Lixie winked. "'Tis a pity. Let me carry the basin."

Lixie Miller led Julianna out into the patio. "Well, if it isn't the famous DelNorte. Please don't try to get up."

"Yes, ma'am. Have we met?"

"Most certainly. Those are my stitches you carry in your forehead."

"You must be Mrs. Miller, the general's widow."

"I'm Lixie, and as of Saturday, I'll be Mrs. Jefferson Carter. What's this about Julianna not letting you have a bath?"

"Don't you start on that, Lixie Miller," Julianna warned as she handed him a cup of water.

"She tried baking me under a buffalo robe. Now my dirty clothes are soaked with sweat."

Lixie tugged the towel off his forehead. "You are a little worse for wear. I've seen cowboys who have gotten a spur caught in the stirrup and been dragged across the prairie that look better than you."

Julianna chuckled.

DelNorte shook his head. "If I have one more pretty woman come in the door and tell me how horrible I look, I'm going to sew a flour sack over my head."

"Would you like a fresh shirt after you wash up?"

"I'd love one, but my clothes are still in El Paso."

"There's an emporium three doors down. I will go buy you one," Lixie announced.

"I'm afraid they stole my silver. I'm temporarily out of funds."

"Then you are a charity case. I will buy the clothes. You can repay me later."

"I don't normally accept—"

"Gifts from strange women? DelNorte, you have never met

anyone stranger than Lixie Miller. Now hush. It's our Christian duty to feed the hungry, tend the sick, and clothe the naked."

"DelNorte," Julianna cautioned, "do not try to answer her. You will only end up embarrassing yourself. You cannot outtalk a career army wife."

"What size shirt do you wear?" Lixie asked.

"Usually I just try them on."

"Well, pull what's left of that one off. I'll take it with me."

"Lixie!" Julianna gasped.

Miller threw up her arms. "This is getting nowhere real fast. I will do the best I can. Will you be needing socks and undergarments as well?"

"Lixie Miller, I am going into the other room!" Julianna stalked red-faced back into the apartment.

Minutes later Lixie hiked into the room carrying DelNorte's torn shirt. "We decided the duckings look tolerable just brushed off. I will buy him a shirt, vest, hat, and some socks. Are you going to cook him something to eat?"

"He was not hungry. Besides, I am going to eat lunch with my father."

"He came? He really showed up? How delightful! Gracie told me about the scene at the depot in El Paso. That is so much the Lord's way of doing something, isn't it? Where is he? I want to meet him."

"He is at the depot."

"What in the world is he doing over there?"

"He is looking for bandits. It is a game Paco plays."

"Playing with his grandson? That is so heartwarming."

"Actually he is waiting for me to make up my mind whether to forgive him for a lifetime of neglect and take him to Mexico so we can visit my brother one last time."

"Of course you will," Lixie insisted.

"It is not that easy."

"Sweet Señorita Ortiz, you are much too young and lovely to have your life ruined with bitterness and hatred."

"You do not know what I went through."

"No, I don't, but I do know the depressing effects of bitterness and hatred. Trust me. Now go on and have lunch with your daddy. The Lord will lead. I'll take good care of Mr. DelNorte for you."

"Remember you are getting married on Saturday."

"Oh, my," Lixie crooned. "So I am. I believe his name is Carter, isn't it?"

"Go on," Julianna motioned. "Buy some clothes for the celebrated DelNorte."

As soon as Lixie swept out the door, Julianna combed her hair back over her shoulders and tugged at her silver and turquoise earrings as she glanced in her small mirror over the counter. *Señorita Ortiz, you will be one of many New Mexico ladies who will be very, very happy when Lixie Miller gets married on Saturday.*

The stores along Railroad Avenue faced north. Nothing faced south. Nothing but the depot, the rail yard, and the tracks. The commercial district of Lordsburg was primarily limited to one side of one street. No one seemed to care.

The buildings all had verandas or awnings facing the street, and pedestrians could stroll in the shade from shop to store to saloon. The rest of town was not carefully planned because everyone had assumed that as soon as the railroad construction was completed, the town would die off.

It didn't.

Located on crossroads between the mines in the Pyramid Mountains and those in the Burro Mountains and the Southern Pacific tracks, Lordsburg found its place as a minor supply depot. It was most well known for the Hernandez Brothers' Bell Foundry and as a cloister for those expatriated from more civilized areas. Strolling along the shaded sidewalk could be wayward daughters and rebellious sons from any family in the States and northern Mexico. No one ever planned to stay long—just until they were summoned back from banishment. The most permanent residents were the self-exiled ones.

Julianna Ortiz knew most of the people in town who had been there a week or more. Sometime during each day she would meet them all on the crowded boardwalk on the south side of Railroad Avenue.

"Miss Ortiz, what delightful earrings. I must buy a pair just like them!"

Julianna turned to see two older women in identical long purple gingham dresses with matching bonnets. One had gray hair. Ortiz spoke to the one with bright red hair. "Thank you, Barbara. How are the Berry sisters today?"

"I was just telling Hollister that we need to stop by your store and look at the new fall collection of jewelry."

"I do not think I have many new pieces since you spent the afternoon looking at them last week."

"You don't have the jade pieces yet?" Barbara asked.

"I almost had them. They seem to be slow getting here."

"Oh, dear. You would think a town on the S.P. would get better service," Hollister mused.

"We are probably not the highest of priorities."

Barbara brushed her red bangs off her gray-brown eyebrows. "That is very true. I told Hollister just the other day that if we wanted to find husbands, we would have to move to someplace like Tucson or San Diego, didn't I, dear? In a remote place like this, the choices are quite limited, as you well know."

"I believe you are right about that. Perhaps you would enjoy living next to a fort," Julianna offered.

Hollister Berry nodded. "You know, I was thinking the same thing myself."

"Hah! You two don't think I know when you are teasing me? We'll stay in Lordsburg," Barbara blustered. "Once Lixie Miller is married on Saturday, we only have the Señorita Ortiz to compete with. The way I figure it, once we find you a husband, we will be next in line."

Julianna smiled, nodded, and tried to scan those entering the dining room of the Sonoran Hotel. *These two sixty-something-year-old sisters are the most optimistic women in town.*

"Are you looking for someone?" Barbara asked.

"I am sorry, I was going to meet someone for lunch at the Sonoran, and I lost track of the time. I am afraid I am a little late."

"A man, no doubt," Hollister said.

"Yes, my father."

"Well, I'll be. I didn't know you had a father!" Barbara said.

"Everyone has a father, dear," Hollister commented.

"I didn't know Señorita Ortiz's father was still alive. Somehow I thought your parents were dead."

"Mother passed away years ago."

"And he's been a widower all these years?" Hollister asked.

"Oh, he remarried." *On more than one occasion.* "I have not seen him . . . in a while. He lives in Texas."

"No foolin'? So does our father," Barbara boomed.

"He's ninety-four years old," Hollister reported, "and lives in Ft. Worth."

"Shoot, he owns Ft. Worth!" Barbara bellowed. "I surely do like them earrings. Are you sure you don't have another pair?"

"None exactly like these, but many that are quite similar. Excuse me, ladies, but I had better find my father. He will not want me to keep him waiting."

"I sure do like those earrings."

"Barbara, would you like to buy this pair?"

"You'd sell them to me right off your ears?"

"It is my business to make the customer happy."

"Did you hear that, Hollister? Now you just don't get that kind of service in a big town."

Julianna pulled off the studded earrings and handed them to the red-headed woman, who held them up to her ears. "What do you think, Hollister?"

"They look quite lovely, dear."

"I knew it. I have an eye for jewelry, you know."

"Yes, except perhaps the earrings made of dried armadillo hide," Hollister reminded her.

"I told you never to mention those!"

Hollister Berry winked at Julianna. "Oh, I'm so sorry, sister. I must have forgotten."

"What do I owe you for these?"

Julianna patted Barbara Berry's hand. "Because of the unblemished turquoise, these are $2.00. But why not wear them and see if you really like them? Then you can stop by the store in the next day or two and settle up."

"Do you see what I mean, Hollister? That's exactly what I'm talking about!" Barbara Berry spoke so loudly that several people on the sidewalk stopped to listen. "No jewelry store owner in the country will treat a girl as nice as Señorita Ortiz. That is exactly why we will always live in Lordsburg."

"We'd better hurry ourselves, dear, or we'll be late."

"Do you two have an appointment?" Julianna asked.

Hollister glanced around at the sidewalk, then leaned closer to Julianna, and whispered, "There's a cockfight Saturday night at Tres Alamos, and Mr. Gomez has a new rooster. He said we could watch the rooster practice this afternoon."

"Yep," Barbara said. "You don't bet on a horserace unless you study the ponies, if you catch my drift."

The Berry sisters pushed their way through the crowd as Julianna entered the lobby of the Sonoran Hotel. The dining room was three-quarters filled, but she did not see her father.

I should have gone over to the depot and walked him here. That way he would not get lost, and . . . She tugged at her earlobes. . . . *I would still have my earrings.*

She sat on the round leather sofa near the entrance to the dining room in the hotel lobby. A large cowboy with a bullet belt across his chest meandered up to her. "Miss Ortiz, how is Guillermo? I hear he got himself into a little trouble down in Mexico."

"Yes, Tuffy, he is in a lot of trouble."

He stared at her for a minute. "I don't reckon I've ever seen you without purdy earrings on."

She tugged at her earlobes. "I, eh, just sold the pair I was wearing."

"Things is that bad, huh?"

"No, no. A customer liked mine better than those in the store."

"If there's anything we can do, me and some of the boys, well, we could ride down there with you if you need us to."

"Thank you, Tuffy. There is not too much we can do right now but pray."

"I ain't never been too much of a one for prayin', ma'am."

"Did your mother ever pray?"

His face lit up. "Yes, ma'am, she surely did."

"Was she a good woman?"

"I reckon she was the best mama there ever was."

"But she didn't teach you how to pray?"

He looked down at black boots starting to separate at the soles. "She taught us, all right."

"Please pray for Guillermo for me when it comes to mind."

"Do you think the Lord will listen to me?"

"Pray like your mama taught you, and El Señor will listen."

"Yes, ma'am, I think I will. But I was serious. If you need some boys with guns to help them prayers get answered, I can round you up a few."

"Thanks, Tuffy. If I think of some way you can help, I will let you know."

"We're goin' out on the fall gather a week from Saturday. So if you want something, it will have to be before then."

"I will remember that."

She watched the large man part the crowd as he ambled out to the sidewalk. *A crew of cowboys with guns to help my prayers get answered. And he did not even see anything incongruous with the idea.*

Paco burst into the lobby soon after Tuffy cleared the doorway.

"*Niño*, you are just in time to eat lunch!"

"I was here earlier, but I did not find you, so we went to play rock tag."

"Rock tag? Do you and Bonita throw rocks at each other?"

"No," he laughed. "That would be a dumb game. Bonita never misses anything she throws a rock at. This is tag, and the only safe place is a rock big enough to stand on with two feet."

"I see. Are those your clean feet, or did you leave the clean ones at home and wear a dirty pair?"

"Aunt Julianna, I am so poor that I only have one pair of feet."

"Yes, but you have a pair of new shoes."

"I am saving them."

"For what?"

"For the wedding."

"Yours or mine?" she teased.

"Are you going to marry DelNorte?" Paco asked.

"Of course not. That was a joke."

"Where are your earrings?"

Julianna pulled her hair up to the front of her shoulders so that it would hang across her ears. "Miss Berry talked me into selling them to her, and I did not have time to go back and get another pair."

"Which Miss Berry?"

"Which one do you think?"

"They will not go well with her red hair."

"That is true. Would you like to be the one who tells her that?"

"No." Paco grinned. "I will say they look lovely."

"Smart boy. Now go to the tub in the alley behind the hotel and wash your hands. Then you can eat with your grandfather and me."

"He is gone," Paco announced.

A lump rose in Julianna's throat. "What?"

"I forgot to tell you. He is gone and told me to tell you he would not be here for lunch, but he will see you before the train leaves at 6:00 P.M."

She stood straight up. "He left? Where did he go?"

"We were at the depot, and he was playing find the bandit with Bonita and me. Then two men rode up and asked if he knew where Guillermo Ortiz was. They talked in Spanish. He told me he must go see someone near Shakespeare about some treasure. He said that it would help Uncle Guillermo and that you would understand."

Julianna's shoulders felt heavy as she slumped back down on

the leather couch. *I cannot believe you did this to me again, Papa. Surely you are not still running after wild stories of treasure and gold. You had me convinced. I wanted to believe those sad eyes of yours. Oh, Papa, how I wanted to believe you were different. I will never, ever let you do this to me again.*

A very dark-skinned, yellow-haired, barefoot girl ran into the lobby. She was wearing a violet dress over blue denim jeans.

"Hi. Do you like my new hair? Paco said it makes me look like a cocker spaniel, but I think I look like a sunbeam."

"Bonita, what happened to your hair?"

"Look, it is a wig!" The girl pulled off the long blonde wig. "Isn't it funny?"

"Where did you get that?"

"I found it. Someone threw it away."

"It was down in Larga Seca," Paco reported. "I think someone threw it from the train."

"Why do you say that?"

"There was a pillow there too that said Southern Pacific on it. But the dogs had ripped it open and scattered feathers everywhere." He glanced into the crowded dining room. "Are we going to eat lunch here?"

"No, I have changed my mind. I want to go tell the marshal about the wig," Julianna said.

"It's mine. I get to keep it," Bonita insisted.

"Yes, it is, but I need to talk to him."

Bonita twirled the long blonde wig in her hand. "I wonder if Mama will let me wear it to the wedding."

Julianna and the children hurried along the crowded boardwalk toward Marshal Yager's office.

"Darling, why would you want to cover up that beautiful black hair of yours?"

Bonita bit her lip and then rubbed her nose with the palm of her dirty hand. "So I would not look so much like an Apache."

"That is dumb," Paco said. "That wig makes you look like a sad dog instead of a beautiful Indian maiden."

Bonita looked up at Julianna and flashed a wide, white-toothed grin.

Julianna held open the screen door on the front of the marshal's office. "Paco Ortiz, if Indians and women ever get to vote in this territory, I do believe you *will* be governor."

Lixie met them on the sidewalk in front of the bank. She insisted that Paco and Bonita eat with her. Julianna watched in amazement as Lixie Miller pulled off her hat, placed the blonde wig on her head, and then strolled south arm in arm with two giggling children.

Julianna unlocked the jewelry store and peeked back toward the apartment. *I must open the backdoor. It is too stuffy.*

She paused by a case of silver earrings and selected a pair with two long, dangling silver feathers on each one. She slipped the posts into her ears and fastened them. *If business gets slow, I can just stroll up and down the sidewalk modeling my wares. I do not think anyone ever noticed my earrings until they were gone.*

She shoved open the curtain door, strolled over to the sink, and poured herself a cup of cold coffee. She plucked the last apple from a basket that hung above the counter. She bit into the fruit and sipped the coffee.

Papa, I had hoped to have a nice meal at the Sonoran Hotel. Now I am drinking bitter, cold coffee and eating an apple that has gone to sauce at the core. That is the story of you and me. Some plots never change. Always major expectations and major disappointments. I cannot believe I let you take me in like that again. Julianna Ortiz, when it comes to men, you are the most naive woman ever born. You believe everything they say.

Even when it is in a letter.

Coffee and apple in her hands, she strolled out to the patio.

The first thing she saw was Roberto Alvarez with his hands raised.

Then Laredo Nisqually.

And Jack Burkeman.

"He has two guns, *hermana*!"

She glanced at the rocking chair in the shade where DelNorte sat with a new white cotton shirt buttoned at the collar and a new hat pushed far to the back of his head. He held a cocked Colt peacemaker in each hand.

She took a bite of apple and chewed it slowly. "Yes, and he has a forehead that looks like a map to a lost gold mine. Hello, DelNorte."

"Miss Ortiz."

"You know him?" Burkeman quizzed.

"Oh, yeah, she slowed me down in Guadalupe so that you three could get away. I know your tactics," DelNorte said.

She took a sip of cold coffee. "What are you all doing here?"

"We came back for something else to eat," Burkeman said, "and he was lying in ambush for us."

"He just sits in that chair and tells us how my cousin and the Iturbe brothers got off easy," Laredo informed her.

"He is goin' to kill us, *hermana*," Alvarez warned.

"I hope he does not do it in my patio."

"It's no joke," Burkeman insisted.

DelNorte waved a gun at her. "He's right, Miss Ortiz. I intend to kill all four of you."

"She had nothing to do with it," Roberto Alvarez insisted.

"I'm afraid it's too late to be noble. You should have thought of that before you involved her in the first place."

"If you are going to kill me, can I finish my apple?" she asked. "I have not had much to eat today."

"Certainly."

"Thank you."

"You're welcome."

"*Hermana*, this is no joke. Our lives are in danger."

"I believe you, Roberto. But so far I am having a very lousy day. Dying might improve it. It is never bad timing for going to heaven."

"Well, some of us might be headed the other direction," Laredo retorted.

"I can see your point," she said. "Perhaps now would be a good time to settle with El Señor. He is as close as a heartbeat."

"How can you preach at us at a time like this?" Alvarez said.

She took another bite of apple. "How can I not preach at a time like this?"

"There is one other option," DelNorte offered.

"What is that?" Laredo replied.

"If you return my saddlebags with all the papers and the silver, I just might let you off alive."

"But we cannot do that," Alvarez protested. "We told you. It was all stolen at Hachita."

"Then go steal it back. You are valiant border *banditos*, aren't you?"

"But people at Hachita are just crazy killers," Jack Burkeman stormed.

"I believe you have too low an estimation of yourselves. Or was Guillermo Ortiz the only brave one?" DelNorte challenged.

"There is bravery, and there is suicide," Laredo insisted. "That would be suicide."

"Get those hands higher, Alvarez!" DelNorte shouted.

Roberto raised his hands. "Are you saying you will let us all go free if we promise to return your saddlebags and silver?"

DelNorte laughed. "Oh, two of you will go free."

"Two of us?"

"Yes. If you are not back with my saddlebags in twelve hours, I will shoot the one I keep here. If you are not back within twenty-four, I will shoot the other and then come looking for you."

"But there are only three of us," Laredo said.

"I count four who were in on stealing my saddlebags."

"Julianna had nothing to do with this," Roberto insisted.

"She is Guillermo Ortiz's twin sister. What more do I need to say? I will keep her and Laredo here with me. I will shoot him first. The woman with the silver feather earrings I'll keep alive for twenty-four."

"Two of us riding into Hachita?" Burkeman ranted. "You might as well kill us all right now."

"Good idea. Perhaps I'll start with you."

"You two try. It is our only chance!" Laredo insisted.

"How do we know you will not kill them the minute we ride off?" Alvarez quizzed.

"How do I know you will even go to Hachita? You might ride off for Colorado . . . or even Idaho and never be seen again."

"This is crazy," Burkeman complained. "You are just playing with us. Two people can't ride into Hachita and come out alive."

"Three of you made it yesterday. I'll tell you what. I really want my saddlebags and those papers back. So I will let three of you go and just keep one. I'll keep Laredo, since he is the one who took my saddlebags in the first place."

"Go on, boys, make a break for it," Laredo cried. "He has made up his mind to kill me, and there is nothing I can do about it. I am a dead man."

"I cannot take *hermana* to Hachita," Alvarez insisted. "There are things worse than dying that can happen to a woman in that town."

"That leaves only one option," DelNorte said. "You leave the woman with me."

"I cannot do that!" Alvarez said.

"Go on," Julianna urged. "You can get the saddlebags back. I know you can."

"*Hermana*, this is crazy. The man is insane. The blow to the head has made him deranged," Alvarez insisted.

"If I were you, I would not mention the blow to the head," Julianna advised.

"You're going to let the three of us go, and then you're going to kill Julianna if we don't come back within twenty-four hours?" Burkeman quizzed.

"Yep. Then I'll come after you three."

"This is not good," Burkeman murmured.

"Go on. I am ready to meet my Maker. I am not afraid," Julianna insisted.

"We cannot walk out on you," Alvarez declared.

"Maybe we can get the saddlebags back," Laredo said. "We do have friends in Hachita."

"They were the ones who stole from us and promised to filet us if we ever set foot in town again," Burkeman snarled.

"I say we have to try," Laredo insisted.

"*Hermana?*" Alvarez asked.

"How can we help Guillermo if we are all dead? You must succeed," she replied.

"You will not harm her for twenty-four hours?" Alvarez challenged.

"That's right. I won't lay a hand on her."

Alvarez started for the alley door. "We will be back, *hermana*. We will not let you down."

"I am counting on it."

"Go on before I change my mind," DelNorte growled.

"You are not goin' to shoot us in the back when we turn to go, are you?"

"That's a chance you'll have to take, Laredo. I want you to be the last one out the door."

All three men sprinted out into the alley. DelNorte shoved his guns back into his holster.

"Do you mind if I lock the door?" Julianna asked.

"Go right ahead." He nodded.

"Are you hungry?" she said.

"I'm starved."

"Are you strong enough to walk into the kitchen while I cook?"

"I'm not sure I can even stand up."

"I did not think so." She walked over to his chair. "Give me your hand. I'll help you."

He struggled to his feet. She pulled his arm around her shoulder. "Lean on me." She walked slowly as he shuffled along beside her.

"How was lunch with your father?"

"He did not show up. He left."

"I'm sorry."

"I was not completely joking when I said I felt ready to die."

"I know. I could tell it in your voice."

"I like your new shirt."

"Thank you. I like your new earrings."

"Do you expect to ever see your saddlebags again?"

"No, but I don't expect to ever see those three again either. It will be a good trade."

"They thought you were going to kill them."

"How about you, Señorita Ortiz? Did you think I would kill them?"

"No, I knew you would not."

"How did you know?"

"'It is not the words a man selects or even the tone of his inflection, but rather the heart and soul of the words that communicate true meaning.'"

He pulled his arm away from her and propped himself on the table. "Why did you say that?"

"It seemed to fit."

"No, why did you use that exact phrase?"

"I, eh . . . I heard that a long time ago, and it stuck in my mind. Why do you look at me like that?"

"Julianna, I'm sure we've known each other somewhere. There was a time long ago when the exact same thought fluttered in my head."

"Word for word?"

"Yes."

"That is strange. We must think alike. But if you do not take it easy on Lixie's stitches, it will be a New Mexico dust storm that flutters in your head."

Six

Julianna's long white apron covered most of the lavender summer wool dress as she diced peppers, onions, and pimentos at the counter. "I did not get to the meat market yet today, so you will have to survive on eggs. Do you like them spicy?"

"Yes, ma'am. I like everythin' spicy."

Julianna gave him a quick look.

"I mean food, that is."

"I know exactly what you mean, Señor DelNorte."

"Julianna, you are easy to talk to. I must admit I'm again surprised."

"What surprises you? I am but a simple, predictable Mexican woman."

DelNorte shook his head and laughed.

"Oh? You think different?" She waved the paring knife at him. "When you are quite through being amused at me, you can tell me why you are surprised."

"You are anything but simple. You are so complex that you don't even understand yourself."

She sliced the washed potatoes very thin, looking back at him. "Just because I cannot figure myself out does not make me complex. It only makes me dumb or naive. Others have figured me out very quickly."

"The others are wrong."

"Tell me, DelNorte, what makes Julianna Naomi Ortiz so surprising?"

"Lordsburg is a plain, little railroad town in the midst of cattle country, gold and silver mines, and disgruntled Indians. It's the kind of town most people pass through on their way to somewhere else."

The onions made her eyes water. She wiped the tears on her blouse sleeve. "What does this have to do with me?"

"You have no family, no roots here in Lordsburg. I'm surprised you selected this town."

"Guillermo used to run the saloon next door."

"Which makes your presence even more astonishing. I would think you'd be more comfortable far away from saloon life. I've heard the heart and soul of the words when you say, 'El Señor.' He is your Lord and Savior, isn't He?"

"Yes, He is, but why is that a surprise?"

"The photograph on the wall behind the sofa."

"You examine everything?"

"I suppose it's a habit of mine."

"We had a photographer take our picture last Easter on the front steps of the new church."

"It's a Baptist church."

She stopped slicing and brushed her long, thick black hair over her shoulder. "Oh, so that is it. You are surprised that a Mexican is a Protestant."

"There's more."

"I feel like a turnip being examined at the market."

"Not a turnip, Señorita Ortiz. You're a successful business-woman. Not many women in New Mexico run their own jewelry stores."

"I have very low expenses and very few needs. Most could not be content with such meager profits. Besides, I told you all about myself and how my mother's cousin helped me start the business."

He sat straight up. "When did you tell me that?"

She licked her lips and continued at the sink. "Last night."

"When I was unconscious?"

"Yes. I have that effect on many men."

"It doesn't count," he blurted out. "You have to tell me again."

"It counts to me, DelNorte. Now finish the story of the amaz-ing Señorita Ortiz."

"Miss Ortiz is an intelligent and educated lady. I can see that in her speech and vocabulary. That would not surprise me, but the fact that such a woman can act so calm and cool when confronted by a potentially violent scene such as what just took place in your patio . . . well, I watched you and decided you'd do to ride the river with."

"DelNorte, my twin brother has been bringing violent scenes to my doorstep, like a cat brings a mouse, since he was twelve. I learned long ago that if I am scared to death, I do not think clearly. So you found a Mexican Protestant Christian businesswoman, who does not faint when a gun is drawn, living in Lordsburg, New Mexico—about this you are surprised?"

"I'm surprised to find a very attractive Mexican Protestant Christian businesswoman, who doesn't faint when a gun is drawn, living in Lordsburg, New Mexico, who is not married."

"Hah! Why does my marital state even cross your mind? You, of all people?"

"What do you mean—me, of all people?"

She turned and tossed a peeled potato at him. He caught it with one hand. "Now you have the hot potato. Why is the famous DelNorte, who is obviously advanced in years, not married?"

He tossed the potato back. She caught it with one hand. "The answer to that is apparent. What kind of woman would want to be married to a man in my profession?"

"Just exactly what is your profession?" she quizzed.

"You see? No woman could live with such a mystery."

"You would not even tell your wife what kind of work you do?"

"Perhaps not. What kind of husband, what kind of father would that be?"

"You have told me why no woman should marry you, but you have not told me why you do not want to marry."

"You caught that, huh?"

"Yes, I am the surprising Señorita Ortiz, remember?"

"And when will the surprising Miss Ortiz get married?"

"Never."

"You have taken vows?" he laughed.

"I will raise Paco and then be an old lady."

"I know something about Señorita Ortiz. I think that you once loved someone who hurt you deeply, and you decided all men are deceitful liars. Am I right?"

You are wrong, DelNorte. I decided all people are deceitful liars. "Why is it, DelNorte, that women who do not marry have to have some troubled relationship in the past? I do not think the matter is that simple."

"You didn't answer my question."

"Yes, there was a time when I gave my heart and was deceived and lied to. It hurt me deeply. It hurts still. But that is not the reason I will not marry."

"You see, I did know something about your past," he boasted.

"And I know many things about your past," she countered.

"Oh? What have you heard?"

"You were a spy for both the North and the South during the war and somehow pulled it off so that they both love you."

"You have read some old newspapers."

"And that while working at a customhouse in Baltimore after the war, you were engaged to be married to Ramona Hawk."

DelNorte roared with laugher. "Miss Ortiz, you've been spying on me. How did you find that out so quickly? Not that it is any big secret."

"Never underestimate the curiosity of several women."

"Several women?" he asked.

"I have friends who know many people in Washington."

"Well, all of that is true. It was a very, very long time ago and brings up a character lapse that I would rather not be reminded of."

"Oh?"

"I fell for a line, Señorita Ortiz. I've tried never to let that happen again."

Julianna spread a dollop of lard in the iron skillet and watched it sizzle. "Then I have some news for you about your former fiancée. I think you were still unconscious when I first heard that Ramona Hawk has escaped from the Detroit Prison for Women."

DelNorte leaped to his feet, then staggered back, holding his head with both hands. "When?"

"I see there is still some fire in the bones."

"Julianna, this is strictly business. When did she escape? Yesterday?"

"No, that is the amazing thing. She escaped two weeks ago, but the prison officials kept it quiet. They hoped to recapture her before the public found out."

"Two weeks? The fools! The complete fools!"

"Yes, but let me give you some information that the authorities have not pieced together. You see, I know Ramona Hawk too."

"Many in New Mexico do."

"I believe that it was Ramona Hawk and two accomplices who robbed Fieldman's Wholesale Jewelry in El Paso yesterday."

"She does like to steal jewels. Did you see her?"

"No, but before this beautiful blue lump was stamped on the back of my head, I heard her laugh."

"How do you know her laugh?"

"Have you ever been used by Ramona Hawk?"

"What do you mean?" he asked.

"You know exactly what I mean, DelNorte. She has a special little laugh—one that says, 'You are nothing, and I am victorious.' There is no sound quite like it, and I am convinced that once it is heard, one never forgets."

"You are right, Julianna. Why didn't you tell me this before?"

"Before what? You just woke up."

"You think she's still in El Paso?"

"There is more to the story. When I came to, Mr. Fieldman said the woman had long blonde hair."

"You think she dyed her hair?"

"Could be. But there is one other explanation. Last night— actually it was early this morning—while I was sitting up with you, I stood by the front window and watched the street. A woman and two men rode right down Railroad Avenue and did not stop. It was too dark to tell who it was, but I believe the woman was a blonde, and she was straddling a horse. Besides Gracie Parnell, Ramona Hawk is the only woman in New Mexico I know who does not ride sidesaddle."

DelNorte set his hat lightly on the back of his head. "You think she passed through Lordsburg?"

"About an hour or so ago Paco and his friend Bonita were playing west of town along the tracks. Bonita found a blonde wig."

"I've got to get to the telegraph office."

"Why?" She scraped the potatoes, onions, and peppers into the sizzling pan.

He looked at her for a long moment. "That's precisely why I'm not married, Julianna."

"The secretive DelNorte? You cannot make it across the room by yourself, let alone the street. Write it out, and I will take it over."

"Who's on the key during this shift?"

"I do not know. Maybe Mr. Cushman."

"Where's he from?" DelNorte asked.

"He has a deep Southern accent."

"Are there any telegraph operators you absolutely trust?"

"Mr. Holden, of course, but he is out of town. And Gracie. My good friend works part time. I would trust her with my life."

"Good, because I might have to do the same. Can you go get her and bring her here?"

"Yes. It will take a few minutes. You will have to watch the skillet."

He cupped his hands and blew into them. "She has jewels and is on the New Mexico border. Maybe she wants to sell them and take U.S. money to Mexico."

Julianna broke six eggs into a pottery bowl. "But why come to Lordsburg? Does she want to see you?"

"She doesn't know I'm here, or she would never have come. Go get your Gracie."

Julianna beat the eggs with a fork. "You are beginning to sound like a U.S. marshal, DelNorte."

"I can assure you, Señorita Ortiz, that I'm not a U.S. marshal."

"I will go get Gracie." She started toward the display room.

"Julianna, is this the only jewelry store in Lordsburg?"

She paused in the doorway. "It is the only one for miles."

"Have you ever purchased jewels from Ramona Hawk?"

"No, never. But she has, Mr. DelNorte, stolen much from me! And I do not mean just jewels."

Julianna sprinted across the jewelry store, pulling off her white cotton apron as she ran. The front door swung open. Rev. and Mrs. Howitt stepped inside.

"Oh, dear," Mrs. Howitt said. "You look like you're in a hurry."

"Yes, an emergency came up."

"Don't let us keep you. Dear Posey decided she wanted to buy another of your one dollar rings," the preacher explained.

"I will be back soon."

Rev. Howitt opened the door for his wife. "We'll come back later."

"That would be good," Julianna agreed.

Mrs. Howitt stared at the apron in Julianna's hand. "Señorita Ortiz, is there anything we can do to help?"

Julianna brushed the hair back off her eyes. She felt the dull pain from the lump on the back of her head. "Yes, there is. Rev. Howitt, could you watch my store for me? I will only be gone a few minutes."

"Certainly. And I'll try to read the prices correctly." His Adam's apple bounced up and down with every word.

"How about me, dear?" Posey Howitt offered. "Can I take your apron for you?"

Julianna shoved it into the small woman's hand. "Yes, thank you. There's an injured notorious gunfighter by the name of DelNorte in my kitchen. Would you put on the apron and go finish cooking him some eggs and potatoes?"

Mrs. Howitt's face lost what little color it had gained from the New Mexico sun. "Oh, dear."

Rev. Howitt grinned. "I'm sure she's teasing you again, sweet Posey. Isn't that right, Señorita Ortiz?"

"No, Rev. Howitt, I'm not. Welcome to Lordsburg."

Grace Parnell huddled at the table with DelNorte while Julianna escorted Rev. and Mrs. Howitt back into the store showroom.

"My, he is certainly a nice gentleman," Mrs. Howitt said, "once you look past the stitches. He has quite an appetite."

"His views on transubstantiation seem quite orthodox," Rev. Howitt reported.

Julianna raised her eyebrows. "You were discussing theology?"

"Quite the enigmatic fellow indeed. Do you have any idea where he was educated?" Howitt asked.

"Harvard."

"My word, Harvard Divinity School?" Rev. Howitt gasped.

"The university, I believe."

Mrs. Howitt stepped closer to Julianna and whispered, "Is he really a notorious gunfighter?"

"All I can say is, when other gunmen along the border hear he is coming to town, they leave."

"I believe we've had more adventures in Lordsburg in half a day than we did in ten years in Plainfield, Wisconsin," Posey said.

Just then Paco and Bonita burst through the front door.

"Can we go over to Tío Burto's?" Paco shouted.

"He's going to ring my bell!" Bonita proclaimed.

Mrs. Howitt gasped. "He's going to do what to this child?"

Julianna laughed. "The Hernandez brothers have the bell foundry on the south edge of town. They name their bells after ladies, and they were casting one named Bonita when she moved to town. She is quite convinced they named it after her."

"And today they will ring it for the first time," Paco explained.

"My, that is pretty yellow hair," Rev. Howitt remarked.

Bonita jerked off the wig. "Do you want to wear it?"

"Oh, my no," he stammered.

Julianna motioned the children to the door. "Yes, you may go."

"Can we have some crackers?" Paco asked.

"Yes, but let me get them. DelNorte is busy with Gracie."

Bonita stared at the heavy green curtain dividing the rooms. "What are they doing?"

"He is giving her a telegram to send."

Paco scratched his arm and then rubbed his flat nose. "In the kitchen?"

"He is too weak to walk over to the telegraph office."

Gracie Parnell was sitting across from DelNorte at the table when Julianna entered the kitchen. Their voices dropped as she approached.

"Excuse me, Paco and Bonita need a snack." She grabbed the cracker tin.

"I'm through," Gracie declared. She accompanied Julianna back into the store.

"I presume you got that all down?" Julianna inquired.

"Not without swearing eternal secrecy."

"He is hard to understand."

"Not anymore."

"And you are not going to tell me about him?"

"No. He said he would tell you."

"But when?"

"He just said, 'Please don't tell Julianna. I want to tell her myself.'"

"Meanwhile you know some juicy tidbits."

"Sweet Julianna, what I know could get me shot!"

"Are you in danger?"

"No, I'm happily married."

"Gracie, that is not what I meant."

Parnell flipped her hair back off her forehead. "It isn't?"

Paco tugged on his aunt's skirt. "Tía Julianna, DelNorte is calling you!"

Grace hurried out the door and across Railroad Avenue. Julianna watched until she disappeared into the depot, then turned around. "What did DelNorte say?"

"I believe he needs something," the preacher reported. "But my darling Posey went to see."

Julianna buzzed into the kitchen. DelNorte stood over the stove scraping more eggs onto his plate.

"Where is Mrs. Howitt?"

"Someone was at your backdoor," he mumbled. "Good eggs."

"Sit down before you fall over. You look weak."

When Julianna reached the doorway to the patio, she spotted Mrs. Howitt sprawled near the alley door. A man with a gun squatted next to her.

"What are you doing?" Julianna shouted as she rushed toward them.

He glanced up. "*Hermana*, who is this lady?"

"Roberto? What did you do to her?"

"Nothing." He stood up. "I rapped on the door and called out to you. But you did not hear me, so I beat a little louder with my gun barrel. After a few minutes this lady opened the door, looked at me, and fainted. Maybe it was the drawn gun. Who is she?"

Julianna knelt down and raised Mrs. Howitt's head to her lap. "The preacher's wife."

"What is she doing here?"

"What are *you* doing here?" Julianna challenged.

"I have been asking myself the same question. Is DelNorte still here?"

Julianna stroked the woman's thin cheeks. "Yes, he is."

Roberto rubbed his thick mustache. "Are you safe, *hermana*?"

"Of course."

"We did not believe his story about harming you, but it was a good excuse to leave alive."

"Roberto, I am surprised you are back. I think he was very serious about wanting you gone."

"We ran into trouble near Shakespeare."

Julianna patted the woman's face. "Mrs. Howitt?" She looked back up at Roberto. "Now what kind of trouble did you get yourself into?"

Roberto glanced down at the unconscious woman. "I need to talk to you alone."

"Is this about my brother?"

"Yes, and it is about your father, *hermana*."

"What do you mean, my father? Did you see him?"

"Yes."

"Where is he?"

"In an arroyo east of Shakespeare."

"Is he hurt?"

"Not yet. That is what I must talk to you about. It is extremely important . . . and private."

Julianna motioned toward the woman. "Help me carry Mrs. Howitt into the house."

Roberto lowered his voice. "DelNorte is in there. He will shoot me on sight. You heard him say so."

Julianna stood. "Just a minute. Stay with her." She scampered over and stuck her head into the apartment. "DelNorte, Mrs. Howitt has fainted, and I have asked Roberto Alvarez to carry her in here. Do you promise not to shoot him?"

DelNorte picked eggs out of his teeth with his fingernail. "What are they doin' back so soon?"

"I think it is just Roberto, and he wants to talk to me. He has a message about my father."

"Tell him to keep his gun holstered."

"I will tell him. Thank you."

When Julianna returned to the patio, Posey Howitt was sitting up, but Roberto was gone. She helped the woman to her feet.

"Oh, dear, I must have fainted. When I came to, three armed men were staring down at me. I overheard you talking to Mr. DelNorte, and they took off."

"Three men? There was only one before."

"Oh no, there were three men with guns drawn. That's why I was so startled."

Julianna stepped to the doorway and peered into the alley. Jack Burkeman, Laredo Nisqually, and Roberto Alvarez crouched behind crates and barrels. "*Hermana*, we have to talk!" Roberto called out. "Without DelNorte listening."

"I need to help Mrs. Howitt."

"Hurry, *hermana*. If he comes out that doorway, we will shoot," Burkeman asserted.

"Do not shoot anyone. Just wait."

Posey Howitt leaned against a rough wooden post. "Who are those men? Friends of DelNorte?"

"No, they want to kill DelNorte. They are friends of my brother. Let me help you inside."

"Friends of your brother? I'm confused."

"Yes, dear. It is a requirement for living in Lordsburg."

DelNorte, gun drawn, met them at the door. "Where's Alvarez?"

"In the alley with Burkeman and Nisqually. They said if you went through that door, they would shoot you."

"They think that's goin' to stop me?"

"Those turkey tracks across your forehead are going to stop you. You cannot walk ten feet on your own, and you know it."

"I think I'm going to faint again," Posey said.

"No, dear, you cannot do that. You have already fainted today. Only one faint a day is allowed unless you are pregnant."

Mrs. Howitt teared up.

Julianna hugged the thin woman's arm. "Honey, that was a bad joke. It was very thoughtless. Forgive me."

Mrs. Howitt nodded and patted Julianna's hand.

"What's going on here?" Rev. Howitt scooted across the long apartment. "My sweetie, what happened?"

"I got a little startled by a gun."

"Mr. DelNorte, I must insist that you put away your revolver. It's frightening my wife."

"Not *his* gun," Posey protested.

The preacher surveyed the patio. "Whose gun?"

"The men who are friends of Señorita Ortiz's brother who want to shoot Mr. DelNorte."

"I'm sure you have that mixed up a little, my darling. This heat makes our heads swirl at times."

"No, that about sums it up right. You might want to take her back to the Holdens' to rest," Julianna suggested.

"Señorita Ortiz, are you back there? This is Marshal Yager."

Julianna glanced at DelNorte.

"It's okay. Let him come back, " DelNorte offered. He shoved his gun into his holster.

"We are back here," she called out.

Marshal Yager charged through the doorway.

"Julianna, I believe you were right. I got word from Shakespeare that a lady straddlin' a horse and answerin' Hawk's description was seen south of there." The marshal glanced at the

Howitts and lowered his voice. "I reckon it's her. But I don't know why she didn't jump over to Mexico."

"I guess she wants to buy something with those jewels before she crosses the border."

"What would she buy?" Julianna questioned.

"That's a mystery."

"Marshal, do you think she's coming back to Lordsburg?" DelNorte asked.

"I don't think so. She doesn't have any friends to hide her here. I'd say she's in Hachita or on the way there."

"That's what I'm thinkin'," DelNorte put in.

"I'll telegraph the army."

"Don't bother," DelNorte cautioned. "Some boys in blue will get killed in Hachita, but they won't catch Hawk. The army has never been able to capture Ramona Hawk. How did she get captured last time?"

"It was Lixie and Bonita," Julianna offered.

"And before that?"

"Gracie and Colt."

"Where is this leading?" the marshal asked.

"Ramona Hawk is only captured when she thinks there's no threat of being captured. Send a posse or the army, and she'll disappear faster than an Apache on the desert. The best they can do is contain her while someone deals with her face to face."

"How come you know so much about Hawk?" the marshal asked.

DelNorte glanced over at Julianna and then back at the marshal. "Because I was engaged to her at one time."

"I have to go talk to, eh . . . someone about my father, if you two will excuse me." Julianna hustled out into the alley.

"Over here, *hermana*," Alvarez called from behind a barrel.

Laredo kept his revolver pointed at the alley door.

"What took you so long?" Burkeman asked.

"I had to persuade DelNorte not to come out and shoot you," she replied.

"He would never make it through the door," Alvarez boasted.

She pointed down the alley. "Who said he was going to use the door?"

Gun drawn, Jack Burkeman crept out toward the street. The other two kept low behind the barrels and crates.

"What is the message from my father?"

"The message is not from your father. It is from Ramona Hawk," Alvarez said.

"She is in Shakespeare?"

"Southwest of town. You do not sound surprised, *hermana*," Alvarez added.

"I had an idea she was in the area."

"We thought she was in prison," Laredo mumbled.

"We were on our way to Hachita to retrieve DelNorte's saddlebags and save your life when we came upon a woman camped all alone at the springs at Yucca Flat," Alvarez explained.

"Yucca Flat? You were not headed for Hachita. You were going to Mexico."

"And leave you in danger?" Alvarez protested. "How could you think such a thing, *hermana*? We were going to circle around and sneak up on Hachita."

Julianna glanced out at the street and noticed a pig looking down the alley. "Paco's not here, Buddy. He is at the foundry."

The pig trotted off.

She turned back to the three gunmen. "And the woman turned out to have friends?"

"We were ambushed," Laredo griped.

"Yes, I imagine you were. The three of you robbing a lone woman was not so easy as you expected."

"She had two men with her," Alvarez explained.

"And they had another man tied up. When we got close, we recognized your father!" Laredo said.

"Ramona Hawk has my father tied up?"

"Yes. It is true," Roberto replied.

"Why? He cannot possibly be a threat to her."

Roberto Alvarez stood and shoved his revolver back into his holster. "As far as we can tell, Hawk sent her partners to Lordsburg this morning to find Guillermo. They asked at the depot and found your father. When they found out Guillermo was in a Mexican jail, they told your father some big story about jewels and how it would help your brother if he would come with them."

"What does she want with my father?"

"She does not want him. She wants Guillermo," Alvarez explained.

"Why? Now I am really confused."

"Guillermo has done business with her in the past," Laredo answered.

"What kind of business?"

"She would buy what we had to sell. He always met with her in secret. He would not discuss the details with us, but she usually paid in jewels and jewelry," Laredo replied.

Julianna swatted at two flies that buzzed near her head. "So what have you stolen that she wants?"

"She insisted on talking only to Guillermo," Laredo explained. "She said she would turn us loose if we came back here and told you to get Guillermo out of jail. She said to bring him to her in two days or else," Alvarez reported.

"Or else what? She kills my father?"

"That is what she says," Laredo replied.

"This is insane."

Alvarez stepped toward the patio door and tried to peek around Julianna. "Hawk said, 'Go tell *La Tonta Señorita* that we have her father.'"

"She called me 'The Foolish Miss'?"

"Do you know Ramona Hawk?" Alvarez asked.

"I have known her for many years. But I cannot get Guillermo out of jail."

"Perhaps with the proper diversions and dynamite, we can do it," Laredo proposed.

"I cannot do that."

"What choice do you have?" Laredo asked.

She studied Laredo's deep brown eyes. "How do I know you are not lying to me? You might not have seen Hawk or my father and are just using this story to get me involved."

"*Hermana*, how could you think such things about us?" Alvarez exclaimed.

"I find it very easy since you three have lied to me for years and for two days have tried to enlist my support to blast Guillermo out of prison. How do I know it was not you who kidnapped Father?"

Alvarez's voice lowered. "We told Hawk you would not believe us. So she sent this." He handed her a coin.

"A gold eagle with a hole shot through it. The date on it is 1852. My father still carries that?"

"Not anymore," Laredo said.

"On the day I was born he shot the hole in it."

"He told me to tell you he was sorry for getting you in this fix," Roberto added.

"He is sorry? If he had stayed in town, he would not be in trouble now."

"He said he had hoped to help Guillermo without dragging you into it."

"It is a little late for that."

"What are we goin' to do?" Laredo asked. "Are we goin' after Guillermo?"

"I do not know. I have to think about it." She turned back to the alley door.

"What about us?" queried Laredo.

"Do not wait out here because I will not be able to restrain DelNorte much longer. Come back in an hour."

"Shall we get some dynamite?" Roberto asked.

"Do you have any money?"

"No."

"Then, by all means, do not get any dynamite."

DelNorte was leaning over the porcelain basin when Julianna reentered the apartment.

"What are you doing?" she asked.

"Vomiting. I shouldn't have tried to eat."

"You need to lie down."

"I need to get well quick."

She grabbed his arm and led him to the sofa. "Lie down."

"I left you a mess."

"Not nearly the mess that I have with my brother."

She placed a damp cloth over his eyes.

"What did Alvarez want?" he asked.

"He had a message from Ramona Hawk."

DelNorte sat straight up. The wet towel dropped to his lap.

"Please lie down, and I will talk to you. Keep your eyes closed. 'It is when your eyes are closed—'"

"'That you really hear someone's heart.'" He collapsed on the sofa.

"Yes." *DelNorte, I do not appreciate your reading my mind so easily.*

"Where is she?"

"Beyond the springs at Yucca Flat."

"She could be in Mexico by now."

"Yes, but she has my father."

He peered out from under the wet towel. "Why?"

"She thinks she can force me to get my brother out of jail by holding my father hostage."

"Can she?"

"That is what I am debating. I am now in a bind over a father that did not bother seeing me for twenty years and a brother whom I vowed never to help again. It is not 'heaven that is hounding me but the plots of Hades,' I am afraid." She looked up at his gaze. "Why are you staring at me?"

"You keep quoting phrases word for word from my brain. Are you a mind reader, Señorita Ortiz?"

"No."

"Good."

You were very quick to say "good," DelNorte. What exactly is on your mind? "Perhaps we have read the same books."

"Perhaps. What does she want of you?"

"If I get my brother out of jail, she will turn my father loose.

She thinks Guillermo has something she needs before she goes back into Mexico. Why is it there are no choices that I want?"

DelNorte hid under the wet towel. "What do you want?"

"To live a peaceful life in anonymous isolation."

"Sounds like a convent."

"If I were Catholic, I would consider it," she said.

"I don't think so. You have too much fire in your bones, Señorita Ortiz."

Why am I scowling at a man who cannot see me? "You have not known me long enough to say that, DelNorte."

He lifted the towel but kept his eyes closed. "'The depth of a relationship is never—'"

"'—measured in days or hours, but in the knowledge of words never spoken.'"

"This is most disarming, Julianna. Perhaps when my skull was laid open, you read everything in there."

"The answer is not complex," Julianna said. "But it is difficult to explain."

"And what have you decided about your brother?"

"If I do not do something, Ramona Hawk will retreat to Mexico and have no use for my father. She might turn him loose. An old man is not much of a threat to her. But she might kill him just to torment me."

"Why does she want to torment you?"

"That, DelNorte, is knowledge I will probably take to my grave."

A grin broke across his face. "She stole someone you love from you!"

"I will not let you pry out information that is better kept hidden."

"So you will try to get your brother out of jail."

"I know of no legal way to do that. The Mexican authorities made it clear they have no intention of releasing him."

"When is the execution?" DelNorte asked.

"In three days."

"They don't want to kill him too badly. Normally they haul a man out and shoot him on the same date as his sentencing. Perhaps they're hoping for a bribe."

"I asked them if I could pay a fine, and they refused to talk to me. Roberto and the others want me to divert the guards while they dynamite him out."

"Then you would have the Federales on your trail."

"I cannot with Christian conscience do that."

"I can get him out," DelNorte declared.

"Legally?"

"Yes."

"How?"

"Trust me, I can do it."

"You will not tell me how?"

"No."

"What are you suggesting?"

"You take me to Mexico."

"I take you?"

"I will need your help."

"DelNorte, you are in no condition to go anywhere."

"That's why I will need you and Paco."

"Paco too?"

"Most assuredly."

"What can a ten-year-old boy do?"

"He can be the chaperon."

"That is true, but in your condition, you hardly pose a threat to me."

"It was not your safety I was worried about. It was mine."

"Hah! The wound in your head has made you delirious, DelNorte."

"'Your protest was too loud to be—'"

"Yes, I know—'too loud to be well planned. The deaf that only read lips miss the depth of a person's heart.'"

"This is getting quite—"

"Annoying?" she supplied.

"I believe that is the word I was thinking of. Are you going to tell me how you know what I'm going to say?"

"Perhaps on the way to Guadalupe."

He pulled the towel off his face. "So we are going?"

"Only if Paco will come along to protect you from my advances."

He managed a tight smile. "Yes, of course."

"You will make a pathetic passenger."

"Thank you."

"Do you plan to vomit anymore?" she asked.

"If I do," he said, "I will do it discreetly."

"Hah! You will no doubt want me to clean up after you."

"'Do only what satisfies your heart and your Christian conscience.'"

"I knew you were going to say that."

"I knew you knew."

"Perhaps we can stop talking completely and just have the conversations in our minds."

She glanced at him for a long moment.

He didn't say a word, but a slow, wide grin broke across his face.

"We just went down there, and now we are going back?" Paco complained.

"Yes."

"But you said we were never going back."

"That was yesterday."

"Are you going back to the jail?"

"Yes."

"Are you going to get Tío Guillermo out?"

"Perhaps. That will be up to DelNorte."

"What can he do? He is hurt very bad."

"He says he can persuade the authorities to release Guillermo."

"And you believe him?"

"Yes."

"Why? Maybe he is trying to trick you."

"I have chosen to trust DelNorte, but I am not sure why."

"Are you in love with him?"

"Of course not. Why did you ask me that?"

"Bonita said she thought you were."

"She is a ten-year-old Apache girl. What does she know?"

"She knows how to smell a coyote from a mile away."

"Well, yes, that is very commendable. Now go back into the kitchen and wash up."

"And she knows how to shoot an arrow into the mouth of a beer bottle at one hundred feet."

"Okay, you have made your point. Bonita is a talented girl."

"But I can spit farther than she can," he bragged.

"Yes, that does seem to be something you excel in. Go clean up."

Paco glanced out the front window. "Here come Lixie and Gracie. Perhaps I will stay with Lixie tonight."

"You most certainly will not. Go wash up. Supper will be ready soon." She scooted him toward the green curtain door in the back of the display room.

Lixie held the door open, and Gracie Parnell strolled in with a wave of strong rose perfume.

"Guess which one of us just found out she is expecting?" Lixie blurted out.

Gracie blushed.

Julianna clapped her hands to her cheeks. "Since you are over fifty and not married until Saturday, I will guess Gracie."

Lixie fanned the collar of her dress. "Yes, isn't that exciting?"

Julianna hugged Gracie. "I think it is wonderful!"

Gracie stepped back. "You should hear Colt brag."

"Ruthie will have a little sister," Julianna commented.

"Colt insists on a boy."

"Either way, a handsome child, no doubt." Lixie sashayed toward the green curtain door. "How is my patient this evening?"

El Señor, I always feel so plain when I stand next to these two. Perhaps that is my role—to make others look good. "He threw up this afternoon. Now he is asleep, but the stitches look fine."

"He has a concussion. He should keep lying down and not move for several days," Lixie advised.

Julianna let out a deep sigh.

Lixie reached out and took her hand. "What's the matter?"

"We need to go to Guadalupe tonight."

"Why? What for?" Lixie pressed.

Gracie slipped an arm around Julianna's waist. "I understand perfectly. Did he tell you the secret yet?"

"No."

Lixie stiffened her back. Her brown eyes flashed. "Tell you what?" she demanded.

"Oh, well, then I'm still the only one to know," Gracie gloated. "This is so delightful. I'll cherish the moment forever."

"You look very smug," Lixie retorted.

"Thank you." Gracie held the curtain back as they entered the living quarters. "For a few moments I know something Lixie Miller doesn't. It's like the thrill of standing on a high mountain after an arduous hike."

"Enjoy it while you can because I intend to find out quickly." Lixie hiked across the room and surveyed DelNorte. The other two joined her and stared down at him.

"Lixie, do all men sleep with their mouths open?" Gracie asked.

"Why are you two looking at me? Am I an expert on how all men sleep?"

"Come on, Lixie, you've told us about times at a fort when you were the only woman in a company of 175 men," Gracie chided.

"I didn't inspect the enlisted men's barracks at night. Well, not often," she laughed. "Now you and Julianna are hiding things—just to torment me, no doubt. But I want to know why you and a severely wounded man are going to Mexico by yourselves."

"Paco is going with us," Julianna hastened to add.

"Oh, well, of course. I will ask him to keep a close eye on the two of you and report back to me."

"Lixie!" Gracie scolded.

Lixie Miller held her chin up. "Well, he will. I want to know all about this hurried trip . . . and what it has to do with . . . Ramona Hawk."

Julianna pondered Lixie's penetrating gaze. "How did you know it involved Ramona Hawk?"

"I didn't until I watched your eyes when I mentioned her name," Lixie said. "I have never known a woman like Ramona Hawk who can cause such reactions in so many lives."

Julianna moved over to the counter. "Well, sit down. This is going to be a very long story."

Lixie glanced at Gracie. "I knew this was going to be a good day!"

"I will talk while I fix Paco some supper, but if DelNorte wakes up, the story is over."

"I'll cook. You tell us everything," Lixie insisted. She grabbed Julianna's apron from the wooden peg.

DelNorte slept soundly on Julianna's sofa, one arm tucked behind his head, the other flopped to the floor.

Paco ate his third pork chop, two tortillas, and one bite of peas.

Lixie and Gracie scurried out the front door with big smiles.

In the twilight of the hot, sticky day, Julianna paced out back on the patio.

El Señor, this is exactly what I most dislike—others telling me where I have to go and what I have to do. I am going to a foreign country with a severely injured, notorious man I have known for twenty-four hours to get a release for my twin brother, who is obviously guilty, so that we can take him to a desperate murderer and escaped prisoner, who will enlist him to do something illegal for her in order that she liberate my father, who has not really been a father to me. This is like a bad dream that keeps getting worse.

Perhaps I will grab Paco, and we will get on the evening train west and go to Tucson. I will come back in a week and see what has transpired.

A rap at the backdoor caused her to spin around. She hurried across the tiled patio and paused without opening the door.

"Yes?"

"*Hermana*, open up quickly."

"Laredo?"

"Yes. Open up."

"Tell Roberto and Jack that I am going to Guadalupe this

evening, and I believe I can get Guillermo out. But I need to do this without you three tagging along."

"There are more critical things than that. Open up," Laredo insisted.

"What are you talking about?"

"Roberto has been shot."

Julianna unlocked the door and flung it open.

El Señor, this must certainly be a joke. The situation cannot get more complex. I cannot handle anything else!

Can I?

In the shadows Roberto Alvarez was propped up by Jack Burkeman. Dark red blood oozed down his dusty cotton shirt and smeared across his brown vest.

"*Hermana,*" Laredo pleaded, "you must do something. Quick!"

Seven

Laredo Nisqually and Jack Burkeman toted the wounded man into the patio and spread him on the low wooden bench. The vines across the trellised roof of the patio made a variegated light pattern on Roberto's blood-soaked vest.

Julianna bent over and examined the wound. "What happened?"

"Ramona Hawk shot him," Laredo declared.

She stood up. "Is she here in town?"

"No, she's on her way to Mariposa Tank," Burkeman reported. "We caught up with her to deliver the message that you were goin' after Guillermo."

"And?" Julianna prompted.

"Well, *hermana*," Nisqually continued, "Roberto was very distressed that she was holding your father hostage. He thought we could get her to turn loose of him."

"He was wrong," Burkeman added.

She studied Alvarez's pained brown eyes. He reached his left hand up to her, and she grasped it. "You got shot trying to help my father?"

His eyes blinked. "It seemed like the right thing."

El Señor, I have such a difficult time believing this. I trust I have not become cynical beyond reason. But it is more likely that he thought he could cut Guillermo out and deal with her directly. "Keep pressing the bandanna over that wound. Slow the bleeding down. I'll get help."

Burkeman pulled off his hat and fanned Roberto's face. "Perhaps we should move him inside your house."

Julianna continued to hold Roberto's hand. "DelNorte is still there, waiting to shoot the first one of you who comes through the door. Do not even get close to it. There is enough blood on my patio for one day."

Julianna trotted back into the apartment. "Paco, go get Lixie. Tell her there is a wounded man on my patio."

Paco shoved a cracker into his mouth. "Who is it this time?" he mumbled.

"Roberto Alvarez."

Paco peeked out the backdoor. "Did you shoot him?"

She rubbed her temples. "No, I did not shoot him." *Lord, all I ever wanted to do is live in peace in my house, and You allow all of this confusion to come to me.*

Paco ran through the store and into the street. Julianna plucked up a basin and towel. She studied DelNorte's rhythmic breathing. *DelNorte, you are going to sleep through most of this week's adventures. I will probably be able to buffalo the likes of Laredo and Jack, as long as you do not begin to snore.*

Back on the patio, she set the basin on the tile floor beside the wounded outlaw. "Jack, light that lamp hanging above your head. This is crazy. I do not know what you three are doing here. If you are going to go get yourself killed, why does it have to be on my back doorstep? I told you in Mexico I did not want anything to do with you and your plans. You three are like a bad headache I cannot get rid of."

She reached into the basin and brushed her wet fingertips across Roberto's chapped, dry lips.

Taking short breaths, Alvarez glanced over at Nisqually. "What did I tell you, Laredo? She loves us like *una madre*. She scolds us and doctors us at the same time."

Julianna raised her thick, dark eyebrows. "So now I am your mother?"

Jack Burkeman guarded the door to the alley. "You're our angel, *hermana*."

"An angel? That is a laugh."

"No," Roberto said, "think about it. You are as close to an angel as the three of us will ever get."

"It does not have to be that way."

"Are you goin' to preach at us?" Laredo challenged.

"Yes. It is *una madre's* prerogative to lecture *los niños*. El Señor died for your sins too."

"You don't know how many sins we have," Burkeman called out from the alley doorway.

Julianna glanced up at the trellised sky. "He does."

Alvarez's words broke from pained, parched lips. "Why do you tell us this? Why do you care?"

She washed Alvarez's forehead. "Because if you would stop this way of living, I could have a peaceful life. You would not appear at the backdoor with a posse on your tail."

"No posse this time," Laredo said.

"A posse might be easier to handle than Ramona Hawk."

"She is right about that," Laredo agreed.

"There is a woman coming up the alley," Burkeman called out.

Lixie Miller buzzed into the patio, every strand of hair in place, makeup carefully applied. "My dear Julianna, I have never known a woman who attracts so many handsome men."

"Handsome, bleeding, wounded men," Julianna corrected.

Lixie immediately knelt down by the injured man, pulled his bloody hand away from the wound, and ripped his shirt open. "Sweet Julianna, your house is like a war zone. I've been with the ambulance after a battle, and it was more peaceful than your patio."

Julianna stepped back. "Where is Paco?"

"He went to get Gracie."

"Why?"

"Because I might need some help. She and I will take care of this batch. You need to take a trip."

"You are leavin' me?" Roberto asked.

"In very good hands." Julianna turned to Lixie Miller. "What time is it?"

"The train is due to pull out in less than half an hour. You go on and get yourself ready. I'll take care of everything here."

Julianna put a hand on Lixie's narrow shoulder. "But—but you have a wedding Saturday."

Lixie patted her hand. Their rings rattled against each other's at the touch. "I have a wedding in forty-four hours. I'm counting on you being back by then."

"I will be here. I would not miss it for anything."

"Good. Now go on. I'll take care of this."

Julianna tried to brush her long black hair back behind her ears. "I just cannot walk off and leave you here alone."

Lixie opened up the wounded shoulder and peered inside. "Alone? I have two handsome men standing guard and another who desperately needs me. What more could any woman want?"

Julianna gasped at the severity of the shoulder wound. She turned away to see Burkeman and Nisqually staring at her. "You were right about one thing. You are now in the presence of an angel."

DelNorte walked stiffly across the street, his arm around Julianna's shoulder. Paco lugged a small canvas valise.

"How are you feeling?" she asked.

"The ringing pain in my head is not as severe, but my vision remains blurred. The only time my head settles down is when I close my eyes."

"Then keep your eyes closed." She struggled with the dead weight draped on her shoulders. "Are you sure you have the strength to make this trip?"

DelNorte attempted to stand taller. "It's important to me."

"To help me?"

"Yes, and to capture Ramona Hawk."

"'A person is known for the things that drive him to—'"

"'—unexpected behavior,'" he completed.

"It is as if I keep talking to myself."

His words were quiet but strong. "I wish you would tell me why."

"Perhaps later, but only if you will promise to keep your eyes closed."

Paco ran ahead of them, tossed up the valise, and took a flying leap up onto the train platform.

DelNorte shuffled along, his eyes closed. "Is anyone lookin' my way?"

"What are you talking about? Of course they are. Your forehead looks like a grizzly bear has been chewing on it."

He blinked his eyes open. "No, I mean, anyone suspicious. Someone could be trying to trace my movements."

"Why? Who?"

He stopped and shifted his weight back to his own feet. "Do you see anyone suspicious?"

"No one has a gun drawn and pointed at you. Is that what you meant?" She tugged on his arm.

"That's a good start." He began to walk on his own.

She draped her arm in his. "I think the head injury is more severe than you thought."

"You might be right."

She led him to the Pullman car where a uniformed conductor assisted him up the stairs.

Julianna propped DelNorte on a seat next to the window. Paco jumped into the seat across from them. "Can I have this whole seat to myself?" he asked.

Julianna sat down next to DelNorte. "Yes, if no other passengers need it."

"The train is not very crowded. Gracie gave me a book to read."

"Oh?"

Paco held up the paperback book. "*Stuart Brannon and the Circle of Death!*"

DelNorte sat up straight and took a deep breath. "Brannon wins," he said.

"Of course he wins." Paco grinned. "He always wins, but how will he do it this time?"

"You look a little stronger. Are you all right?" she asked DelNorte.

"I'm feeling better than this afternoon."

"Perhaps it was the nap."

"Or the vomiting," Paco added.

"Would you like to lie down? I can sit with Paco," she offered.

"No, this is fine." She noticed a spark in his eyes. "Would it be improper for me to put my head on your shoulder?"

"Hmmm, I do think you are feeling better. With a head that looks like yours, I am not sure anything would look proper. Go ahead."

"Thank you."

"You are welcome."

His head rested lightly against her shoulder. She reached over and patted his knee.

"Am I going to have to keep an eye on you two?" Paco called out.

She jerked her hand back. "What do you mean?"

"Lixie said I was to watch you two closely."

DelNorte opened his eyes but left his head on her shoulder. "Watch for what?"

"Kissing and stuff like that."

Julianna tugged on the lace cuff of her sleeve and glanced over at the ten-year-old. "Read your book. I promise there will be no kissing."

"How about 'stuff like that'?" DelNorte murmured.

Julianna burst out with a laugh. "And absolutely no 'stuff' will happen either."

She could hear other passengers come aboard and watched as they filled some seats around her. Then she stared out the window.

El Señor, time is such a strange phenomenon. For months and years my life was so predictable. I could tell a week ahead of time exactly what I would be doing at any given hour of the day. Now suddenly I have absolutely no control over anything. It is as if I have lived a lifetime in less than two days. I want to run back to the routine, but I do not know why. I cannot remember the last time I had a man's head on my shoulder. Perhaps never. It is not a bad feeling.

So why do I want to run? Why do I want to hide? Why am I so terrified of something outside my routine? Outside my store?

And why is this gray-headed man who yesterday grabbed my shoulder on the boardwalk of Guadalupe, threatening to shoot me, now sleeping on that same shoulder?

A stiff finger tapped her other shoulder. "Excuse me."

The finger belonged to a large lady in a blue gingham dress. She was sitting in the seat across the aisle, holding a big black leather satchel in her lap.

"Yes?"

"Do you speak English?"

"Eh, yes, ma'am." Julianna tried to smile. "What can I do for you?"

"Oh, my, I'm just so nervous. It's good to have someone to talk to who speaks English. You hardly have any accent at all." The woman licked her full, pink lips.

Perhaps it is because I grew up in a home where English was the language spoken. Or perhaps because my mother was American. She watched the woman staring out the window at the Lordsburg station as the train pulled away. "What are you worried about?"

"Oh, your dear husband looks quite sorry. Did he get scalped?"

Julianna reached over and brushed shaggy gray hair off DelNorte's stitches. *It just is not worth the effort to explain.*

"No. He had a work-related accident."

"Oh dear! My Harvey, rest his soul, once drilled a hole right through his thumb."

Julianna winced.

"When you first got on the train, I thought perhaps he was your father, you know, with all that gray hair. But then I looked at you and said to myself, 'Myrtle, that *señora* is not a young lady either. So she must be his wife. Not that you look old. Oh heavens, I didn't mean that. But there is a certain 'seasoning' that age brings to our looks, isn't there?"

Seasoning? That is a strange term for growing old. "I suppose you are right about that."

"That last town looked almost like we're still in the States."

"What do you mean?"

"This is my first trip to a foreign country."

"Are you going to Mexico?"

"Going? Honey, we've been in Mexico ever since the Arizona border. But you bein' one of them, you know all about it, of course."

"Ma'am, we are in New Mexico."

"Yes, that's what I said."

"But New Mexico Territory is in the United States," Julianna declared.

"Oh, no, we crossed the border back at Arizona. I noticed your son is reading English. That's quite commendable. I'm a school-teacher."

Julianna tried to maneuver her shoulders to a more comfortable position. Her back and neck ached. *El Señor, when is something not worth arguing about? No logic would convince her.*

The woman leaned so close Julianna could smell the peppermint on her breath. "I have a rather delicate question I'm dying to ask you. I hope you don't take it as rude."

"Yes?" Julianna glanced down and saw DelNorte's eyes still closed.

"I'm a widow lady."

"Yes?"

"I have heard," the woman whispered, "that Latin men are quite . . . well, some say they are very good at . . . romance."

Julianna burst out with a laugh.

Paco dropped his book.

DelNorte sat up.

The red-faced woman pulled back and fanned her face with her straw hat.

"Are you all right?" DelNorte mumbled.

"Yes, I am. What about you? You had a little nap."

He stretched his long arms out in front of him. "I do feel better."

"Do you feel good enough to wrestle a mountain lion?" Paco asked.

DelNorte glanced over at the boy and grinned. "Probably not."

"In the first scene in this book, Stuart Brannon had to wrestle a mountain lion in his long handles."

"The lion is wearing his long johns?"

"No!" Paco squealed. "Brannon was camping alone and woke up in his bedroll in the mountains with two feet of fresh snow when a mountain lion pounced on him for no reason."

"That's a rough way to wake up. How did he defeat such an enemy?" DelNorte questioned.

"He rolled the animal over to the fire, and the cat got burned and ran away."

"Too close to the flames?"

"Yes. Brannon is very, very smart."

"So is his horse."

"What do you mean?"

"If Brannon just woke up," DelNorte said, rubbing his unshaven chin, "who built up that fire to a blaze? Brannon wouldn't have had time. So it must have been his horse."

Paco's eyes widened. "Mr. Rodriquez has a horse that can draw water from the well. I've watched him."

"Here is my best advice, Mr. Paco. Always ride a horse that is smarter than you. He'll keep you out of trouble."

Paco studied his face. "DelNorte, did you ever have a book written about you?"

This time it was DelNorte who burst out laughing. "No! I don't think that will ever happen. How about you, Paco? Did you ever have a book written about you?"

"Not yet, but I will. It will be called *The Boy Governor of New Mexico*. I'm writing it myself."

"I like the title."

"Thank you."

"You're welcome."

"I want to write down all the exciting things in my life now so I can remember them when I am old like you."

DelNorte laughed again. "Mr. Paco, you are quite an entertaining fellow."

"I believe Mr. DelNorte is regaining his strength," Julianna observed.

"Paco makes me relax."

"And the ladies find me quite handsome," Paco boasted.

"Paco!" Julianna scolded.

"They do . . . except for one Apache girl who thinks only Indian boys are brave and handsome."

"Having a tough time impressin' her, are you?" DelNorte asked.

"She can outrun me and throw rocks better than me."

"I'm sure you excel in some things," DelNorte encouraged him.

"I can spit off the trestle over Arroyo Seco better than her." Paco beamed.

"There you go. The Lord gave everyone special talents."

Paco's eyes widened. "Do you believe in El Señor?"

"I certainly do. And so does Stuart Brannon, doesn't he?"

"Yes, he does! But I do not think it is going to help right now."

"Why not?" DelNorte asked.

"Because the axle busted on the stagecoach, and the team panicked and is racing straight for a cliff."

"Do you think Brannon will get killed?"

"No." Paco grinned. "Aunt Julianna says Stuart Brannon is like okra."

"Okra?"

"Yes. No matter what you do to it, it always survives."

"He reads too much fiction," Julianna mumbled. "Lixie keeps him supplied with books."

"I've heard that all those Stuart Brannon books are true," DelNorte commented.

"I have heard the same thing," Paco replied, "but I think perhaps there are a few stretchers."

By the time the train pulled into the station at Deming, both Paco and DelNorte were asleep. Some passengers disembarked, and others boarded. Julianna stared out the window at shadows, street lamps, and foglike steam from the engine.

Twenty-four hours ago I had made up my mind that I would never see my brother again. Now I am on my way back to Guadalupe. I cannot even guess what the next twenty-four hours will bring. I am not at all sure what You want me to do, El Señor. Sometimes I feel like a rock sliding across the ice. I have no power to control my direction, destina-

tion, or speed. I just go sailing the direction I am shoved. This cannot be
how Your will is determined, can it?

"Wish me luck." The large woman behind her struggled to the
aisle.

"You are getting off here?"

"I change railroads here."

"Are you going north?"

"Yes, I'm going to spend a week with a friend in Santa Fe."

"It is a very nice place. I grew up there. I hope you enjoy it."

"Do you know of any restaurants where English is spoken in
Santa Fe?"

"All of them do, I believe."

"Oh, how delightful! That will keep the culture shock of being
in a foreign country at a minimum. I'm taking notes so I can teach
my class all about Mexico."

"New Mexico," Julianna corrected.

"Yes, yes. It was so nice to meet you. I'm sorry I embarrassed you
with that question."

"That is quite all right. I was just surprised."

"I watched you and your husband visit. I can tell you have a
very close relationship—the way he teases your son. That
reminded me of my father and brothers."

"*Gracias.*"

The woman's eyes lit up. "Oh, yes . . . thank you—*gracias*,
señora. Oh my, I am getting the hang of this."

Twenty-five miles east of Deming, the train slowed so suddenly that
it tossed Julianna forward. DelNorte's head slipped off her shoulder and slid to her lap, but neither he nor Paco woke up. The lamps
in the train were so low it was difficult to see anyone's face clearly.

She could hear the conductor as he entered the front of the car.
"It's okay, folks. The United States Army needed to stop the train.
You can't see 'em too well, but there are sixty-five boys in blue out
on the north side of the tracks. They are searching for someone and
thought he might be on the train."

Julianna pulled DelNorte's hat over his sleeping head. *Why is*

it, El Señor, that I know they are looking for DelNorte? Since I have met
this man, there has been one crisis after another. I do not understand.
But if he does not get Guillermo out of jail . . . then Hawk will . . . This
is insane!

The conductor strolled down the aisle. "We'll get started in just a minute, folks. Just relax." He stopped by Julianna.

"Señora, I noticed your daddy was injured when you got on. How's he doin'?"

Julianna tugged down the hat just low enough to reveal the stitches in DelNorte's forehead.

"My word, señora, it looks like a freight wagon ran over him."

"*¿Habla usted Español?*" she asked.

"No, ma'am, I don't speak Mexican." The conductor marched to the back of the car and exited.

She reached over to lower the window and tried to spot the troops in the desert starlight. *Why is he wanted by the army? A man is sleeping in my lap, and I have no idea who he is. I am a very rational person, but my behavior has become erratic, even questionable.*

The front door burst open. A captain marched in leading two carbine-toting soldiers.

Lord, keep us from all evil.

The captain marched straight up to her. "Are you Señora Ortiz?"

"I am Señorita Ortiz," she replied.

The captain smiled. "I should have figured this is where DelNorte would be. He needs to come with us."

"He is sleeping," she murmured.

"Yes, ma'am, and he looks quite comfy, but this is rather important."

He plucked up DelNorte's hat and handed it to one of the men. "Good grief!" he exclaimed. "What happened to his forehead?"

"He was attacked by assassins. My friends and I doctored him."

"Yes, ma'am. Put your gun on him, Schmitt. As you must have found out by now, DelNorte wakes up grouchy." The captain reached down and shook the man's shoulder.

DelNorte drew his revolver as he staggered to his feet.

Paco sat up and stretched his arms.

"Put the gun away, DelNorte."

"Captain Brinkman? I wasn't expectin' you."

"That's obvious. Levertts is over on the Pecos, so he sent me. Come on, DelNorte, you're wanted outside."

"What is going on?" Paco asked as he scooted next to Julianna. "Are we in El Paso?"

She hugged his shoulders. "No, baby. The U.S. Army needs to . . . eh, talk to DelNorte."

"About what?"

Brinkman grasped DelNorte's arm and turned toward the rear exit.

"Take it easy, Brinkman. Got to get my bearings."

"He is an injured man," Julianna protested.

"Yes, ma'am, but DelNorte dead is tougher than most men who are healthy."

She reached up to grab his sleeve, but caught his hand instead. "What do you want us to do?" she asked.

He squeezed her hand. "Don't worry, darlin'. I'll be right back." He winked.

He and the soldiers walked out into the night.

"Are they going to arrest him? Does the army arrest people, or do they just shoot them? Are they going to shoot him?" Paco questioned.

"They are not going to shoot him. The army does not shoot people they find on trains."

"What if he is a criminal?" Paco pressed.

"He is not a criminal."

"That is what they said about El Paso Pete."

"Who?"

"In the Brannon book. He was the town banker, but really he was an outlaw just pretending to be a banker."

"And then he robbed the bank?"

"Have you read the book?" Paco asked.

"No."

"What did DelNorte mean when he said he would be right back?"

"I do not know."

Paco stared out the dark window. "Why did he wink at you?"

"I am not sure."

"Can you see anything outside?"

"No. It is quite dark."

"What are we going to do?"

"I am going to pray."

"For DelNorte?"

"Yes, and for wisdom. Everything is so confusing. If he does not come back, I am not sure we should go on to Guadalupe."

"He will come back," Paco insisted. "He will keep his word."

"'Sometimes the circumstances of the body do not allow us to follow the promises of the heart.'" *He would have known that one too. She wrote the exact same letters to both of us. Maybe it is good that he went away. Some things about my past are much too painful to discuss . . . ever! Lord, please keep Your hand on us and give me wisdom. Please protect DelNorte.*

"I like DelNorte," Paco declared.

"He is an interesting fellow."

"Do you like him now?"

"What do you mean, now?"

"When I asked you if you were going to marry him, you pitched a fit."

"Paco Ortiz, I did not."

Paco stuck his head out the window. "I think the soldiers are leaving. Where is DelNorte?"

"Perhaps the soldiers took him."

"Took him where? He said he would come back," Paco protested.

The train lurched forward.

The train car door opened, and the conductor strolled in. "Here we go, folks. Just some official army business. The engineer said he will try to make up the time so we won't be too late pulling into El Paso." He came down the aisle and pointed his finger at Julianna. "Señora, you certainly pulled one over on me."

She watched his small, round, dark eyes.

A smile broke across his face. "But it all turned out fine." He ambled on through the car.

Turned out fine for whom? I do not know who to ask, what to ask. Or if I even want to know what happened.

"Where's DelNorte?" Paco whispered.

Julianna took a big, deep breath.

Lord, it is time for things to turn around. I cannot face another crisis. There is a limit of my endurance, and I have just reached it. I believe You have an inflated idea of my stamina and faith. I am trying, but I cannot do this. I am too weak. I just want to go crawl in a hole.

The hand that grabbed her shoulder sent shivers down her back.

"You still got room for me?"

"DelNorte!" Paco shouted. "Where have you been? Aunt Julianna has been very, very worried."

Paco dove across to the facing seat. Julianna scooted over to the window. DelNorte slid in next to her. "So you were worried?"

"I was worried about my father's fate."

"And your brother's?"

"Yes. If you did not come back, I was trying to decide what to do."

"But you weren't too concerned about me?"

"I prayed that you would be treated fairly."

"Thank you. Your prayers were answered."

"I suppose it would be of no use to ask you what they wanted you for."

"Oh, they didn't want me. I wanted them."

She sat straight up and threw her shoulders back. "What?"

"There are two ways of looking at the situation. Either the army stopped the train to find me, or I stopped the train to find the army."

"That is ludicrous. You did not stop anything. You were sound asleep."

"In your lap. Perhaps I was not always sound asleep."

Julianna folded her arms across her chest.

"You made her mad," Paco announced.

"I can see that."

"I am not mad!"

"Let me apologize if I did anything improper," he offered.

"Yes, and you seem to be feeling much stronger."

"A rest and a stroll in the night air seems to do that for me."

"DelNorte, I would like to know what is going on."

"I'm sure you would."

"And you are not going to tell me?"

"Not yet, but I will." He slumped down in the seat and leaned his head on the leather backrest. He propped his hat across his face so that it didn't rub against any of the stitches.

Julianna couldn't tell if his eyes were open or closed. "Are you going to hide under your hat?"

"There's room for two."

She scrunched down and tried to peer under the brim of the hat. "What?"

"Scoot down under here, and I'll show you."

DelNorte put his head close to hers and draped the wide-brimmed black felt hat over both of their faces.

"See."

"Your hat smells of campfires, smoke, and sweat."

"Yes, ma'am, I reckon it does."

"I want to know one thing," she pressed. "You really look much stronger. What did those soldiers say that perked you up?"

"I think it's a combination of finally getting enough rest, my stomach settling down, the fever breaking, and . . ."

"And?"

"A plan starting to work."

"What kind of plan?"

"I can't tell you now."

"It involves more than my brother and father, I think."

"Perhaps."

"That is the best I get?" She started to sit up.

"Wait." He held her shoulder. "Please."

She slumped back down. "Do not use me, DelNorte. I have been used too often." She laid her hand on top of his.

"What was his name?" He laced his fingers into hers.

"Do not start that game, because I am not going to discuss it." She held his hand tight.

"You are a tough one, Señorita Ortiz. Let me give you a quiz. I will start a phrase, and when I stop, you finish it."

"Okay."

"'The true depth of love can only be measured by—'"

"'—the ease and breadth of one's forgiveness.'"

"That's good," he said.

"What does it prove?"

"Let me try another. 'Every classic romance involves—'"

"'—a secret well hidden and never told.'"

"Very good! How about this one: 'Like stars that blanket the skies—'"

"'—thoughts of you mark the parameters of my world and bring comfort to troubled nights.'"

"Okay, Señorita Ortiz, when did you read my mail?"

She shut her eyes. "I will tell you, but you will have to tell me what the deal is with the troops."

"Do you think we can trust each other?"

"I think we can. Do you think so?"

"Yes, but I don't know why I trust you. I have survived for many years by trusting no person. I can't tell you everything you will want to know. Not now. But I will tell you about the troops. I ordered them here from Fort Bayard."

"You ordered them here? One of the telegrams Gracie sent?"

"Yes. I sent them to patrol the border from the customhouse at Deming to the west. Another telegram went to Arizona. Troops there will sweep out of Black Water and across and meet these troops. I want to keep Ramona Hawk out of Mexico."

"Just like that. DelNorte speaks, and the troops move?"

"Yes."

"Are you going to tell me how you happen to have such power?"

"No. But I told you much more than I should have. It's your turn."

"It is a much longer story."

"We have two hours until El Paso."

"Are we going to keep whispering under your hat?"

"Yes."

"Why?"

"So people will be suspicious of what we're doing."

She started to sit up. He held onto her hand. "Please. I was kiddin'. Everyone is asleep. But I didn't want anyone to overhear."

He peeked out at Paco. "Looks like the *niño* is asleep. Funny how kids sleep with their mouths open like that."

As do certain men I know. "I will tell you some, DelNorte, but if I get upset, I might just quit in the middle."

"Okay, that's fair. I'm very curious as to how you managed to read my personal correspondence, and I didn't even know it."

"I assure you, I have never seen your correspondence."

"But you know those phrases word for word."

"Let me shorten the version a bit. I grew up living with my mother's cousin and her husband in Santa Fe. He was a jeweler. Before he retired, he was the most successful jeweler between St. Louis and San Francisco."

"He taught you his trade?"

"As much as he could. I wanted to go to Holland and learn to cut diamonds, but they would not accept a lady or a Mexican. But I did learn much. My sister, Paco's mother, was extremely beautiful and outgoing. Paco is much like her. But I was the shy sister. I watched my sister dance while I sat in the shadows, terrified that some man would ask me."

"I find that difficult to believe. You are a beautiful woman."

"Yes, and you have a concussion. But thank you. When I turned twenty-one, the governor had a big cookout in my honor at the plaza in Santa Fe."

"The governor? I'm impressed."

"My 'Uncle' Paul knows many important people. Anyway, at the party my sister Marga was already quite large with child, so she took it as her task to arrange for every eligible man present to dance with me."

"That's quite a sister."

"She was the most incredible person I have ever met, if you can imagine Grace Parnell's beauty with Lixie Miller's outgoing personality."

"And Julianna's class?"

"Please be still. Your head injury is much more serious than you thought. Anyway, it was a most delightful evening. As it turns out, it was the highlight of my life."

"But something happened?"

"The very next day I received an unsigned letter from a secret admirer."

"How exciting!"

"Are you mocking me, DelNorte?"

"No, ma'am."

"This is a very painful subject. No soul on earth has heard me talk about it."

"I will respect your feelings, señorita."

"Every morning after that there was a letter under the door of the jewelry shop."

"Never signed?"

"No. And every night I would leave a note half under the door in response."

"This must have seemed very romantic to you."

"The letters I received were beautiful." Julianna took a deep breath and held it.

"Are you okay?"

Tears rolled down her cheeks. "Yes. I must keep talking. I need to tell someone. They were the most beautiful and loving letters I had ever read in my life."

"That's where you learned all those expressions?"

"Yes."

"So this thief somehow read my mail, and then he sent those lines to you? That's not a totally bad thing. The heart makes us do strange things."

Julianna kept her eyes closed as she talked. "This was not from the heart. After thirty days he wanted to meet me."

"A month. This secret letter-writing went on for a whole month?"

"Yes. I was so enthralled. No one had ever spoken to me like that before . . . nor since. I was twenty-one but emotionally probably no more than fifteen."

"So he wanted to meet you?"

"In private."

"Without your relatives around?"

"Yes. He had a very private question he wanted to ask me."

"To marry you?"

"That is what my heart told me."

"Where did he want to meet you?"

"At the jewelry store. He did not know where our house was."

"I'm sensing a cloud on the horizon. He wants to meet inside a room filled with jewelry?"

"I know. I was a foolish girl."

"Were you in love with him?"

"Yes. As much as I knew what that word meant."

"Were you ready to marry him and ride off with him that night?"

"I believe I would have ridden off with him whether married or not. El Señor was very kind to me in that way. He protected me from my own sinful desires."

"Did you have a visitor at the jewelry store?"

"Oh, yes, I had a visitor."

"And what was the all-important question?"

"At the point of a gun I was asked for the combination of the big safe."

"Oh, Julianna, that's cruel beyond measure. How did this *malo hombre* come up with my correspondence?"

Julianna bit her lip. "It gets worse."

"Did he harm you?"

"Not physically. But emotionally I suppose I have never recovered."

"What happened?"

"I do not know if I can say this without bursting into tears."

"Then stop right there."

"What?"

"Julianna, I don't want to stir up your old pain."

"DelNorte, I have gone this far, and you are going to have to put up with my blubbering."

"Okay. What happened?"

"I know that you were engaged to Ramona Hawk, and those expressions were part of your correspondence."

"That's true."

"That is why I know them so well."

"I don't follow."

"The one who wrote them to you was the same one who wrote them to me."

"What?"

"It was not a young man who was secretly courting me. It was Ramona Hawk deceiving me so she could gain entrance to the safe at the jewelry store."

"She's the one who showed up that night?"

"Oh, yes. She laughed and laughed. I cried."

Julianna laid her head on his shoulder. He patted her hair but said nothing.

"I was so naive that I not only fell for a line, but I fell for a line penned by a woman and did not even know it. I gave my heart to a phantom created by a thieving woman. That is why I know those expressions. Like you, I memorized every one. Try as I may, I cannot get them out of my mind. They remind me a dozen times a day that I can never trust my heart."

He said nothing.

"Are you stunned?"

"Julianna, I appreciate your telling me this. I guarantee I will tell no soul, ever."

"Thank you, DelNorte. You see, we do have more in common than you thought. We have both listened to her words that touched our hearts and deceived us."

"It's incredible that we ever met."

"If Laredo had not stolen your poke, we would never have met. If you do not mind, I really cannot talk about it anymore."

"Perhaps at some future time? I would like to discuss it more with you. There is more to the story you should know."

"I am very sleepy. I have needed to tell that story for nine years. Now I can rest."

"Earlier you offered your shoulder for me to sleep on. I will offer you the same."

"Do we have to hide under this hat?"

"No." He sat up and carefully tilted the hat to the back of his head. He put his left arm on the back of the train seat, and she laid her head on a hard-muscled shoulder.

"Thank you for listening to my pitiful story," she murmured.

"I like listening to you, Julianna. You have a strong, musical voice that is very easy to listen to. 'It carries a depth of feeling—'"

"'—like wild rose petals on a fresh mountain stream.'"

"Yes. Soon we will only nod and know what the other one is about to say."

"Perhaps you will need new lines to use on me, DelNorte. I have heard all of Ramona Hawk's lines."

"I have been thinking that myself. Now go to sleep. Once we get to Mexico, I doubt if there will be any time to rest."

She yawned. "Can you really get my brother out of jail?"

"That will be the easy part."

"And the difficult part?"

"Trying to keep us all alive."

"You have the entire United States Army poised against one woman?"

"The woman is Ramona Hawk, but she's not alone."

"The two men?"

"It's bigger than that."

"She has a gang?"

"It's bigger than a gang."

"How big?"

"That's what I was trying to find out when Laredo stole my poke."

"I am very confused."

"Get some sleep."

"I think I will. I am suddenly so exhausted I cannot keep my eyes open."

His arm slipped around her shoulder and gently hugged her.

"DelNorte, you will not do anything improper while I sleep on your shoulder, will you?"

He jerked his arm back. "No, ma'am."

"Good." Julianna reached up and pulled his arm back to her shoulder.

Eight

Julianna and Paco huddled at a bench on the train platform in El Paso while DelNorte disappeared into the dimly lit night.

Why did I feel a need to tell him all of that? It sounds even worse when I say it aloud. I cannot believe I said those things. He was shocked. Astonished. I am sure he will want to run away now. But I am surprised that I do not want him to run away. Why do I want to impress such a man? There is no reason to trust him any more than any other. And I have never trusted any man, except "Uncle" Paul. Maybe Colt Parnell and Jefferson Carter, but only because of the women they are associated with. I was deceived by a woman, and therefore I trust no man. El Señor, do You understand my heart? I have no idea why it operates as it does. Perhaps it has been damaged beyond repair.

In the distance she heard the clomp of hooves and the squeak of carriage wheels.

All I know is that that nap was the best rest I have had in ten, maybe twenty years. Such a sense of peace, of being at home. Home on a train? On the shoulder of a mysterious, wild, strong man with gray hair and a battered forehead?

The carriage pulled up by the depot.

"Come on, Paco. DelNorte is here."

He raised his head off her lap. "Can I stay here and sleep?"

"No, come on."

"Carry me," he whined.

She pushed him to his feet and hugged his shoulders. "You are very funny, *niño*. Soon you will be big enough to carry me. Come on, I'll carry the bag."

They hurried toward the long black leather carriage. DelNorte waited beside the team of black horses.

Julianna squinted at the rig. "What is this?"

His reply was soft, deep. "A hearse."

"But why?"

He took her arm and helped her up the carriage step. "It might help us get your brother out of the prison."

She grabbed the cold iron rail and paused. "How does one rent a hearse in the middle of the night?"

"You telegraph ahead of time." He continued to clutch her arm.

In the distance she heard a yell and a gunshot. Then silence. "You had this trip all planned? I thought it was my idea."

"It was, darlin'. You and I have similar ideas, remember?"

"This is very strange. I trust the hearse is not a premonition of someone's death."

"I reckon we'll find that out in the next thirty-six hours, won't we?" he said.

"Where do we sit?"

"Up front with me."

"Are you going to turn loose of my arm long enough to let me climb up there?"

"Sorry."

"Are you?"

"Not really."

Julianna pulled herself up to the thickly padded leather seat. Even with the warm night and thick dress, it felt cold as she sat down.

"Can I lie down?" Paco mumbled as he climbed up behind her.

The carriage rocked as DelNorte plopped down beside them. "You can crawl in the back if you'd like," he offered.

"But I promised Lixie I would keep an eye on you two."

DelNorte laughed. "I certify that I will keep everything proper."

"And what about you, Aunt Julianna?" Paco asked.

"I certify nothing." She stretched her arms and yawned. "You will just have to take your chances."

"I am going to lie down in the back, but I could be watching when you least expect it."

"That's a deal, partner. That coffin is just an empty box."

Julianna tried to peer into the darkened compartment. "A coffin? This is becoming quite bizarre."

"Do you have a pillow?" Paco called out.

"There's an old wool blanket inside the coffin. Pull it out, and you can roll it up and use it for a pillow."

Paco's voice softened. "I am going to leave this flap unfastened."

"A blanket? What else do you have back there?" she quizzed.

"There's a black dress your size and a veil," DelNorte said. "But I can't figure out when you'll be able to change."

"My, you do have a plan!"

"Yep."

"And you should know that I can . . . see . . . you." Paco's voice faded.

Julianna glanced back. "I think our chaperon is asleep."

DelNorte slapped the lines on the lead horse's rump. The long coach rambled out into the dark street. "How about you, Señorita Ortiz? You look sleepy."

She forced her eyes wide open. "No, I am all right. Do you want me to drive?"

"What?"

She held onto his arm. "I do know how to drive a carriage. I can drive, and you can crawl in the back and take a nap with Paco. Why are you staring at me like that?"

"You mean it, don't you?"

"About driving? Yes, of course."

"Let's get started to Guadalupe. If I doze off, you can drive."

Julianna yawned so widely her jaws ached. "Perhaps if we visit, we will stay awake."

"That sounds good. What would you like to visit about?"

"Perhaps we can take up where we left off. Do you mind if I rest my head on your shoulder?"

"As long as Paco doesn't clobber me." DelNorte's laugh was soft, easy.

"Thank you." Julianna took a deep breath and let it out slowly. She closed her eyes. "Before I fell asleep, you said you had more to tell me about your correspondence with Ramona Hawk."

"Maybe it would be better to wait until you are more awake."

"No, no. It is too dark to see anything anyway; I thought I would rest my eyes. I am quite . . ."

"Quite what?"

"Eh . . . quite awake," she murmured.

For several moments they listened to the clopping of the horses' hooves and grinding squeak of the wheels.

"You still quite awake?"

"Hmmmm."

"In that case, perhaps now is the time to mention the years I spent in prison."

"In person? Yes, well . . . go on. What did you do in person?" she mumbled.

"And I suppose you want to know what happened to my wives."

"Knives? I did not know you carried a . . ."

She thought she felt his arm around her. Or maybe it was her cloak. Then she remembered she wasn't wearing a cloak.

"And I did not rob that train, no matter what you hear."

"No . . . no, I do not like beer either."

Julianna thought it amazing how soft the hard, muscled shoulder had become. Her eyelids were heavy, and her whole body slumped against his shoulder.

The voice was as deep as the Rio Grande in the spring. "Guadalupe."

Julianna sat straight up. In the east, light led the sun to the horizon above the river. The air felt a little cold, her neck stiff. She rubbed her eyes. "What?"

"I said, we are in Guadalupe."

"But I thought . . . Did I sleep?"

"Yes."

"Did you talk to me?"

"Yep. Don't you remember?"

"No, no, you have to tell me everything all over."

"Even the part about when I found the 300-pound lady and the orange cat in my tent?"

"You what?"

"Or was it a 300-pound cat and an orange lady?"

"Are you teasing me, Mr. DelNorte?"

"I didn't say much. I figured you needed the sleep."

"I apologize for that." She rubbed her stiff shoulders. "I had no idea I was so exhausted."

"Darlin', no one ever has to apologize to me for sleepin'."

"I cannot believe we are already in Guadalupe. I do not even remember the customhouse."

He reached over and began to rub her shoulders. "We didn't use the customhouse. I crossed upriver."

She closed her eyes and let out a deep sigh. "Oh . . . oh my, DelNorte, you do know how to rub shoulders. Why did we not go through the customhouse?"

He continued kneading her collarbone. "Because as far as the Mexican and American governments are concerned, we are not here."

"Where are we supposed to be?"

"In Lordsburg."

"We are in Mexico illegally?"

"That's the least of our worries, darlin'. Let's go get Guillermo."

Several men dressed in white pants and shirts hiked down the dusty street with bundles of mesquite wood on their shoulders.

"What do we do? What do I do?"

"Wear the black veil, at least."

"What do you mean?"

"In the back, remember? Wear the veil over your head and act grief-stricken."

"I do not understand."

"Trust me."

By the time DelNorte parked the hearse in front of the jail,

Julianna had the lace veil pinned over her long black hair, and he wore an ill-fitting black frockcoat.

"How can I look sad when I do not know what is going on?" Paco asked as he climbed down next to them.

"What is your favorite animal in the whole world?" DelNorte asked.

"Buddy."

"Is he your dog?"

In the morning light, the wrinkles in Paco's long-sleeved white shirt made it look like a treasure map. "No, he is a pig that belongs to Mrs. Sinclair," Paco replied. "But me and him are very good friends."

DelNorte put his arm around the boy's shoulders. "Just imagine how you will feel when Buddy dies."

"This is silly," Paco muttered. "Pigs live a long time, you know. Why are we doing this?"

"I can get them to release your Uncle Guillermo easily enough, but they need an excuse to tell those that inquire. If people think he died in prison, perhaps that will satisfy them. Just hang onto your aunt's arm and look down at the top of your shoes. Pretend that you are in a play, trying to convince the audience of your sorrow."

"I am a very good actor, you know."

"Yes, you are. You play the part of a ten-year-old very convincingly," DelNorte said. "Very few can tell you are actually thirty."

"I am not thirty!"

"I keep forgetting. You see how convincing you are? Come on, grieving family." DelNorte led them to the courtyard gate at the prison and rang the bell. The three-foot-thick wall stood fourteen feet high. The iron bars on the gate were no more than two inches apart. Two uniformed guards appeared, carrying battered Winchester 1866 carbines.

"*¿Qué quieres?*" the taller man asked.

"We want to see the *carcelero*," DelNorte said.

The guard switched to English and stared at the stitches in DelNorte's forehead. "You are crazy. He is asleep."

DelNorte pulled a folded piece of paper from his brown leather vest pocket and handed it between the bars. "He will wake up when you give him this note."

The guard refused to take the paper. He turned to leave. "Come back later," he mumbled.

DelNorte rattled the gate and growled, "I guarantee that if you do not give him this note, you will lose your job by noon. ¿Comprendes?"

The man spun around and pointed the barrel of the '66 at him. "Don't you threaten me!"

"I just did."

"What is your name?"

"DelNorte."

The guards looked at each other. Both lowered their weapons. One reached out for the note. "Why didn't you say so?" He slapped his partner's arm. "Unlock the gate and usher DelNorte and his friends into the carcelero's office. I will awaken him."

They ambled across the swept dirt courtyard. The interior walls of the compound towered over them and kept out the morning light.

"It stinks in here," Paco complained.

"Prison is not a lovely place," Julianna replied.

The guard ushered them into a small office with an enormous oak table. The only light filtered through a smudged small-paned window. The room reeked of stale cigar smoke.

"You mention the name DelNorte, and they jump?" she whispered.

"I have dealt with them before."

"I can see that, but I do not know why."

"The warden is a nice fellow. He sided with Diaz, and so he is in a good position for a while. But there is always rebellion in the northern districts."

"I thought all was quiet now."

"Good. Just keep on thinking that."

A wide wooden door swung open, and a short, hatless man with a crumpled tan uniform and wild black hair staggered in.

"DelNorte?" He glanced at Julianna and Paco.

He shook the warden's hand. "They are with me and are reliable."

"How is everything with the president?"

"Very good. He pinched his back, you know, and it's been bothering him all summer."

Julianna studied DelNorte's face. *Which president? Of Mexico? Of the U.S.? How does DelNorte know either?*

"I didn't know that," the warden replied.

"Sorry to wake you up, Don Travelo, but I'm working on a tight time schedule. Every minute counts."

"DelNorte, I would be insulted if you didn't ask me to help. What happened to your head?"

"The Iturbe brothers like to play with knives."

"We cut them down and drug them here to jail. I knew it was you who tied them up. What do you want me to do with them?"

"That's up to you, Don Travelo, as long as I don't have to testify and—"

"And your name is not mentioned. Yes, yes, I do know that much. There was a nice reward."

"For you and your men," DelNorte offered. "Buy Christina a nice gift."

The warden's eyes lit up. "Yes, I will do that!" Don Travelo waved DelNorte's note in front of him. "The prisoner, Guillermo Ortiz, is yours, of course. How do you want to handle it this time?"

Julianna stared at the small man. *This time?*

"In a coffin."

"You have a hearse?"

"Yes. And a grieving family."

"*Excelente*. I will meet you at the alley door. Have the grieving widow at the back of the hearse."

"Grieving sister," Julianna corrected.

"Oh, yes. There will be the standard provision?" he asked DelNorte.

"Of course."

"Very well. Give me a few moments."

"Thank you, Don Travelo."

"For you, DelNorte, it is only a small payment of my debt."

When they reached the hearse, they climbed up onto the driver's seat.

"How did I do?" Paco asked. "Was I convincing?"

"You were superb!" DelNorte exclaimed as he drove the rig down the narrow alley next to a tall adobe wall.

"I do not think we were needed at all," Julianna said. "One word from DelNorte, and jail doors fly open. Much like the book of Acts."

"Much less noble and easier to explain than Peter's release," he said.

"What is the standard provision the warden asked for?" Paco asked.

"If your uncle is ever seen in Mexico again by the federal troops, they will shoot him on sight, and no one in the United States or Mexico may protest in court."

"Are you serious?" she pressed.

"Yep."

"What was in the note?" Paco asked.

"A professional secret," DelNorte answered.

"What are you professional at, Mr. DelNorte?" Julianna probed.

He grinned. "At keeping secrets. Now if you two could just weep and wail a little as they bring the body out."

Paco looked up and down the alley. "There is no one around to hear the weeping."

"The guards that carry the casket will need to hear it. Just think of Buddy run over by a train."

"I am not good at faking tears," Julianna said.

"Do the best you can."

The thick solid oak side door creaked open. Two uniformed soldiers retrieved the casket and took it inside. The sun had broken down the alley when four soldiers carried the rough wood casket back out. DelNorte, Julianna, and Paco waited silently for several moments.

Finally the four soldiers carried the heavy coffin to the hearse. Don Travelo now wore a tall plumed officer's hat. The chinstrap hung barely below his lower lip. DelNorte backed up to give them room. The heel of his boot crushed Julianna's toe.

"Ohhh!" she sobbed. "You did that on purpose."

The guards carrying the casket paused. "No, no, señora," the heaviest one explained, "we did not kill him on purpose. He died in his sleep. He was very healthy yesterday. It is very strange, but we did not kill him."

"You killed my Buddy!" Paco wailed.

"The lad was very fond of his Uncle Guillermo," DelNorte said.

"Yes, I can see that. I am very sorry," the guard added as they slipped the casket into the back of the hearse.

DelNorte fastened the back door.

"Señora Ortiz, I am very sorry for this untimely situation," Don Travelo added in a loud voice. "We had hoped to keep him healthy until his execution."

The warden and the guards slipped back inside the prison. DelNorte assisted Julianna and Paco into the rig.

"Is Uncle Guillermo really in there?" Paco asked.

"I certainly hope so," DelNorte said.

"Can I open it up and see?"

"Not until we're completely out of town."

"You stepped on my foot on purpose, Mr. DelNorte," Julianna fumed.

"Now, darlin', it was sort of an accident."

"Sort of?"

"I didn't mean to step on it that hard."

"You could have broken my toes."

"But I don't believe I did."

"That's not the point."

"The point is, we have your brother, which is one step closer to getting your father released."

She unlaced her high-top shoe. "Are you sure we have my brother?"

"Yep."

"How can you be so sure?" Julianna tugged off her shoe, straightened her white stocking, and rubbed her toes.

"Because the *carcelero* had the fear of DelNorte in his eyes," Paco blurted out.

Julianna pulled off the veil and folded it. "But what if it is the wrong prisoner?"

"Open up the casket, Paco."

Paco climbed into the back compartment and tugged off the pine lid. A bound and gagged man sat straight up, hollering through the gag.

DelNorte turned around and pointed at the man in the back of the hearse. "Ortiz, keep your voice down, and we'll pull off the gag. If you attract attention, the Federales will shoot you. Do you understand?"

The man nodded.

"Pull off the gag, Paco."

Paco yanked down the twisted towel.

"*Hermana*, I knew you would do it. I knew you could get me out! All of those words yesterday were just a decoy to throw off the guards."

"They were all quite true, Guillermo."

"But you changed your mind?"

"Circumstances have come up that demand your presence elsewhere," she explained.

He nodded toward Paco. "Untie me, *niño*. You are looking very handsome, like your Tío Guillermo. What kind of circumstances, *hermana*?"

Paco glanced up at DelNorte. He shook his head.

"You will find out soon enough," Julianna replied.

"Hurry, *niño*, I want out of these ropes. Where are Roberto, Jack, and Laredo?" Guillermo said.

"Roberto got shot," Paco told him.

"Shot?"

"He is in our patio."

"Did he try to rob you, *hermana*? I will kill him myself if he did."

Julianna stared at her brother's thin face and thick, drooping mustache. "He was shot by Ramona Hawk."

"No!" Guillermo peeked out of the back of the hearse as if searching for someone. "She is out of prison?"

"I see you are surprised," Julianna observed.

"I did not know she would be coming back."

"She wants to see you," DelNorte called back.

"I am not going."

"You have no choice," Julianna said.

"Untie me, Paco!" Guillermo growled.

"Leave him tied, *niño*," Julianna said. "At least until we deliver him to Ramona Hawk!"

"You are turning me over to her? *Hermana*, don't do this. Ramona Hawk is crazy. She will kill me."

"Now why would she want to do that?" DelNorte asked. "Besides, you were going to die soon anyway. Why not let it be out in the nice open air for a noble cause."

"*Hermana*, who is this undertaker you hired? He looks familiar. He did a very convincing job, but now he is acting strange. None of this is his business. Untie me."

"He is not an undertaker."

"Who is he? I demand that he stop and untie me at once. I am Guillermo Ortiz!" he shouted.

"Put the gag back in his mouth," Julianna commanded.

"What? You cannot—"

"Yes, I can. Guillermo, I did not get you out of prison. I could not have done it if I had wanted to. You owe your release to this man."

"Mister, what is your name?" Guillermo asked. "Would you like to join my gang? We could use a good man."

For the first time, DelNorte turned around and looked straight at the bound man.

Guillermo Ortiz turned white. "DelNorte? Oh, sweet *hermana*," he implored, "what happened to his head?"

"The Guillermo Ortiz gang hired the Iturbe brothers to ambush him."

"They did? We did? Oh, Julianna, have mercy on me and let the firing squad shoot me. You turn me over to DelNorte? Is there no compassion left in you?"

"Lie down and be quiet," DelNorte growled. "If he says another word, gag him, Paco."

Guillermo Ortiz flopped down in the coffin and folded his tied hands across his chest.

The Rio Grande can slow to a trickle south of El Paso in the fall. There are times when it disappears completely into its underground channel. This was not one of those times. The lazy, muddy water flowed from bank to bank.

"Are we going to drive across the river?" Paco asked.

"Yep," DelNorte replied.

"Why? What is wrong with the bridge?"

"The people at the customhouse do not want to deal with us."

"You mean, they will arrest us?"

"No. They don't have the nerve. But they would rather not have to explain us."

"I do not understand," Paco protested.

"That's okay. Some things are too difficult to understand."

"Like propitiation?" Paco blurted out.

DelNorte stared at the boy. "Did he say propitiation?"

Julianna grinned. "Yes. Paco is very interested in theology."

"If I were not going to be governor, I would probably be a theology professor," Paco announced.

"Well, Li'l Professor, I'll give you a letter of recommendation to Harvard Divinity School if you like."

"But you must finish college first to be accepted," Julianna added.

"I think it is easier to be governor."

DelNorte turned the rig down the embankment to the Rio Grande.

"You have to untie me," Guillermo shouted from his position in the pine coffin. "I cannot swim all tied up like this."

"You won't need to swim. I'll drive us across."

"But what if the rig tips over?"

"Then stand up," DelNorte instructed. "The water is no more than two feet deep here."

"Make him untie me, *hermana*."

"Guillermo, I do not make DelNorte do anything."

"Surely he cannot resist your charms."

DelNorte laughed.

"I am sorry, *hermano*," Julianna said. "You can see he only laughs at my charms."

"That's not true," DelNorte said.

She nudged his arm. "You were laughing."

"Yes, but not at your charms. I was laughing because he might be more right than he knows or than I will admit."

"You see, *hermana*, I could tell!"

"Are you going to marry my Aunt Julianna?"

"Paco!"

"Well, are you?"

"Yep, I believe I will," DelNorte replied.

"He is not!" Julianna insisted.

"Will you two make up your minds and then untie me!" Guillermo hollered.

"My mind's made up," DelNorte said.

"And so is mine," she snapped.

"Yes, but I know something you don't."

"What is that?"

"I'll tell you at an appropriate time."

"What is an appropriate time?"

"When we are alone."

"That can be arranged," Guillermo offered. "Untie me, and Paco and I will go for a hike."

"No, we won't," Paco insisted. "Mrs. Miller is going to pay me one cash dollar for keeping my eye on them."

"Well, you watch them. I will go for a walk," Guillermo suggested.

"I do not think so," Paco said.

DelNorte slapped the lines on the lead horse's black rump. "Hold on and watch your feet. Water rose up to the floorboard last night when we crossed."

The pair of horses slowed as they waded into the water. A breeze drifted from the north. Julianna felt the wind chap her lips. When the hearse's narrow wheels hit the river, they plumed the water straight up like a fountain. The vehicle jolted across the rocks, and Paco clutched the iron rail.

Julianna held onto DelNorte's arm. "Are you sure this is safe?" she asked.

"Did I say anything about it being safe? It's just necessary," he replied.

"Untie me," Guillermo shouted.

DelNorte whipped the lines on the horses' rumps as the wheels lugged down in the river sand.

"Are we getting stuck?" Paco asked.

"No, we won't get stuck unless we stop, and we aren't stopping," DelNorte replied.

When they reached the center of the sixty-foot-wide river, DelNorte stood and shouted at the team.

"Tío Guillermo jumped out!" Paco yelled.

DelNorte reined up the team and handed the lines to Julianna. "He was tied hand and foot. He'll drown!"

He scrambled through the back of the hearse while Julianna and Paco stood on the leather seat and peered around the corner.

"There he is," Paco shouted.

Julianna spied Guillermo sitting in the river, only his neck and head above water. His wet black hair was plastered down over his ears.

"Help me, *hermana*," he cried out. "I cannot stand up."

DelNorte jumped into the water and waded over to the outlaw. "Ortiz, I can't understand how you could have lived this long. It could only be the prayers of your righteous sister."

"I thought if I landed on my feet, I could hop back to Mexico."

"Where they will shoot you on sight."

"They would have to catch me first."

"Which isn't very hard since you are tied up."

"Perhaps we should just leave him," Julianna called out.

"*Hermana*, this is no time for jokes."

"I am not joking. Tied up with your head above water, sitting on an international boundary. It does sound like an interesting dilemma," she called out.

"Don't tempt me," DelNorte hollered back. "Come on, *hombre*, time to get back in your coffin."

DelNorte reached down under Ortiz's armpits and jerked him straight up out of the water.

"I am not as dumb as you, DelNorte." He whipped his hands from behind his back and slammed a river rock into DelNorte's head.

DelNorte tried to duck. The blow glanced off the side of his head and ear. Bright red blood trickled down his neck. DelNorte staggered back in the water.

"Shoot him, *hermana*," Guillermo shouted.

"Shoot him? You are a complete idiot, Guillermo!" she cried as she leapt down into the slowly moving river. Water soaked her long skirt and wicked into her shoes and socks.

"Stay there," DelNorte commanded.

"You need help," she protested.

"Not with him!" With blood dripping into his ear, DelNorte lunged at Ortiz. His clenched right fist landed on the outlaw's chin, almost lifting him completely out of the water. Ortiz staggered and collapsed, sinking under the water.

DelNorte glared down at the bobbing body as Julianna waded to his side.

"It's tempting to leave him," DelNorte said.

"You have a new wound."

"That's the story of my life, darlin'." He reached down and yanked up the unconscious man by the collar and struggled to hoist him to his shoulder. "I should have done this to start with."

Julianna splashed alongside DelNorte to the back of the hearse, where he tossed Guillermo Ortiz into the open wooden coffin. "It's much more difficult to keep some men alive than to kill them," he said. Then he turned to Julianna. "You got a little wet, Julianna. Let me help you up. Did you jump in the water to save me or your brother?"

"I would not have jumped in the water for him."

"I appreciate the offer of help."

"How did he get loose?"

"The water made the ropes around his wrists expand."

"You need to take care of that wound."

"Don't reckon it's as bad as the other, but my ear will sting for a week."

"You are all bloody," Paco observed.

"Some docs say that lettin' a little blood can make you healthier. If so, I should be the perfect specimen."

She reached under the seat for the black silk veil. "Would you like this for a bandage?"

DelNorte splashed water on his face and head, smearing blood like the first fall rain on a dirty window. Rolling the silk scarf into a three-inch-wide bandage, he wrapped it around his forehead.

"Let me tie it," she offered.

"You need to get out of the water."

"DelNorte, whatever was going to get wet is wet already. Let me tie it."

He bent over. She grabbed the ends of the silk scarf. "Tie it tight," he said.

"Does it hurt, DelNorte?" Paco hollered from the front of the hearse.

"Like a stagecoach ran over my head," he replied.

"Have you ever had a stagecoach run over your head?" Paco challenged.

"Not yet." DelNorte retrieved his hat that was bobbing in the water next to the carriage wheel. He tossed it into the hearse. "Julianna, let me help you up."

"Perhaps I should help you."

"No, I need you to drive. I will shove from down here. I reckon the wheels are sanded over by now. It will be tough to get out."

Her skirt felt like it weighed fifty pounds as she crawled out of the water and up into the seat.

"You are getting me wet," Paco complained.

Her scowl sent him scampering to the back of the hearse. "I guess we are all a little wet," he muttered. He peered out at DelNorte, who stood by the left rear wheel. "You look like a bandit with a bandanna on your head. A Mexican *bandito*."

"This is a new style," DelNorte replied. "Everyone in El Paso is going to be wearing them." He leaned around the wheel and shouted, "Now go ahead, darlin', and slap that lead line. I'll shove this wheel."

Julianna beat on the horses' rumps.

DelNorte shoved.

Paco shouted.

But the hearse didn't budge.

"We are stuck!" she shouted.

"You're right about that."

"What are we going to do?" she called back to him.

"We'll unload everything and carry it across. Maybe then we can get the hearse unstuck."

"Even Uncle Guillermo in the coffin?" Paco queried.

"Yep."

"Maybe they will help us," Paco called out, pointing to the Texas side of the river.

Two dozen mounted cavalry with carbines across their laps watched the scene.

"Oh no!" Julianna cried. *El Señor, this is not good. We are all going to jail.*

"You Mexicans turn around and go back," a blond-headed lieutenant shouted. "You enter this country illegally, and you will be immediately arrested. *¿Comprendes?*"

DelNorte sloshed his way to the front of the wagon. "Fellas, glad to see you. We're going to need some help to pull this wagon out."

"You got a dead body in that hearse?" a sergeant shouted.

"Nope. He's unconscious, soaking wet, and lying in a coffin, but he's not dead."

"What's going on here?" the lieutenant shouted.

"I'll explain, but first we could use some help."

"Mister, you will be arrested the minute you reach this shore. My troops will not assist you."

"Oh, they are going to assist me all right."

"Who do you think you are?"

"Maybe I should come over and explain," DelNorte called out.

"I told you, I'll have to arrest all of you once you set foot here."

DelNorte waved at Julianna and Paco. "Wait here," he said and waded toward the soldiers.

"I warned you, mister!"

"You're lucky I'm a patient man," DelNorte replied.

Julianna watched from the hearse in the middle of the Rio Grande as DelNorte reached the shore. There were two dozen Springfield Trapdoor carbines pointed at his head when he sloshed out of the water.

Julianna could not hear the discussion. But when they were finished, she saw the lieutenant salute DelNorte and then shout instructions to his men. *A uniformed officer salutes him?*

Six soldiers rode into the water, and within minutes they managed to drag the hearse to the Texas shore. The lieutenant led them all downriver.

Julianna wrung the water from her skirt and tugged at the laces of her high-top black shoes. "How is your head?"

"It's been better."

"You cannot keep getting your head injured."

"I'll agree with you on that."

"Does it hurt badly?" she asked.

"Yep."

"Do you want me to drive?"

"Yep."

She studied his steel gray eyes. "Are you serious?"

"Do I look like I'm joking?"

"I did not think you would actually let me drive."

"Neither did I." He handed her the reins.

"Do you want to crawl into the back and sleep? I can have Paco come up and ride with me."

"I might just retie Guillermo and sit in the corner. If you come to a *cantina*, let's buy something to eat."

"I suppose this is not a good time for finishing our conversation about our mutual correspondence with Ramona Hawk."

He crawled into the back of the hearse. "No, I don't reckon so. But we have a whole lifetime for that."

"Mr. DelNorte, you are taking much for granted."

"That's true. If I get hit in the head again, I might not see another sunrise."

"Lie down and get some rest."

"First things first," he muttered. DelNorte hovered over Guillermo, retying the leather straps.

Ortiz tried to raise up. "I should have hit you harder," he growled.

"And I should have let you drown. I surmise we both made mistakes today. I don't intend to make any more."

"Why did you not shoot, *hermana*? I told you to shoot. I begged you to shoot," Guillermo croaked.

Julianna looked over her shoulder at her brother. "I strongly considered it, but I did not know how I would explain your death to Father."

"I meant to shoot DelNorte."

"Why on earth would I want to do that?"

"You are really going to take me to Ramona Hawk?"

"Why does she want to see you?"

"I have helped her out in the past. She needs Guillermo Ortiz and his gang. What can I say?"

DelNorte eased down in the corner of the wagon. "You can tell me why you're scared to death to go see her. The feeling must be mutual. She shot up your gang, and you will look very impressive when delivered gagged and bound in a coffin."

"You are not going to take me to her like this!"

"It depends on what happens between here and there. If you continue to act the fool, I will not only gag you but nail the lid on the coffin."

"That is not funny."

"There was no humor intended. You know I'll do it."

The road by the river was level and reflected the bright Texas sun. The black leather seats began to warm. River water streamed out of Julianna's dress, and the rhythm of the rig gently rocked them.

"I think DelNorte has gone to sleep," Paco reported.

She glanced over her shoulder. "Good. Let him rest."

"Stop the rig and untie me," Guillermo called out.

Julianna lifted her thick black hair off her neck and fanned it out. "Gag him, Paco, before he wakes up DelNorte."

"Paco, how would you like to ride with my gang?" Guillermo whispered.

Paco crawled back to the man in the coffin. "It would not look good on my resumé."

"What resumé?"

"When I am governor of New Mexico."

"But think of how it would impress the girls. You could say, 'I rode with the notorious Guillermo Ortiz.'"

Paco glanced up at Julianna. "Then I would grow up and be just like you?"

"Yes, yes, that is it," Guillermo boasted.

"So someday I can be shot on sight in Mexico or be strapped in a coffin riding to Hachita?"

Julianna burst into laughter.

"Well, well . . . you are so smart that you will turn out even better than your famous uncle."

"Yes, I will." Paco turned to Julianna. "I think I will gag him now."

"No, wait. I see *hermana* has twisted your mind. I will be quiet. But it is very uncomfortable in here because I am so wet."

"Yes," Paco replied, "I believe that usually happens when a person jumps into the water."

"*Hermana*, are you sure this is our nephew?"

"Can I nail down the coffin lid?" Paco asked.

"No. The banging might wake up DelNorte."

"Can I come up and sit with you?"

"Yes, of course."

Paco crawled up to the seat and plopped down beside Julianna. "This has been a very exciting day."

"Yes, and it is not even noon yet."

"Did you see those officers salute DelNorte?" he whispered.

She slipped her arm around his shoulders. "Yes, I did."

"Why did they do that? Is he in the army?"

"That is one of many questions I want to ask him."

"He said you will have plenty of time to ask."

"What do you think he meant by that?"

"He said he was going to marry you."

"That is nonsense. We do not even know each other."

"How long should you know someone before you marry them?" Paco asked.

"Are you planning on getting married soon?" She grinned.

"No! Not me!"

"What kind of question is that for a ten-year-old? Ask me ten years from now," she insisted.

"Must you know the person for a year?" he pressed.

"I certainly think that might be good—even a little longer."

"Colt only knew Gracie a few weeks before they got married."

"That was quite unusual."

"And Lixie has only known Jefferson Carter for a month or so, and she is getting married Saturday."

"Yes, well, there are some exceptions."

"I think DelNorte is exceptional. Don't you?"

"Paco, I do not wish to proceed with this conversation."

"Okay. Let's talk about how Stuart Brannon will get out of the snake den."

"He is in a snake den?"

"He had to jump in there to save the orphans."

"I suppose he did."

"Did you know that if you are quick enough, you can grab a rattlesnake by the tail and pound its head into a rock and kill it before it bites you?"

"No, I did not know that. Paco, do not believe everything you read in those books."

"This was not in a book. The other day down by Arroyo Seco, Bonita and I found a rattlesnake about three feet long. She grabbed it by the tail and smashed its head on the rock."

"Oh, my. She is a very brave girl."

"And very thrifty. She took it home to Mrs. Miller to fix for supper."

"And what did Lixie say when she saw the snake?"

"I think the words were, 'Get that thing out of my house, and get it out right now!' Did you ever eat rattlesnake, Aunt Julianna?"

"Yes, I have, with your mother when we were young."

"What does it taste like?"

"Tortoise, but a little stringier."

"You ate a turtle?" he gasped.

"Your mother and I hiked from Mexico up to Santa Fe while the war was being fought in the valley. We ate anything we could find just to stay alive."

Paco sat still for a moment. "I miss my mother."

Julianna put her arm around his shoulders and hugged him. "*Niño*, I miss her too. I miss her every day of my life."

The *cantina* stood by the side of the road like a giant cow pie dropped from the sky. The brown adobe building had so many additions it was difficult to tell its shape. Ivy covered some of the walls. Others were bare.

"Are you sure you want to eat here?" Paco asked.

"We will just buy some tortillas and meat and eat in the wagon."

"Shall I stay here?"

"Do you mind?"

"I would rather stay here than go in there."

"It is small and dark-looking, but there is nothing to fear, I am sure. You keep the shotgun handy. If Guillermo tries to escape, fire the gun."

"At Uncle Guillermo?"

"No, in the air. I will come out and capture him. Do not shoot at anyone."

"Do you want the shotgun?"

"You keep it. El Señor will protect me."

"If I hear a commotion, I will come to your rescue."

"Thank you, Paco."

"You are welcome."

The inside of the small building was so dark Julianna could see nothing at all when she first entered.

"What do you want, lady?"

"Some tortillas, meat, cheese, and fruit would be nice." She squinted her eyes. Several men lined a rough wooden bar. "Do you have food for sale?" she pressed.

"Sure, lady. Maybe you'd like to visit with the boys here while I fix up your food."

"You can wait with me, darlin'," one hooted. "I've been real, real lonesome."

"I will wait outside."

"You expect me to haul it out there?"

"If you want to be paid, you will."

"Who do you think you are?" one of the cowboys challenged her.

"You do not want to know the answer to that," she replied.

"She was not afraid to walk in here, boys," an older Mexican man put in. "That tells you something."

"I will wait with the others," she announced.

The big man glanced at the door. "What others?"

"I assure you, you do not want to know that either."

"Hmmm, a mystery lady. Maybe we should go investigate," he replied.

Several of the men followed her out into the west Texas sunlight. She could now see their shallow, bloodshot eyes and smell the sweat on unwashed bodies.

"You drivin' that hearse, lady?" one asked.

"Yes."

"You hauling bodies?" another quizzed.

"What I am doing is not your business," she snapped.

They followed her to the front of the hearse where Paco stood on the leather seat. He pointed the short-barreled shotgun at the men. "Can I shoot them?" he hollered.

Several of the men scattered.

"No, no one else is to be shot . . . yet. We have to get on down the road, remember?"

"Did you get us any food?" Paco asked.

"The man will bring it out," she answered.

"She's got two dead bodies back here," one of the men reported. "One has his head busted open, and the other is hogtied and drowned like a rat!"

"Good grief, lady, who are you?" the big man quizzed.

The older Mexican man spun back toward the *cantina*. "I do not want to know, and neither do you boys. Get in here!"

The men drifted back with him toward the *cantina*.

When she sat down, Paco shoved the shotgun into her lap. "I am glad I did not have to shoot them. That gun hurts my shoulder."

"I am glad too. Thank you for defending me, Paco."

"You are welcome. Who did they think you are? It was like they were afraid of you."

"I am not sure. If they come out here again, we will drive off."

"Without our food?"

"Yes, if we have to."

In a few minutes, the older Mexican man scurried out with a basket of food.

"Where is the *cantina* owner?" she asked.

"I volunteered, Señorita."

She opened the green valise. "How much do I owe you?"

"Nothing. I paid for it," the old man insisted.

"I need no charity."

"It is a gift. We have mutual friends. I know who you are and have a message for you."

"What is the message?"

"You are not to meet Artiz at Blossom Wells. The Federales are planning an ambush there. You are to meet him at Verdicito Springs."

"Verdicito Springs?"

"Yes, and they will only wait until Saturday. It is very dangerous to wait longer. He said to tell you not to worry. He has the gold with him."

"Thank you."

The old man tipped his wide sombrero. "*De nada*, Señorita Halcon."

"He thinks you are—"

Julianna clamped her hand over his mouth before Paco could complete the sentence. She slapped the lead lines and trotted the team back onto the roadway.

Paco leaned close and whispered, "He thought you are Ramona Hawk!"

"Yes."

"I wonder why? Ramona Hawk looks very pretty, and you look, well . . ."

"Yes?"

"You look like an aunt," Paco said.

"So you keep telling me."

"Why did he think you were Ramona Hawk?"

"Perhaps because I have two dead bodies in the back."

"They are not dead."

"They did not know that. What other woman would go around with dead men in her wagon?"

"Can we eat now?" Paco asked.

"First wake up DelNorte."

Nine

DelNorte crawled over the seat and plopped down next to Paco as the hearse jostled along in the yellow-brown west Texas dust.

Julianna held the lead lines in her left hand. "How is your head?"

The blood on DelNorte's ear was now dried, and he pulled off the veil bandage. "If I get it busted one more time, I think I'll just cut it off and sew me on a new one." He eased his hat down on the back of his head.

"Then you could get one that did not have gray hair," Paco suggested.

"And no wrinkles around the eyes. No broken nose. No scar under the ear. That would be nice. Then I would look only fifty instead of sixty." DelNorte dug into the sack and rolled a large flour tortilla around the cold beef and green peppers and ripped off a bite with his teeth.

Julianna chewed on a plain rolled-up tortilla. "Is that General Artiz whom Ramona Hawk is to meet?"

"Yep," DelNorte replied.

"Why?"

DelNorte took another bite of tortilla. "I can only guess."

"Is it a secret?" Paco asked.

"Perhaps," DelNorte replied.

"How do you know so many secrets?" Paco quizzed.

"That too, I suppose, is a secret," Julianna said. "Would you like to drive?"

DelNorte took another bite of hot peppers and meat. "Nope."

"I did not think that men liked to have women drive them around."

"Why would you think that?" DelNorte asked.

"You never see women driving the men. It is always the other way."

"That's because the women never ask to drive," DelNorte said.

"Is Artiz the general that opposed Porfirio Diaz?" Paco asked.

DelNorte looked at the boy. "That's the one. The general believes he can capitalize on Diaz's need to consolidate power in Mexico City."

Julianna felt uncomfortable with her socks still soaking wet. "You mean, start another revolution?" *How I would love to pull off these wet socks and go barefoot like Paco. That would shock DelNorte.*

"Maybe more than a revolution," DelNorte explained. "Maybe a new country. The Republic of the North."

"The old Rio Grande Empire?" she questioned.

"Thoughts of it never die."

"My father told us of it when we were very young—that is, when he was home."

"The old Mexican at the canteen told you to meet the general at Verdicito Springs?"

"He told Ramona Hawk to meet Artiz there. He said there were federal troops at Blossom Wells."

"I can't imagine more than thirty or forty soldiers this far north," DelNorte said. "Unless . . ."

"Unless what?" Paco asked.

"Unless that train from Monterey did not carry cattle as the invoice stated," DelNorte mumbled.

"What train? What invoice?" Paco quizzed.

"Nothing." DelNorte chomped on his tortilla.

"If General Artiz has gold, what does he want with Ramona Hawk's stolen jewels?" Julianna asked. "Here, Paco, you drive for a while."

He took the lead lines. "What are you going to do?"

"Dry my socks. I am going to pull them off and hang them

across the handrail. Do you have anything against a person being barefoot?"

Paco looked down at his dirty toes. "Nope."

"And you, DelNorte?"

"I'd guess the general doesn't want the jewels. If she had what he wanted, she wouldn't have bothered with your brother or father. I think she wants to buy something with those stolen jewels and sell it to the general."

Either he did not hear me, or he is ignoring me. "For a big profit, no doubt." She tugged off her high-top, lace-up boots.

"Perhaps your brother has contacts who could supply whatever she needs," he added.

Julianna slowly peeled off both white stockings. "What does General Artiz need?"

"The support of the people," DelNorte answered.

"Maybe he wants a printing press," Paco shouted. The team broke into a trot.

Julianna looped the wet socks over the iron handrail on the hearse. "Why a printing press?"

Paco handed her back the lead lines. "Stuart Brannon once said that all you need for a revolution in Mexico is bullets, guns, and a printing press."

"Bullets and guns sound more likely."

DelNorte kicked the coffin hard. Guillermo Ortiz sat straight up. "I was asleep," he growled.

"*Es almuerso, amigo.* I will unfasten your hands and let you eat," DelNorte said, "as long as you tell me where the stolen guns are."

Guillermo yawned. "What guns?"

DelNorte shoved him back down into the coffin. "These tortillas must have been made by a woman from Monterey. You know how good they make tortillas," he said.

Guillermo propped himself up on his elbows and stared at the food.

DelNorte took a slow bite and licked his lips. "I know of a customer who is looking for guns. Someone said you had a few."

"You want those guns?"

"Yep."

Guillermo pointed to the coffin. "All of this is because of those guns?"

"So it finally dawned on you?"

Guillermo Ortiz struggled back up and burst out laughing.

"What's so funny?" DelNorte questioned.

"Naturally I thought the worst. I thought you would shoot me or that Ramona Hawk had a bounty on my head. You merely want those guns? How many do you want?"

"All of them."

"If I give you all of the guns, will you still take me to Ramona Hawk?"

"There would be no need then, would there?" DelNorte said.

"Okay. I will let you have some guns."

"All the guns and all the bullets you stole with them."

"All right, now untie my hands. I am hungry. Oh, *hermana*, you do not know how many things I was worried about. The guns? They are yours. I should have known." He shrugged.

Julianna called back to her brother, "I am amazed that you give them up so easily."

"Easily? *Hermana*, you call this easy? Pass me one of those peppers. Not that one, Paco—one of the yellow ones."

"Where are the guns?" DelNorte demanded.

"Ha! I will lead you there, but I will not tell you ahead of time. The water—hand me a canteen. Wait, I will go with you. Hawk will pay for the guns. She always does. In jewels. Those are my guns, and I should get the jewels."

"Your guns?" DelNorte roared. "You stole the guns. I could shoot you right now, and you would get nothing at all."

"Nor would you."

"Then it looks like we are partners."

"Yes, I suppose. Do you have any tomatoes? I could use a tomato."

"We must get the guns immediately and head to Mariposa Tank. Ramona Hawk is holding Father as ransom," Julianna informed him.

Guillermo scooted to the front of the hearse. "Father? Our father? What is the old man doin' over there?"

Julianna studied the scruffy appearance of her brother. "I believe he was worried about his son Guillermo."

With his hands still bound, he wiped crumbs off his chin and mustache. "Why did he go over there? Why not come see me in prison in Guadalupe?"

Julianna watched his brown eyes dance. "Like his son, he is not too welcome in Mexico," she said. *Guillermo always looked more like Marga's twin than mine.*

"He came to get Aunt Julianna to help get you out of jail," Paco said.

"He came to see you?"

"Yes."

"Has he changed?"

"Perhaps a little. He was concerned about you anyway."

"How did he get captured by Ramona Hawk?"

"I am not sure. I would like to think he was helping you. But it might be he got captured thinking he could cut in on your dealings with Hawk."

"Evil lady has the father, so the sister comes and springs the brother out of jail so they can team up to save the father," Guillermo roared. "This is quite a story."

"It is not as exciting as Stuart Brannon jumping in a snake den to save the orphans," Paco blurted out.

"This story isn't over," DelNorte cautioned. "It just might get a little more exciting."

"When we get to Lordsburg, I think I will stay with Lixie," Paco announced.

DelNorte patted Paco's shoulder. "Too much excitement, partner?"

"Too much sitting on my—"

"Paco!" Julianna scolded.

"Yes. Too much sitting on my Paco."

"We will take the train to Lordsburg. We can get there by two o'clock."

"The train?" Guillermo brightened up. "Then you will have to untie me after all."

"Don't count on it," DelNorte said.

No air moved in the baggage car, and there were no windows to lower. Julianna sat on a crate next to a long pine box and fanned herself with an invoice.

"This is not funny, *hermana*. Open the lid!" The voice was muted but urgent.

"I assure you, none of us is laughing," she replied.

"I can hardly breathe."

"Then stop wasting air by talking. The railroad was quite generous to allow us to ship the coffin for free."

"And they only charged me half-price," Paco said. "I wonder why that is? Am I only half a person? I think it is an insult."

"We're all sitting on crates, and so I reckon it doesn't matter," DelNorte said. "So nice to let the grieving family ride with the deceased."

"I will be deceased if you do not open up and give me a drink," Guillermo ranted.

"You ought to be getting used to that box by now," DelNorte remarked.

"I do not have to show you where the guns are."

"And we don't have to take the lid off. What do you think would happen if we nailed it down and shipped it to Boston?"

"*Hermana*, would you please make this insane man open the lid and give me a drink?"

Julianna pulled the lid off the pine coffin. Sweating through his dirty white shirt, Guillermo struggled to sit up. "Thank you. I do not know what you see in DelNorte. He is a vicious man."

"No," she mused. "Just look at him. With a stitched forehead and a busted ear, he looks rather pathetic to me."

DelNorte nodded. "Thank you, ma'am."

"You are quite welcome. I think you need a vacation. Whatever it is that you do, it is a strain on your health."

"I reckon you're right about that. I hear Mariposa Tank is nice this time of year."

Paco borrowed a wagon from the Hernandez Brothers' Bell Foundry and drove it up to the side of the railroad platform.

"Tío Burto said to be careful. There is a bell in the back, crated for shipment."

"If we get lost, we can unpack it and ring for help," DelNorte quipped.

"How can we get lost? We are only going a few blocks," Paco scoffed.

"You never know." DelNorte winked. He slid the coffin to the back of the wagon and then drove them to the alley behind the jewelry shop.

"You better let me check out who is still in the patio. Laredo and Jack are just crazy enough to try to kill you," Julianna cautioned.

DelNorte offered his hand to help her down. "You have such nice friends. Paco, help your uncle out of the coffin."

Guillermo Ortiz, still bound and hobbled, struggled to his feet. "That is the absolute last time I will get in a coffin."

Julianna raised her eyebrows.

"Alive, that is," he added.

Julianna hiked to the alley door alone. She banged on the rough, unpainted door. It opened slowly. Two wide brown eyes peered out through the crack.

"Hi, Bonita!" Julianna called out.

The door swung open. The ten-year-old girl was barefoot and still wearing a gingham dress over her denim trousers. She stepped back and grinned.

"What are you doin' at my house?" Paco called out as he scampered off the wagon.

"I am watching a man." Bonita stared up at Guillermo Ortiz.

Julianna strolled into the patio. "What do you mean?"

"Mama wanted me to watch Mr. Alvarez while she did some things for the wedding."

"Where are Jack Burkeman and Laredo?" Julianna asked.

"I don't know."

DelNorte untied Guillermo's feet and led him into the patio.

"Who is that?" Bonita asked.

"That is my Uncle Guillermo," Paco announced.

"Why is he tied up?"

"So he couldn't get out of the coffin."

"Paco, go ask your Uncle Burto if we can use this wagon for the rest of the day and till noon tomorrow."

"Can I go with Paco?" Bonita asked.

"Yes, that is fine."

Julianna marched into the apartment. Roberto Alvarez slept in Paco's bed, shoulder bandaged, his mouth open.

"Is he dead?" Guillermo called out.

Alvarez's eyes flew open. "Guillermo! *Hermana*, I knew you could do it!"

"Where are Laredo and Burkeman?" Guillermo asked.

"They took off," Alvarez replied. "Said they had had enough, what with you in front of a firing squad. They said there was no way *hermana* could get you out of jail."

"Where did they go?" Guillermo barked.

"They had no money. Where do you think they went?" Alvarez shrugged.

"How long ago did they leave?"

"This morning after breakfast."

Guillermo spun around, waving his bound hands. "Aye, they are fools."

"Did they go get the guns?" DelNorte asked.

"I suppose. That is all that is down there that is worth a dime."

"Where are they?" DelNorte asked.

"Are you taking me with you?" Guillermo said.

"Yep."

"We have a cache near Antelope Pass. That is all you need to know."

"So they'll take the guns and go to Arizona?" DelNorte quizzed.

Guillermo rubbed his wrists as he paced the room. "If they can find the guns."

"What do you mean? We helped bury them," Alvarez blurted out.

"But none of you saw me move them," Guillermo replied.

"Move them? You moved them?" Roberto Alvarez lay back down. "You would hide them from your friends?"

"I am the leader of the gang. I am supposed to do things like that."

"You were in jail facing a firing squad and did not even send word to us that you moved the guns?"

DelNorte tramped over to the bed. "Alvarez, do you feel well enough to hike over to a room at the hotel?"

"I cannot believe he moved the guns! Maybe I should have gone with Laredo and Jack."

"And leave me in Mexico to be shot?" Guillermo challenged.

"*Hermana* would not cooperate with us."

Guillermo stormed toward the patio. "Fortunately she found someone with more courage."

DelNorte pulled Alvarez to a sitting position. "We've got to get you to a hotel room, *amigo*."

"I do not think I can walk across this room."

"In that case, I will go get the coffin," Guillermo threatened and stalked out to the patio.

"The coffin?"

"We have a coffin on the wagon," Julianna said.

"I think perhaps I can walk," Alvarez mumbled.

The wagon rolled north out of Lordsburg by 4:00 P.M. and skirted the desert to the west of the Pyramid Mountains. The road was no more than two dusty trails that ran straight as arrows toward the mountains of Mexico. There was no wind. The dust from the wagon wheels hung like ground fog. Julianna held a parasol over a hatless DelNorte. Guillermo sat in the back on top of the closed coffin, his feet chained to the bell crate. Heat settled down on all three as the sun lowered toward the Peloncillo Mountains to the west.

Julianna dozed, her head bobbing on her chest.

"Were you ever in an earthquake?"

Her eyes blinked open. "Did you say something to me? An earthquake?"

"Were you ever in an earthquake?" DelNorte asked.

"No. Were you?"

"I was in California about fifteen years ago when that bad one hit."

"I think I nodded off. Did I miss some of the conversation?"

"No."

"Why are we talking about earthquakes?"

"Because you remind me of an earthquake."

"Oh?"

"Earthquakes give no warning. You can go about your life day after day, year after year, in the same routine. Then in a split second, an earthquakes hits. Within moments your life, your home, your future are totally changed forever."

"And I am an earthquake?" she probed.

"Yep."

"Why, DelNorte, you say the nicest things! Now do not flatter me so. I venture to say your life has never been dull, boring, or routine. I am amazed you even noticed my impact."

"That's not true. There was a time when my life was very boring."

"When?"

"When I was ten or eleven years old."

"Where did you live at that age?"

"You think I'm going to fall for that?"

"Yes, I do. And what did your friends call you at that age?"

"Ha! You can be a more creative snoop than that," he laughed.

"You did not answer either question."

"Washington. Butch."

"You lived in Washington Territory?"

"I lived in Washington, D.C."

"I never knew of anyone who lived in Washington, D.C., except politicians."

"Me neither."

"And they called you Butch?"

"Yep."

"Why?"

"Because the boy on the place next to us had the same name as mine. It got confusing, and since he lived there first, I got the nickname."

She reached over to hold his arm. "Oh, by the way, what was that boy's name?"

"I can't remember. That was a very long time ago."

"This is a game, is it not?"

"What's a game?"

"Seeing how long you can string me along without telling me anything personal about yourself. Do you do this with all women, or am I the only one gullible enough?"

"I reckon I treat them all the same—if there were any others to treat."

"That is a relief. I will not take it personally. So I am an earthquake."

"Yep."

"The last two days have been more like a flood to me," she said. "I am caught up in a current of a mighty power and pushed along in directions I would rather not go, and I cannot do anything about it."

"A flood and an earthquake—that's quite a partnership."

"You and me are partners," Guillermo hollered from the back of the wagon. "You should not keep me bound like this," he grumbled.

"You tried to bust open my skull."

"That is the trouble today. People are not willing to forgive and forget. Everyone holds a grudge."

"That was just this morning," DelNorte reminded him.

"You see what I mean? Where is the generosity of heart? Where is the forgiving spirit? Where is simple Christian trust?"

"Oh, I trust the Lord, Ortiz. It's people that I have problems with."

"You are beginning to sound like *mi hermana*."

"Compliment me all you want, Guillermo, but you're still shackled to that bell."

"We should have unloaded that bell at the foundry," Ortiz called out.

"We did not have time," Julianna said.

"This is dumb. I am the famous Guillermo Ortiz, and yet I have no gun and am chained to a bell in the back of a wagon."

Julianna continued to hold DelNorte's arm. "If it were not for DelNorte, you would be the famous Guillermo Ortiz facing a Mexican firing squad and a volley of .45-.70 bullets."

"You cannot leave me chained to this bell without a gun when we face Ramona Hawk. That would be murder, DelNorte. Your Christian conscience would not permit it."

DelNorte peeked back from under the parasol at the unshaven face of Guillermo Ortiz. "I'm wondering how you know anything about a Christian conscience."

"Then you have not had to listen to *mi hermana* preach. She has been my conscience for all of my life."

"It has not done much good," Julianna commented.

"Do not belittle yourself, *hermana*. Perhaps it is your prayers that prevented my becoming worse."

"And Mother's prayers."

"Yes . . . yes." He said no more.

Finally Julianna glanced back. Her brother's eyes looked shallow. There was no swagger in his face now.

Guillermo's voice dropped. "When I was young, Papa and I would be camped out in the mountains in some godforsaken place, and I used to cry myself to sleep. I missed her and you girls so much."

Julianna tried to study his deep, dark eyes. "You never told me that before."

He took a deep breath and looked away. "I do not know why I am telling you now."

Lord, I do not know if I can believe him. My heart says I should, but my heart has lied to me many times. "I will not unshackle you, no matter what you say."

"Do you know what I did when I found out Mama died? I hiked out into the Borro Mountains and spent an hour throwing up. I hurt so much I wanted to die. If there had been a cliff, I would have jumped. You and Marga lost a mother that you had. I lost a mother that I never had. You have fond memories of good times together. All I have is memories of Father and me leavin'. It was always a hug good-bye and 'be a good boy.' DelNorte, did *mi hermana* tell you that our mother was a beautiful Christian lady?"

Julianna stared straight ahead over the horses. She could feel the tears trickle down her cheeks.

"I believe she did imply that. It's easy to tell from Julianna that your mother was a very charming lady."

"It is Marga who looked most like Mama," Guillermo said. "But it is Julianna who acts most like her."

Julianna laced her fingers and clutched them tight. "Guillermo, we are thirty-two years old, and you have never told me that before."

"I do not think we have spent as much time together in ten years as we have in this one day."

"You hated me two days ago. You cursed me to Hades when you were in jail."

"I was terrified of dying two days ago. You do not know what it is like to be terrified of dying."

"You are right. Death has always seemed like a sweet release to me," Julianna admitted.

"For those of us going to hell, death is not a pleasant prospect."

"You do not have to go to hell, Guillermo. You know about Jesus. Mama taught you that much. She taught us at the same time."

"Sometimes I think we are meant to be examples—twins who turn out totally different. Good and bad, right and wrong, righteous and wicked. The worse I am, the better that makes you look. Enough of that. If I get any more melancholy, I will crawl into the coffin on my own."

"I will make a confession, Guillermo. I am glad DelNorte saved you from the firing squad. I needed to hear those words."

"Will you unlock these shackles now?"

"No."

"Why?"

"Because I have a goal of keeping DelNorte alive until Lixie's wedding."

DelNorte bumped his shoulder against hers. "I never heard that before."

"You heard it now. You are taking me to the wedding."

"I am?"

"I do not wish to go alone and sit in the old maid's section."

"I thought Paco was taking you to the wedding."

"He is the ring bearer—that is, if I can talk him into wearing shoes. Lixie insists that he and Bonita wear shoes. We shall see."

"When is the wedding?"

"Six o'clock tomorrow."

"I won't be very pretty looking."

"No, you will look pathetic. I hope to generate a lot of sympathy. 'Poor Julianna,' they will say. 'She has to put up with that brawler.'"

"I like the way you tease, Julianna Ortiz."

"I do enjoy teasing you, DelNorte. I wonder why that is?"

"'Sometimes the depth of a relationship is—'"

"'—seen most clearly through the things one allows the other to laugh at,'" Julianna concluded. "She wrote some profound things, even if it was to manipulate. I do not regret memorizing them."

"Julianna, I need to—"

"'The time one takes to contemplate each word reflects—'"

"'—the depth of one's wisdom,'" he completed.

"'Promises that must be squeezed out of the heart with care—'"

"'—cannot be broken by any threat of violence.'" DelNorte turned the horses toward the treeless mountains to the west. The low sun hung directly in their eyes. "Guillermo, is that Antelope Pass?"

"Yes. You should head toward the two boulders on the south."

"I thought the springs were to the right."

"Do you want a drink, or do you want the guns?"

"Maybe both." DelNorte slapped the lines on the horses. They broke into a trot.

"Do you think Jack and Laredo will still be there?" Guillermo called out.

"Do you?"

"Only if they cannot find the guns. I hid them very carefully."

DelNorte shaded his eyes with his hand. "I don't see anything up there."

"They will not be pleased to see us."

DelNorte jerked up his carbine from the floorboard, cocked the lever, and let the hammer down slowly. He laid it across his lap. "Julianna, I really need to talk to you—"

"You have to give me a gun too!" Guillermo shouted.

"You think your own gang will shoot at you?"

"How do they know it is me?"

"Hide behind the bell. You'll be safe."

Julianna slipped her arm into DelNorte's. "Do you think we will ever get a moment to talk in private?" she whispered.

"You mean sometime in the next thirty years?"

"Yes."

"I'm sure we will."

"How about in the next three days?" she pressed.

"I have my doubts about that."

"DelNorte, you know many things about me and my family."

"And you know nothing about me."

"I do not even know your name. Do I have to call you 'Of the North' your whole life?"

"That depends."

"Upon what?"

"How long my life is and . . ."

"Yes?"

"How much you are in my life."

"Hah. DelNorte, are you getting cold feet? You told Paco you were going to marry me. Now you have doubts." She giggled. "Were you teasing or lying?"

"Neither. I was wishing."

"You do not know me, DelNorte, and I certainly do not know you."

"I know of your love for the Lord, your sacrifice for your family, your pain of losing loved ones, your courage in adversity, your kind and sensitive spirit, and your heart-stopping beauty. Just what else am I supposed to know, Julianna Naomi Ortiz?"

"Hah. Now you have broken the spell. Your lines were convincing until you got to the beauty part. Then I knew you were a flatterer."

"'Every once in a while words bypass the mind and bubble up from the spirit and soul of a person—'"

"Yes, yes, and they 'are the most true words ever spoken,' but we both know those wise words were penned by a deceitful woman. So I am not sure how much credibility we should give them."

DelNorte glanced back at Guillermo. "Now where to?"

"Aim for the brown granite outcropping."

"Can we drive a wagon up there?"

"I did."

"It's a wonder you didn't break an axle."

"I wonder if Laredo and—"

Even though the bronze bell was crated, when the bullet slammed into it, it sounded like an alarm for the dead.

Guillermo dove behind the coffin. Julianna dropped the parasol and threw her arms around DelNorte's neck.

DelNorte slapped the lines on the rump of the lead horse and raced straight toward the gun smoke.

"What are you doing?" Guillermo screamed.

"Trying to flush them out."

"You are crazy! Give me a gun."

"I would be crazy to give you a gun."

Julianna saw puffs of smoke from the boulders ahead of them, but the noise of hooves and wagon wheels prevented her from hearing the gunfire.

DelNorte tugged her arms away from his neck and shoved the reins into her hands. "You drive!"

"What?"

He stood up in the tossing wagon with the carbine at his shoulder before she could protest. Within the next thirty seconds, he had cocked the lever and fired seven times. All seven shots showered granite among the boulders. After the last shot, two men on horses galloped toward the Arizona line.

"Slow it down," he shouted.

Julianna tugged back gently on the reins. Guillermo peeked up over the bell crate. "*Hermana*, he is tryin' to get us all killed."

"He chased off Burkeman and Laredo."

"What good is that? If they had known I was in the wagon, they would not have shot."

"You mean, they wouldn't have shot at you. What kind of guns do you have cached up here?" DelNorte quizzed.

"You will see soon enough."

"Rifles, muskets, or carbines?"

"Rifles. They were all rifles," Guillermo informed him.

"What were Burkeman and Laredo carrying on their saddles?"

"Carbines."

DelNorte patted his shirt sleeve on the sweat that rolled across the stitches on his forehead. "Then they found the stash. They were shooting rifles."

"There is no way to know that," Guillermo objected.

"They hit the bell. You couldn't hit the bell from there with a carbine."

"You seem to be quite proficient at hitting that boulder above their heads with a carbine."

"That's because I have some experimental compressed powder under a short 180-grain bullet. I'm used to long range."

"You are sure they found the guns?" Julianna asked.

"Yep. But they didn't get away with many of them—only what they could carry on two horses. They must have left a couple of packhorses loaded down. So I reckon they'll be back."

"I cannot believe they would double-cross me like this," Guillermo mumbled.

"Don't be too hard on them. You were in jail about to die, and Roberto is wounded. Exactly what were they supposed to wait for?"

Julianna drove the wagon straight for the boulders. In the distance two riders crested the hill to the west. "It does not look like they are doubling back."

"They will. No one wants to lose a cache of valuable guns. Drive very slowly around these rocks. It's rough on a heavy wagon like this."

When she had steered around the shed-sized boulders, they saw a faded wagon with a broken axle.

"How did you get that wagon up here?" DelNorte asked.

"We ran down eight driving horses. We wanted to get to Arizona, but this is where it busted."

"What is under the tarp?"

"Some big, ol' machine. The guns were on the back."

"What kind of machine?"

"How should I know?"

"I reckon the guns were buried in that hole."

"Yes, and I do not know how they knew they were there," Guillermo said.

"It looks like the only soft dirt for miles. Where else would they be? They obviously didn't get them all. That hole isn't big enough for more than one crate. That would hold about ten guns."

"And there is the crate." Julianna pointed to a long wood box.

"Where's the rest of them, Ortiz?" DelNorte demanded.

"What rest of them?"

"There was surely more than one crate on that wagon you stole."

"The other wagon went over the cliff. We could not retrieve its cargo." Guillermo scratched the back of his neck. "You would think an official government shipment would have more guns."

DelNorte grabbed Guillermo's collar. "Are you telling me you only have ten guns total?"

"I am telling you that Laredo and Jack have ten guns."

"We came up here for ten guns?"

"Yes. I told you I was quite surprised you were after the guns."

"Why would Artiz go through all this for ten guns?" DelNorte mumbled.

"Why would Ramona Hawk need jewelry to buy ten guns?" Julianna wondered. "This does not make sense."

DelNorte let out a deep sigh. "Hawk must have thought this shipment had lots of guns. They helped get her out of jail because she can work both sides of the border, and General Artiz can't. They thought she could locate the guns."

"What do we do now?" Julianna asked.

"We'll go see Hawk and let Guillermo explain why there are no guns."

"She will kill me," he protested.

"Yes, but maybe we can get your father released."

"This is not good," Guillermo mumbled.

DelNorte stared into the empty gun crate. "What if we find out we can only save one or the other? Are you ready to choose between your father and your brother?"

Julianna dropped her chin. "No one can make that choice."

"You're right," DelNorte agreed. "We must have a plan that saves all of us."

"You will have to cut me free and give me a weapon," Guillermo insisted.

"Not until we are within striking distance."

"We are going to ride up to Ramona Hawk with nothing in the wagon?" Guillermo questioned.

DelNorte waved to the back of the wagon. "Oh, we'll have something. We'll pull a tarp over that bell."

Julianna pointed toward the broken wagon. "The machine. We can load it in this wagon. Covered up, it will look like a full load of goods."

DelNorte hiked to the broken wagon and climbed up in the back.

"*Hermana*, cut me loose," Guillermo urged. "Hurry, while he is busy."

Julianna ignored her brother and watched DelNorte.

"For the love of God, at least let me have a gun."

"For the love of God, my brother, I will try to keep both you and Father alive."

"You do not understand Ramona Hawk."

"I probably understand Ramona Hawk better than almost anyone on earth."

"Paco would love this," DelNorte shouted from the other wagon.

"What is it?"

"A printing press."

"Really?"

"It's brand new, manufactured in Philadelphia."

"I did not know they were that big."

"There's a crate of newsprint too."

"You still want to load it?" she queried.

He pulled the dirt-covered green canvas back down over the press. "Yep."

It took DelNorte and Guillermo, now untied, over an hour to transfer the two crates to the back of the bell wagon. It was almost dark when they got the canvas tied down. On top of the green canvas they strapped the pine coffin.

"I am not goin' to ride up there!" Guillermo insisted.

"Nope. You get to ride chained to the tailgate."

"You expect me to ride on the tailgate?"

"It's either that or the coffin."

DelNorte climbed up beside Julianna. "I figure about twenty-four miles to the Mariposa Tank. At three to four miles an hour, we should make it before sunup."

"And then what?"

"Then we find out what Ramona Hawk has in mind. If we get there when it's still dark, we will have a better chance."

"It will be a long night. I can drive if you want to sleep."

"I got some sleep earlier today. I reckon that's about all I need for a while."

"I would guess that you do not sleep well anytime. Did you know that you sleep with your mouth wide open?"

DelNorte chuckled.

"I thought that might make you mad."

"We sound like a married couple describing how we sleep."

"I am not going to marry you, DelNorte."

"Darlin', now you're breaking my heart."

"You mock me?"

"No, but I would rather you didn't write me off completely."

"I will not marry a man if I do not know his name, his occupation, nor the taste of his lips."

"I reckon we could settle up on one of those right now."

"I thought you would. What is your real name?"

"That wasn't the one I was thinking of."

"Hmm. Why does that not surprise me?" Julianna turned in the twilight, closed her eyes, and puckered her lips.

The wagon bumped and rolled east through the cooling evening. She opened her eyes. *That was coy, Miss Ortiz. You just succeeded in making a complete fool of yourself. Perhaps he did not see me.*

"You're probably wondering why I didn't kiss you."

"Yes, the thought did cross my mind."

"Because I don't deserve a kiss until I answer those other two questions."

"And you are not going to do that?"

"Not tonight."

"Do you believe it will be anytime soon?"

"Yep."

"Just how soon?"

"Maybe a day, a week, a month."

"You do know how to string a lady on, DelNorte. Do you know that I have spent more time traveling with you than with any other man?"

"This has been quite a saga."

"If we survive, I shall write a book."

"What will you call it?"

"*The Man from the North*," she said.

"Oh no, this is your story."

"That remains to be seen. 'History is written by those who survive, and their account—'"

"'—reveals a heart released from death and defeat.'"

Julianna laughed. "I changed my mind. There will be no book."

"Why the change of mind?"

"Because there are too many quotes from Ramona Hawk in my life. I do not intend to share the story with her."

"She seems to dominate your life."

"Two days ago she injured my head and now holds my father captive."

"Has she held your mind captive for ten years?"

"In a way, I suppose."

"You carry a grudge a long time."

"Then you have no idea of the pain that event caused and the loss of self-confidence it produced. For years I hid in my shop and never wanted to go outside. When Paco was five, I would send him to the store for groceries. I was afraid to get to know anyone."

"Are you afraid to get to know me?"

"No, and I do not know why. Perhaps you are so mysterious that I am not threatened. Yet it truly seems like we have known each other for years. I have asked El Señor often about you in the past few days."

"And what has the Lord told you?"

"He says I can trust DelNorte. Why do you think that is?"

"He is kind to you and to me."

"Tell me about your Jesus, DelNorte."

"My Jesus?"

"I want to know about your Jesus. Is He the same as mine?"

"I don't believe I've ever had a woman ask me that."

"'Some questions are best asked in the dark—'"

"'—and answered in the light of day.' Yes, I remember that one too. My Jesus is Lord, Savior, God, Redeemer, Judge, and coming King. Should I say more?"

"You have good theology, DelNorte. Where is He today?"

"What has He done for me today?" he clarified.

"Yes."

"I had two requests for Him today. One, that I would be able to deliver your brother to you."

"He has answered that."

"And two, that I would have a few moments to talk to you alone."

"Like right now?"

"Yes, like right now."

"What did you want to talk about?"

"About loneliness."

"Are you a lonely man?"

"I think that's obvious."

"How long have you been alone?"

"Except for a short engagement after the war, with which you are familiar, I've been alone for twenty years."

"And you are tired of it?"

"I am dying with it. My heart feels dead. I think it's time for me to make some changes."

"Why have you kept on with such a lifestyle for so long?"

"Because I'm very good at it. I'm convinced that my work makes a difference in our world," he replied.

"A work that you cannot tell me about."

She heard a deep sigh. His strong arm surrounded her shoulder. Julianna turned to speak, and suddenly warm, narrow, chapped lips brushed across hers. She kissed him back.

"That will do," he said.

"I am certainly glad I passed the test," she murmured.

"Did I?"

Suddenly Julianna began to cry. She wrapped her arms around herself and sobbed. She felt warm tears cut tracks in the dust on her cheeks. There was pressure against her chest; each breath was shallow.

"Julianna, what did I do? I had no intention of upsetting you. What is it?"

"You kissed me," she wailed.

"Yes, I did. And I'd do it again, but I have never had such a reaction."

"Please do," she sobbed.

"Kiss you again?"

"Yes."

"Are you going to cry?"

She rubbed the back of her hand across her nose. "Probably."

"Why? What's wrong?"

"Why do you assume something is wrong?"

"Because you are uncontrollably weeping."

"Is crying ever under control?"

"No, I suppose not."

"Are you going to kiss me again or not?"

"Yes, and then will you tell me why you are crying?"

This time the kiss was not a light brushing of the lips, but a warm pressure applied to her lips as his hand pulled the back of her head toward his. When he finally pulled back, she began to sob again.

"Julianna, I had no intention of upsetting you. You have no idea how long it's been since I've kissed a beautiful lady . . . any lady."

"I am thirty-two years old, DelNorte," she whispered, "and that was the first time I have ever been kissed."

"Ever?"

"Except for my mother and my sister."

"Your father never kissed you?"

"Never."

"No boyfriends ever kissed you?"

"Never."

His arm went around her waist, and he held her tight. "Now I'm going to cry."

"Why is that? Do you pity me?"

"Because the Lord was so gracious as to allow me to be the first to kiss you. I have never been the first to kiss a woman."

"Not even when you were a teenager?"

"I was never a teenager. I grew up quick. 'There are kisses lightly given that will ride gently on our hearts until—'"

"'—we reach the gates of heaven.' Yes, I loved that one but

never experienced it until just now." She laid her head on his shoulder. "Do you know one thing that baffles me about Ramona Hawk?"

"What?"

"The spiritual sensitivity in her words. I was so caught up in them. How could anyone with such a wicked life write such words?"

"They are not her words, Julianna."

She sat straight up. "You know, for ten years I have read books and books, half expecting to find those wise sayings and lovely thoughts. What book are they from?"

"They aren't from any book."

"But where did she find them?"

"In letters."

"What letters?"

"Letters from me, Julianna."

"From you? But—I thought . . ."

"You thought she sent them to me? I sent them to her. She must have saved them all and used them to deceive you."

"But . . . where did you find such beautiful thoughts?"

"In my heart and soul, darlin'."

"You mean, all these years . . . all those words were from you? From you, not her?"

"I reckon that sums it up."

Julianna slugged him in the arm.

"What did you do that for?"

"I have been in love with you for ten years, DelNorte, and hated myself every moment of it," she sobbed.

He slipped his arm around her shoulders and held her close. "Julianna, I'm truly sorry to cause you such pain."

"Pain?" she wailed. "Pain? This is the best day in my entire life!" She put her head on his chest and continued to sob.

Ten

Time is measured at best by a relative calculation. There are no objective standards of comparison, and the subjective ones sometimes leave people confused.

For seven hours they drove the heavily laden freight wagon through a still New Mexico night under the light of stars hung low.

Occasionally a coyote yipped in the distance.

The horses plodded.

Guillermo slept.

Julianna and DelNorte talked.

And talked.

And talked.

They talked of Virginia and New Mexico.

Of Harvard and jewelry.

Of childhood fantasies and yesterday's daydreams.

Of adobe haciendas and Cape Cod summer homes.

Of the sinfulness of mankind and the Lord's return.

For Julianna Naomi Ortiz, they were the fastest hours of her life.

"Are those lights from Hachita?" she asked.

"I reckon they are. Mariposa Tank should be off to the right about three miles."

"I suppose it is time to put Guillermo up here with us."

DelNorte pulled his arm away from her shoulder. "Yep. You figure he'll give us a fight?"

"You can count on my brother always looking out for himself only. He will do anything and say anything to give himself the advantage. If siding with us is best for Guillermo Ortiz, he will stand with us. But if it is to his advantage, he will shoot us."

"Even his twin sister?"

"I have seen him that angry. But thus far, his shots have always been wild."

He slipped his hand into hers. "He actually fired a gun at you?"

"I have no pride in saying that several men have taken shots at me."

"I guess we didn't cover that part yet."

"But we did make good progress."

He leaned over and kissed her cheek. She reached up and kissed his lips.

Julianna sighed.

"That good a kiss, huh?"

"Oh no, the kiss was distracted and anemic."

"Thank you, ma'am. I surmise you say that to all the boys."

"You *are* all the boys, DelNorte."

"I marvel over that."

"You have no idea what last night did for me. I do not know where we will be tomorrow. I do not even know what will happen today. But I know that I will never be the same. I feel like a new person this morning."

"You feel that good?"

"Sweet DelNorte, for ten long, painful years, I have felt like a total failure. I thought my heart was pathetic and weak if I could be deceived by a woman. Therefore I could certainly not trust my heart to any man. I felt doomed to be the old maid in the jewelry shop, cooking bland suppers and sitting in her patio rocking chair as life rolled by. When I thought of those wonderful letters, my heart would jump, and I would punish myself because I knew they had come from a deceitful woman."

"And now how do you feel?"

"Now my heart is much wiser than the rest of my body. My heart heard your words and refused to let you go. And now El Señor has brought you into my life. How do I feel? Like an old prospector who hit the mother lode, and instantly his whole miserable life is vindicated and forever changed."

"I'm not all that valuable, darlin'."

"No, you are not."

DelNorte chuckled. "I'm glad we got that straight."

"Sweet Del, it is not just you. It is the glorious freedom to trust my heart again. You will never know how restricted I have felt."

"I might know. I've been single for a long time, darlin'." He pulled the wagon to a halt.

"What are you going to do?"

"What do you want me to do?"

"I want you to go wake up Guillermo and put him up here with us, or we will both be in trouble," she said.

"You figure we need a chaperon?"

"Do you?"

"Yep."

The dark eastern sky had started to fade to charcoal gray as DelNorte led Guillermo to the front of the wagon.

"So I get promoted to the front seat?"

"You sit next to sis and behave yourself. I'd hate to have to shoot you in front of her."

"But you'd do it?"

"I would if you put her life or mine in jeopardy. But before you try anything, just who do you think Ramona Hawk will shoot first when she finds out we don't have the guns?"

"She will shoot me," Guillermo admitted.

"Your best bet is to stick close to us until we get you out of this."

"Do I get a gun?" Guillermo asked.

"Not unless things get desperate."

"It will look strange if I have no gun."

"It will look stranger if you're dead and lying out in that coffin," DelNorte replied.

"What kind of story are we going to give Hawk about the cargo?"

"We'll get you to negotiating and then figure out how to overpower them."

Guillermo sat up straight. "I negotiate?"

"You and Julianna. I'll stay hidden."

Guillermo pulled his black hat low across his forehead. "I am liking this plan more and more all the time."

"I am not," Julianna admitted.

"I'll be right behind the seat with a gun pointed at you, Ortiz. I can bring down four or five before they get a shot off. You'll be the first."

"You had better put on a good show, *hermano*," Julianna said. "If she finds out what we have in the wagon before we can capture her, you will be dead." She turned to DelNorte. "So you want me to drive?"

"Yes, Julianna darlin', that's the plan."

"Julianna darlin'? What have you done to my sister?"

"Are you defending my honor, Guillermo? How touching! And I had just told DelNorte how many times you tried to shoot me."

"I was drunk." Guillermo waved his hands as he talked. "That was not for real."

"The bullets were real," she murmured.

"You have a charming sister, Ortiz, and provided that we live through this day, I intend to pursue her," DelNorte announced.

"That is just what I need," Ortiz moaned. "*Hermana*, how could you do this to me? How will anyone take me serious with DelNorte hanging around my sister?"

She patted his ducking-covered knee. "Just who are you trying to impress?"

"This is perhaps the worst day of my life," he groaned.

"And to think, it is just breaking daylight. There is still a lot of day left." Julianna pulled a wide brush from the valise under the seat and began to stroke her hair.

DelNorte hunkered down between the tarp-covered bell and the seat of the freight wagon. Julianna slapped the lines on the horses, and the wagon lurched forward.

"Are you going to keep that carbine barrel in my back the whole time?" Guillermo complained.

"Yep," DelNorte replied.

"You are not a very trusting man, DelNorte."

"I trust your sister."

"Everyone trusts my sister. That is like saying I trust the sun to come up in the morning. It takes very little faith."

"That's true enough, Guillermo."

"So when are you going to allow me to have a gun to defend myself?"

"Whenever Julianna says it's time."

"*Hermana*, tell him to give me a gun."

"I trust DelNorte's judgment in such matters."

"Wait a minute. He will not give me a gun until you say, and you will not say because you trust him? Perhaps . . ." He reached down for the shotgun on the floorboard.

Julianna's boot slammed into her brother's fingers just as the lever checked on DelNorte's carbine.

"Aiyeee!" Guillermo yelped. He sat back up and shook his fingers. "*Hermana*, you have become a very suspicious woman. I remember when you were young, you trusted me."

"I wanted very much to believe all your lies, Guillermo."

"And now your heart has hardened to me."

"It has been kicked too many times, my brother. But yesterday when you talked fondly of Mama and Marga, you softened it some. I think if you continued, things could be different in the future."

"I could never be the brother you want me to be. You have very high standards, *hermana*. Perhaps too high."

"Too high?" she asked.

"Why else would a pretty woman such as you not be married at your age? You will never find a man who can meet your expectations."

"That is not true. I think I have found such a man."

Guillermo glanced back at the man hunkered down with the carbine. "DelNorte, what went on last night while I slept?"

"About thirty years of catching up, I reckon."

Guillermo turned back and stared straight ahead over the team of horses. "DelNorte, can you and me talk man to man?"

"As long as I keep the carbine trained on you."

"I want to talk to you about my sister."

"Would you like me to leave?" Julianna giggled.

"No, but I would like for you to be silent until I am through. DelNorte, as horrible a brother as I have been, I want to remind you that Julianna and I have shared a mother, father, sister, nephew, and most of all a womb with each other. She is the sweetest and most virtuous woman I have ever known in my life."

DelNorte eased the gun back a few inches. "I agree with you on that."

"And I swear to the God of heaven that if you treat her badly, I will track you down. I know you think of me as a petty outlaw, and there is an awfully good chance I could not finish you off, but you need to know I would try. I have done very few good things in my life. That is no one's fault but my own. But *mi hermana* is a jewel. Just because a man has spent his life doing wrong does not mean he is incapable of doing right."

Julianna reached over and threaded her hand into Guillermo's arm.

DelNorte pulled the gun away from Guillermo's back. "Partner, that's something I fully agree with. If I mistreat her, I deserve to be shot."

Guillermo lifted her hand and kissed her fingers.

"You know, if I live through this day, it will truly be the best in my entire life," she murmured.

Guillermo pushed his hat back. "Do not make any wedding plans yet, *hermana*. There is a rider waiting for us."

"Is it Hawk?" DelNorte asked.

"It looks like a man," Julianna replied.

"Last time she was caught, she was dressed as a man. Is it Ramona Hawk?"

"No, and he has a gun pulled."

"I'm staying hidden. You two negotiate. We need to see your daddy alive before they know what's under here."

"Now would be a good time, DelNorte," Julianna murmured.

"Grab the shotgun, Ortiz," DelNorte ordered. "Sis said now is the time."

By the time they neared the waiting rider, daylight had colored the sky a light gray. DelNorte was out of sight, and Guillermo Ortiz had a shotgun across his lap. The desert was nothing but yellow-brown dirt and widely scattered yucca. The hills ahead of them showed no signs of vegetation.

The man with the iron-framed Henry rifle glared out from under a wide, low hat. "She said you would bring the goods," he called out.

"Where is our father?" Guillermo asked.

"With Hawk," the man replied.

"And where is she? She said to meet her at Mariposa Tank," Julianna said.

"She changed her mind."

Guillermo stood up, holding the shotgun and blocking DelNorte. "What do you mean?"

The Mexican waved at the mountains. "She said you should meet her at Blossom Wells."

"We are not crossing the border. The Federales are at Blossom Wells," Guillermo insisted.

"That is crazy. There are no troops there."

"Did she not get the word from General Artiz that the rendezvous has been changed to Verdicito Springs?" Julianna called.

"You do not know what you are talking about!"

"I do not care what happens to you or to General Artiz, and I certainly do not care what happens to Ramona Hawk, but I very much care about my father. And there are Mexican Federale troops at Blossom Wells."

"I do not believe you." The man's beard was so full Julianna could not see his lips when he spoke.

"That is not the point," she called out. "The deal was, we deliver the wagonload of goods to Mariposa Tank as instructed. We expect Father to be released."

"And to be paid in jewels," Guillermo added.

"You must follow me to Blossom Wells," the man shouted. "We are wasting time."

"None of us will get anything at Blossom Wells. The Mexican

troops will get the jewels, these goods, have us dig our own graves, and then shoot us," Guillermo insisted.

"You must come with me, or she said your father dies."

"You must bring him here alive, or you will not get the contents of this wagon. And if Ramona Hawk does not deliver these goods to Verdicito Springs, both the Federales and General Artiz will be tracking her down," Julianna threatened.

The man stood in the stirrups and yelled, "If you do not follow me, your father is a dead man. She is a vicious woman."

Julianna flipped her wrist at the man. "In that case, go ahead and shoot this one, Guillermo. It will be partial vengeance for our father's death."

Both big hammers were cocked on the ten-gauge. The gun flew to Guillermo's shoulder.

"You are crazy," the man protested.

"You lift that Henry, and you are dead," Guillermo screamed.

The man sat down in the saddle, the gun in his lap. "I have more important battles than this one," he said.

"We will wait here at the Tank until the sun is straight up," Julianna announced. "If you are not back then, we return to Lordsburg with the goods."

"You do not make the demands around here," the man shouted.

"We just did," Guillermo growled.

"It is impossible to find Ramona Hawk and return in that length of time," the man groused.

"You are wasting valuable time," Guillermo said.

"You would abandon your own father?"

"Abandon? Do you have any idea what we went through to get here? Tell Ramona Hawk that we have done exactly what she asked, and that the Ortiz twins demand that she keep her word."

"No one makes demands of Ramona Hawk," the man warned.

Julianna reached over and patted Guillermo's arm. "Count to ten, *hermano*, and then shoot him if he is still in range."

"*Uno.*"

"I cannot go back without you!" the man screamed.

"*Dos.*"

"She will kill me!"

"*Tres.*"

"You have no idea what you are doing!"

"*Quatro.*"

"You are making a big mistake."

"*Cinco.*"

"I think the mistake is yours. You cannot outride the shotgun blast now," Julianna said.

"*Seis.*"

The man turned and spurred his black horse. Julianna put her hand on her brother's arm. "Let him go."

Guillermo lowered the shotgun. "Of course."

"You two did a fine job," DelNorte said as he crawled out from behind the seat. "Is that the first time the twins have stood side by side against a foe?"

Guillermo released the big hammers on the shotgun. "No," he murmured, then sat down beside her. "Once when we were six."

"We were seven," Julianna corrected.

"When we were seven, Father came home drunk and hit Mother in the mouth." Guillermo stared out across the empty desert.

"We took him on side by side," Julianna said. "We told him we would beat him up if he ever hit Mother again."

"Two seven-year-olds?"

"We meant it," Guillermo added.

"What did he do?"

"He sat down and cried," Julianna said.

"And never struck her again," her brother announced.

"Guillermo, that was a long time ago."

"I had almost forgotten it until just now."

"DelNorte, do you think Hawk will come back to the Tank?" Julianna asked.

"Yes."

"By noon?"

DelNorte clutched the lead lines. The heavy wagon jolted up

the barren incline. "I think she'll be here in an hour. She wouldn't want to be very far in front of us. That was a bluff. She doesn't want to cross that border without the guns."

"The guns we do not have," Julianna reminded him.

"Will we set a trap?" Guillermo quizzed.

DelNorte eased the hammer down on his carbine. "Yes, but she'll expect us to set a trap."

Julianna slipped one arm into her brother's and the other into DelNorte's. "She does not know you are with us."

DelNorte brushed his shaggy gray hair off his swollen ear. "She might assume Burkeman and Nisqually are around."

"True enough," Guillermo agreed. "What does that mean?"

"It means she'll set a trap for our trap."

"And what will we do?" Guillermo pressed.

"We'll set a trap for the trap she set for our trap."

Guillermo glanced at Julianna "Are you following this, *mi hermana?*"

"I have no idea what he is talking about."

"Do you have a plan that will keep yourself and three Ortizes alive?" Guillermo asked.

"I reckon we'll know that in the next couple of hours," DelNorte murmured.

Mariposa Tank was a pool of runoff water collected in a hard granite basin just south of Hachita Peak. In the spring it was almost six feet deep. By late August it stood a foot deep in a good year. Some years it was dry by the middle of September.

Guillermo Ortiz hiked around the edge of the pool and stared at the horseless freight wagon parked out in the middle of the pond. "This is crazy, *hermana.* I do not understand it."

"Good. Perhaps it will confuse Ramona Hawk as well," Julianna said.

Guillermo waved his arm. "I see a dust cloud to the south."

"Can you tell how many riders?" DelNorte quizzed.

"Is there a wagon?" Julianna asked.

"Nope."

DelNorte pulled cartridges from his bullet belt and shoved them into the loading gate of his Winchester '73 carbine. "She's expecting to take this wagon."

"The Hernandez brothers might object."

"The government will replace it."

"Which government?" she asked.

"Ours."

"It would take two or three at least to stir up such dust," Guillermo remarked.

Julianna turned back to the wagon in the water. "I suppose we should get ready."

"Why do I have to be the one?" Guillermo complained.

"Because I have a wedding to go to at six o'clock."

"If we do not do this right, it will not matter."

"You can do it, *hermano*."

"Well, here goes." Guillermo raised the shotgun to his shoulder and fired a round straight up in the air. At the sound of the blast, Julianna held DelNorte's Colt peacemaker up, cocked the hammer, and fired. Again Guillermo fired the shotgun. This time Julianna fired off two shots in the air. Then they hiked to the edge of the Tank and stared down the gradual slope to the south.

"They are galloping," she observed.

"Yes, but two circled to the east. Two are coming up the hill."

"That is what DelNorte said would happen. Now go on."

"I am not looking forward to this, *hermana*."

"It is only water."

"It is only water?" he mocked. "Somehow I feel like a fool."

Guillermo reloaded the shotgun and laid it by the side of the Tank. "Boots and all?"

"Of course."

He sloshed out into the water and then stopped.

"Hurry."

"I cannot believe I am doing this," he mumbled.

"You are not doing anything yet. Sit down."

Guillermo plopped down. The water covered his ducking-clad legs and wicked its way up past his belt. "It is a little cool out here."

"Are you bragging or complaining? Now go ahead—lie down and roll over. Toss your hat out by the wagon."

"What?"

"It will look more authentic if it is floating in the water."

"What if that isn't them?"

"Then we have had a dress rehearsal. Think of it as being baptized. It is not as cold as the Rio Grande that autumn when Marga and I were baptized."

Guillermo Ortiz leaned straight back until the water flooded over his chest and face. When he came up, he gasped for air, his wet black hair hanging straight down over his ears and eyes.

She placed the two empty shells next to the shotgun. "Now come over here, half in the water, half out."

Guillermo crawled until his shoulders and head rested on granite. He lay on his stomach, his nose to the rock. His right hand gripped the shotgun. DelNorte's gray silk scarf covered with dried blood in hand, Julianna knelt beside her brother. She splashed a little water on the sleeves and bodice of her dress.

"That is it?" Guillermo grumbled. "That is all the water you are going to use?"

"That is sufficient."

"Are they still coming?"

"Two of them."

"And the others?"

"They must be trapping our trap. I trust one of the four is Father."

As the galloping hoofbeats thundered up the bare mountain slope, Julianna soaked the rag. The surface of the pond turned red. She smeared Guillermo's face with several drops and then dripped some on the granite slab next to him.

"Here they are," she whispered.

"Who is it?"

"Hawk and the Mexican we saw earlier."

Lord, help us now. I want no one killed, but I do want justice. She thought of the day she heard of Marga's death, of her sister's battered, stripped body lying out on the desert road by a mesquite tree.

"Oh, no," she cried out. "No! El Señor, no, no, no!" Tears streamed down her face.

The riders reined up at the edge of the granite.

"Help me," she screamed. "They shot Guillermo. Help me!"

A short woman in tooled-leather split skirt dismounted and stalked toward her, a long-barreled Colt .44 in her right hand. The man stayed on his horse, his carbine pointed at Julianna.

"Who shot Guillermo?" Ramona Hawk shouted as she approached.

"The Apaches."

"I didn't see any Apaches."

"You never see Apaches until it is too late. They stole the horses and killed Guillermo!" Julianna shrieked.

"How come they didn't kill you?"

"They saw you approaching. Help me!"

Hawk kept the revolver trained on her. "Help you what?"

"Help me pull him out!"

"He's dead. Who cares where he is? I don't see any Indian tracks."

Julianna glanced up at the bearded Mexican. "For the love of mercy, help me!"

The man dismounted.

"Edwardo, where do you think you're going?" Hawk growled.

"Even the enemy is allowed to care for their dead."

"Wait. It's a trap."

"By a dead man and a woman?"

"Where are the others?" Hawk demanded.

"I suppose Nisqually and Burkeman are in Arizona by now."

"And Alvarez?"

Still sobbing, Julianna pointed at the coffin on top of the freight wagon. "You finished him off."

"He was a fool. Like you and your brother, he was a fool!"

Edwardo waded out into the water and tugged at Guillermo.

"Where is my father?" Julianna wailed.

Edwardo glanced to the boulders to the north.

Julianna clutched Ramona Hawk's skirt. "Where is my father?"

Hawk kicked at her, and Julianna grabbed the woman's boot, twisting it sharply. Ramona stumbled into the shallow water. Julianna grabbed her black hair, yanked it back, and pushed DelNorte's Colt into the woman's back. At the same moment, Guillermo caught Edwardo by the collar and shoved the cocked shotgun in his face.

"I told you it was a trap!" Hawk screamed as she flailed in the water.

"Where's my father?" Julianna cried.

"Dead, if you don't let us go!"

Julianna shoved the woman's face under the water and jerked it back up again. "I said, where is my father?"

"Bring him out!" Hawk hollered.

From behind the boulders to the north, a broad-shouldered Mexican shuffled out, his hand on the back of Trubidicio Ortiz's collar, his revolver at the old man's head.

"Here is your father. Say good-bye to him. Turn me loose, or he's dead," Hawk growled as the water dripped off her face and chin.

The old man rubbed his chin. "Guillermo, what mess have you got your sister into this time?"

"Me?" Guillermo kept the shotgun trained on Edwardo. "You are the one who got yourself caught. And this is Julianna's plan."

Mr. Ortiz threw his shoulders back. "Let them shoot me, but save your sister."

Julianna stared at her father. *He would give his life for me? He would never even give me a moment of his time before, and now he will sacrifice himself for me?*

As Julianna's hand sagged, Ramona Hawk flew up out of the water, her head slamming into Julianna's stomach. Julianna dropped the gun in the water, staggered back and fell, sitting in the water next to the wagon. Hawk swung around with one motion, grabbing Julianna's long black hair and holding her own dripping-wet revolver to Julianna's temple.

"Your gun is wet," Guillermo warned.

"You want to take a chance on it?" Hawk sneered.

"Turn her loose, or I will kill this man."

"Kill him. What is he to me?"

The terrified Edwardo glanced over at his comrade, who held Mr. Ortiz. "Do something, Miguel!"

"Your sister and your father will die before your eyes, Guillermo Ortiz, and all you will have to show for it before a bullet strikes you is one dead Mexican. Is that worth it?" Hawk screamed.

"I will shoot him!"

"Then shoot him! Shoot both the Mexicans, for all I care! They mean nothing to me."

She yanked Julianna to her feet. Both women stood with wet dresses dripping. "Just like old times, sweetheart—you and me. Have you gotten any good love letters lately?" Hawk jerked Julianna back through the water and slammed her against the wagon. "Shoot the old man!" she commanded.

"No!" Edwardo screamed. "He will kill me."

"Shoot him," Hawk shrieked.

DelNorte flung the coffin lid into the water as he sat up. His hand gripped Hawk's shoulder; his carbine pressed against her back. "It's a voice from the grave, darlin'," he snarled.

Hawk spun around with a curse. "DelNorte!"

Julianna's fist crashed into Ramona Hawk's small, narrow nose, causing her to stagger back and drop her revolver.

Blood smeared across Hawk's wet mouth. "You broke my nose!" she cried out.

"Yes, and it felt very, very good. It felt so good, I will probably have to repent tomorrow."

DelNorte looked over at the Mexican holding Mr. Ortiz. "It's your move now, Miguel. You pull the trigger on the old man, and four people will be on their way to heaven or hell in a matter of seconds. Maybe there's an alternative."

Miguel's hand shook as he held the gun and choked out the words, "What alternative?"

"We can do some trading. You don't care if we take Hawk and send her back to prison, do you?"

Miguel glanced at Edwardo. "We would not care if you shot her right now. She obviously has no loyalty to General Artiz."

"What do we get?" Edwardo blustered.

"You get to live. What else do you want?" Guillermo growled.

"We have to show up with something for the general."

"We get the jewels," Julianna declared. "They were stolen from a friend of mine."

"And you get the contents of the wagon," DelNorte offered.

"Are you serious?" Miguel asked.

"Yes. We take Hawk and the jewels. You take the wagonload of goods."

"We will take it!" Edwardo hollered. "Do it, Miguel, do it!"

"How do we know he will not shoot us as soon as I turn loose of the old man?" Miguel questioned.

"Because he is DelNorte," Edwardo insisted.

"Turn Mr. Ortiz loose. Guillermo, release the other one. Then you and your father go get the horses. Let's pull this wagon out of the Tank."

Miguel retrieved his hat. "Can we look at the goods?"

"Leave your weapons lying on the granite," DelNorte instructed.

They laid the carbines down and waded out to the wagon.

"Can I at least wash the blood off my face?" Hawk asked.

"I reckon so." DelNorte released his grip on her shoulder, and she squatted down in the shallow water. He leaped down into the water.

As he splashed, Ramona Hawk swooped out of the water with a dripping .44 Colt revolver in her hand. She cocked the hammer and pointed it at DelNorte. Julianna leaped in front of him just as Ramona Hawk pulled the trigger.

With the barrel only inches from Julianna's stomach, the revolver made a loud click but did not fire. Hawk cocked the hammer and immediately squeezed it again.

This time the click of an empty chamber coincided with the impact of Julianna's fist glancing off Hawk's chin. Hawk staggered and lost her footing, her head crashing into the iron wagon wheel. Hawk dropped unconscious into the shallow water.

DelNorte grabbed her arms and dragged her out of the water. "I can't believe you did that," he said.

Julianna followed him to the granite shore gripping her right hand. "That I slugged her twice? I cannot believe that either. I have never hit anyone but Guillermo in my life. I think I broke my knuckles."

"I can't believe you jumped in front of me to take that bullet. I don't know if I could have lived, knowing that you gave your life for mine."

"Before you make me a heroine, remember that we fired the last three bullets in that gun before they rode up. The plan was that she would probably try to grab my gun, and it would be empty. I knew when she came out of the water with your gun, it was empty."

"How did you know that was my gun?" DelNorte asked.

Julianna tried wringing out her heavy skirt. "It was a Colt peacemaker with walnut grips."

"So was Ramona's."

"What? No, no, she had a—" Julianna stared at his eyes. "It was?"

"Yep." DelNorte waded back out to the wagon and felt around under the water. He pulled up another revolver. "Both had seven-and-a-half-inch barrels and walnut grips."

"That is her gun?"

"Identical to mine." DelNorte aimed the gun over his head and pulled the trigger. Flame and smoke spewed out as gunfire echoed off the granite rock.

Julianna burst out laughing.

"You think it's funny that you almost got killed?"

"DelNorte, I must laugh, or I will faint. Perhaps 'acts of heroism are merely—'"

"'—stumbling into the exact location where God is about to work.'"

"Did you really write all of those?" she asked.

"Yep. Some of them are kind of naive, aren't they?"

"How would I know? I am queen of naive. To me, they are wonderful."

"This is incredible!" Edwardo shouted from the back of the wagon.

DelNorte clutched his carbine in front of him. "Sorry, there are no guns, but you made a deal for 'the contents of the wagon.'"

"Guns?" Miguel hollered. "Who wanted guns? The general has guns. He needed this printing press."

"Paco was right!" Julianna whooped.

"We want the bell too!" Edwardo called out.

"The bell belongs to the Hernandez brothers."

"I am sure the general will buy it. How much?"

DelNorte glanced at Julianna. "What do you think?"

"Forty dollars," she announced.

"We will bring you back the money when we bring back the wagon."

"What if you don't come back?" DelNorte asked.

"Sell our horses and saddles. They are worth more than that."

"You got a deal, *amigos*."

Miguel stared into the crate. "What is this bell's name?"

DelNorte stepped to the edge of the water. "What do you mean?"

"Everyone knows the Hernandez brothers name their bells for ladies. What is the name of this one? That is the first thing the general will ask us."

"That bell is named Julianna," DelNorte proclaimed. "It has a sweet, innocent sound that, once heard, is never forgotten."

It was well after 2 P.M. when they left Mariposa Tank. They rode the horses down the slope to the barren Playas Valley and then turned north. The Mexicans pointed the wagon south. Trubidicio Ortiz led the way on a tall black horse. His new suit was now soiled, the black tie lost, and his collar sweated through. His crisp new felt hat revealed several new creases and was jammed down to his ears.

Guillermo Ortiz rode behind him on a sorrel with a bald face and one large white spot on its right rump. He sat tall in the saddle, shotgun across his lap, the reins of the third horse in his hands.

Ramona Hawk slumped in the saddle of the gray gelding. Her

once-soaked leather skirt had now dried stiff. Her feet were tied in the stirrups. A rope around her neck was tied to the saddle horn. Her hands were tied behind her back, and her mouth was gagged with a gray silk bandanna. A black straw hat tilted to the right on her head.

The last horse was a big brown gelding. DelNorte sat behind the saddle with his long legs in the stirrups. Julianna sat immediately in front of him, side saddle, with her legs off to the left. She held his carbine in her lap. His arms surrounded her and held the reins.

"What is she humming?" Julianna asked.

"Ramona always hums 'Dixie' when she feels helpless."

"I cannot believe I slugged her."

"Twice."

"Ten years of frustration. The amazing thing is that I feel no guilt."

"There are times when evil must be opposed with whatever force is necessary. In my line of work, I couldn't survive a day with my conscience if I didn't believe that."

"Ah, yes, the enigmatic DelNorte."

"And the outlaw's twin sister. We do make a pair."

"Do you think now would be a good time to tell me your name and your line of work that allows your conscience peace with God while you are shooting people?"

"I shot no one today."

"That is true."

He glanced up at the declining sun. "Do you think we can still make it for the wedding?"

"You are changing the subject. But it is doubtful that we will make the wedding. Besides, I am a mess. My clothes are dirty and wrinkled, my hair stringy, and I am sweaty and grimy."

"That's true," he mumbled.

"That's true? All you are going to say is that's true?"

"What did you want me to say?"

"You are supposed to say, 'Julianna darling, you are a flower in the desert, always a beautiful blossom to behold.'"

"Oh, okay. 'Julianna darling, you are a flower in the desert, always a beautiful blossom to behold.' There—is that better?"

"No, because we both know I am sweaty and grimy."

"True enough, darlin', but so are the rest of us."

"Yes, but you are not due at a wedding."

"I thought I was going with you."

"Are you really going with me? I was just teasing. I thought you would refuse."

"I didn't, did I?"

"No. That is good. Two of us sweaty and grimy. I hope Gracie coaxed Paco into wearing shoes," Julianna said.

"We have a long ride ahead of us, darlin', before any of us has to worry about the wedding."

"Are you comfortable?" she asked.

"Maybe if I just held on a little tighter, I'd be more relaxed."

"I see," she giggled.

"And my neck is a little stiff. I thought perhaps I'd lean forward a bit and just rest my lips on the back of your neck."

"By all means, if it makes the trip more bearable for you."

"But my lips are so chapped, perhaps they would feel better over here . . . or over here . . . or maybe here!"

"My, Mr. DelNorte, you do have active lips."

"Are you complaining?"

"By no means."

"Good, 'because the lips never caress anything that—'"

"'—the heart has not pondered with fondness.'"

DelNorte sat up and chuckled. "Are we ever going to stop quoting my old letters?"

"I will never mention them again if it hinders you from, eh, resting your lips on the back of my neck."

"You like that, do you?" He snuggled closer.

"I believe I love you, DelNorte."

"And I know I love you, darlin'."

"I suppose I will either have to marry you, or I will need to spend the rest of my life repenting of my thoughts."

"Are you proposing?" he chuckled.

She sat up and leaned forward. "Most certainly not, DelNorte. You have been making overtures at marrying me for several days. I merely assumed you were a man of your word."

"That I am. How about you?"

"Yes, I am certainly a woman of my word. I think I made myself quite clear. I will never marry you unless I know your name and your occupation."

"You have to know a man's job and his name? You're mighty particular." He laughed.

"Yes, I have always had rather high standards, which many assume is why I have never married."

"And just how many fellas have you had to refuse because of this narrow attitude of yours?"

"How many? You mean in the past ten years or in my entire life?"

"How about your whole life?"

"One."

"Fairly handsome fella, no doubt?"

"Actually he was not much to look at—gray-headed and well-worn by the time I met him. And his forehead was stitched up with green thread, and his ear purple and swollen."

"You had pity on him, I presume."

"Yes," she giggled. "He was rather pathetic, but he did have one redeeming quality."

"Oh?"

"His soft, sweet kisses on the back of my neck."

"I hate to hear a woman your age beg like that." He leaned forward and kissed her neck. She jerked forward, out of his reach.

"I am not begging!"

"Oh? What do you call it?"

"Just small talk."

"Small talk? Why are we engaged in small talk?"

"Because it might keep me from having even more to repent over tomorrow."

The sun was low on the Pyramid Mountains when they drew even with Shakespeare. Then they paralleled the railroad tracks west into Lordsburg. The street in front of the church was crowded with parked carriages and tied horses.

"It looks like everyone in Lordsburg is here," Julianna commented.

"It looks like everyone in southern New Mexico is here," DelNorte said. "I hear organ music. I reckon we're too late."

Guillermo Ortiz rode back to them, still leading Ramona Hawk. "What now, *compadre?*"

"I want you and your father to take Hawk to the marshal and get her locked up."

Mr. Ortiz rode up alongside his son. "This has been a revolutionary trip for me."

"It has been a revealing one for me as well," Julianna said. "It has been healing beyond belief. El Señor has been so gracious to me I could cry."

"Don't cry, darlin'. It might smudge your makeup," DelNorte teased.

"Very funny. Buddy the pig is cleaner than either of us."

"I suppose he is at the wedding."

"Maybe he saved us a seat."

"Are you two really going to the wedding?" Guillermo asked.

"Yes, if we can hide at the back."

DelNorte slipped down off the back of the horse. "Guillermo, when you turn in Ramona Hawk, I want you to say that she was captured at Mariposa Tank by the Ortiz twins. Don't mention my name."

"Are you serious?"

"It's important that I'm not mentioned. There is a very large reward posted, I'm sure. You split that between *tu hermana* and yourself."

"You do not want any of it?"

"No. Remember, don't mention me. It was Guillermo and Julianna Ortiz who captured Ramona Hawk and freed their father."

"I like the sound of that," Guillermo reveled.

DelNorte walked over to the old man. "Mr. Ortiz, I have a question for you. I would like permission to marry your daughter."

The old man grinned. "You have my permission."

"I am not going to marry him," Julianna insisted.

DelNorte turned to Guillermo. "And I'd like your blessings too, *hermano*."

Julianna slipped off the horse. "I said, I am not going to marry him—unless . . ."

"You certainly have my blessing, but you remember what I said."

"You will track me down and kill me if I mistreat her?"

"I meant it."

"So did I," Julianna hollered. "I am not marrying this man until he tells me his name and his occupation."

DelNorte winked at Mr. Ortiz. "We have just a few minor wedding details to work out."

"You sound like a married couple already," the old man said.

Guillermo spurred his horse and led Ramona Hawk toward Railroad Avenue. His father followed behind. DelNorte shoved the carbine into the scabbard and tied the horse off to the back of a long black carriage.

"Maybe we didn't miss much. I can hear the organ processional," he said.

"That is the recessional! We have missed everything," she moaned.

"In that case, we can just stand out here by the pony and watch them all come out."

Within minutes they were surrounded by the wedding party and most of the citizens of Lordsburg. After giving their regards to the bride and groom, they slipped to the back of the crowd and up the church steps.

"She looks beautiful," DelNorte said.

"May I look that good at her age."

"How old is she?"

"Older than my mother would be if she had lived," Julianna declared.

"Where have you been?" Paco cried out. Bonita tagged along behind him.

"Oh, we had to go out and capture Ramona Hawk," Julianna reported.

"You did? By yourselves?"

"The Ortiz twins captured her," DelNorte said.

Paco's brown eyes widened. "Really?"

"Yep," DelNorte said. "I just backed them up. You can read the paper in the morning, and it will say that Ramona Hawk was captured by Guillermo and Julianna Ortiz."

"That is wonderful!" Paco shouted. "It will look very good on my resumé when I run for governor."

"I get to be the governor's wife!" Bonita exclaimed.

"You do not," Paco insisted.

"You promised. I gave you my watermelon last night, and you promised I could be the governor's wife."

Paco shrugged at DelNorte. "What can I say? It was a good bargain at the time."

"Where are your shoes?" Julianna asked.

"Mrs. Miller said I did not have to wear them after all."

"I kept falling down in mine," Bonita remarked. "And now I have to stay at your house for five days."

"Your mama and Jefferson need a little time together, honey," Julianna said. "I hear they are going on the train to Tucson."

"I do not know how she will get along without me."

"I am sure she will miss you very much."

"Mama cried at the wedding," Bonita said.

"And I would have cried if I had gotten here sooner."

Bonita stared down at her bare toes. "I think Mama's shoes are too tight. That is why she cried."

"Rev. Howitt did a very nice job, you know, for a man from the States," Paco announced.

"I'm glad to hear that." DelNorte slipped his arm around Julianna. "Your aunt and I were just going to see him."

"We are not!" Julianna insisted.

The crowd around Lixie and Jefferson Carter buzzed as they neared their carriage. Julianna and DelNorte waved from the top step of the church. Suddenly Lixie tossed her bouquet toward the front door of the church. Julianna reached straight forward and caught it.

Everyone clapped.

"You are going to get married next!" Paco shouted.

Julianna scowled at DelNorte. "I doubt it."

He tugged her around to face him. "I'm employed jointly by the Department of War, the Department of State, and the President of the United States as Director of Covert Investigations from Brownsville to San Diego. My Christian name is Benjamin Savant."

"You are a spy?"

"I prefer Director of Covert Investigations. I love you, Julianna Ortiz. Will you marry me?"

"What are my choices?" she asked.

"Marry me, or I'll have to shoot you."

"You are so smooth-talking. How can I refuse?"

"Some have."

"I will not."

"You haven't known me very long."

"Benjamin Savant, I have been in love with you for ten years." Julianna threw her arms around his neck.

Their lips were still touching when a small, barefoot girl tugged the bouquet from her hand. Bonita giggled and then beat Paco over the head with the white daisies.

For a list of other books
by this author
write:
Stephen Bly
Winchester, Idaho 83555
or check out his website:
www.blybooks.com

The Belles of Lordsburg

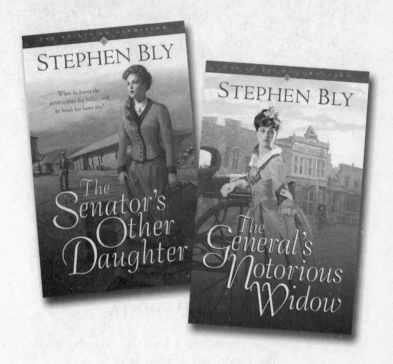

Their pasts held only pain and heartbreak. Now three women of the Lord struggle to find His peace for their futures.

Lordsburg, New Mexico, is a dusty little railroad town with few trees, treacherous heat and no luxuries. But it's perfect. Perfect for those who need to hide from the world. Perfect for a wayward daughter with a secret that could ruin her father's precious political career. Perfect for a widow desperately trying to escape the scandal surrounding her husband's death. Perfect for a young woman whose past prevents her from seeing any joy in the future.

For the belles of Lordsburg, this forgotten town is the refuge they need to open their hearts to all that God has for them.

Book 1: *The Senator's Other Daughter*
Book 2: *The General's Notorious Widow*
Book 3: *The Outlaw's Twin Sister*

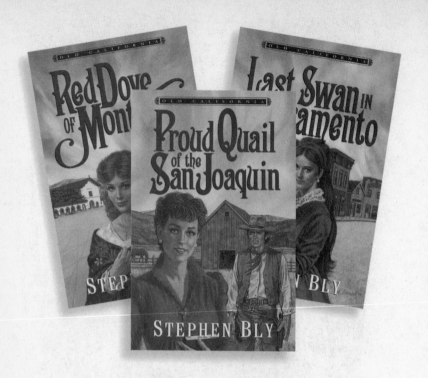

OLD CALIFORNIA

They were women of courage in a land and time that would test the strength of their faith

Though at 19 Alena Tipton is a confident entrepreneur, her heart is restless to fulfill its divine calling. But it could lead her away from the place—and the man—she loves.

Martina Swan's marriage was supposed to be perfect. So why is she fighting a devious bank and outlaws by herself, with the most difficult battle—learning to forgive and love again—still ahead of her?

Christina Swan is still seeking to find her place, her man, and her calling. The answers will come in one incredibly surprising way after another as she struggles to be obedient to God's leading.

BOOK 1: *The Red Dove of Monterey*
BOOK 2: *The Last Swan in Sacramento*
BOOK 3: *Proud Quail of the San Joaquin*

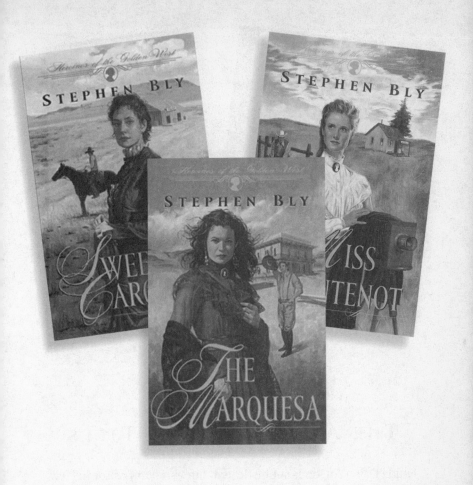

HEROINES OF THE GOLDEN WEST

They've come West for completely different reasons, but what Carolina Cantrell, Isabel Leon, and Oliole Fontenot are about to discover is that moving to Montana Territory will change their lives, their dreams—and their hearts—forever. With robberies and shootouts, love and romance, life in Montana is anything but dull for these Heroines of the Golden West.

THE AUSTIN-STONER FILES

Lynda Dawn Austin is sophisticated. Life as a book editor in New York City has prepared her for just about everything—except a certain charmin' rodeo cowboy and the rugged territory he's guiding her through. Join them as they travel the West in search of lost manuscripts, stolen chapters with treasure maps, and missing authors.

Now if only they can find everything they're looking for before danger finally catches up with them!

BOOK 1: *The Lost Manuscript of Martin Taylor Harrison*

BOOK 2: *The Final Chapter of Chance McCall*

BOOK 3: *The Kill Fee of Cindy LaCoste*